THIMBLE DOWN

A Mystery

by

PETE PROWN

Copyright © 2013 Pete Prown

Cover background illustration copyright © Unholyvault | Dreamstime.com

Cover design by Baxendell Graphics

ISBN: 1482510383

ISBN 13: 9781482510386

Dramatis Personae

At the Perch

Dorro Fox Winderiver: *Bookmaster of Thimble Down (door-oh, winn-da-river)*
Wyll Underfoot: *A young thief (will)*

In the Village of Thimble Down

Sheriff Forgo: The law in Thimble Down
Cheeryup Tunbridge: Daughter of the village seamstress
The Mayor: Mayor and magistrate of the hamlet
Osgood Thrip: Thimble Down's wealthiest citizen
Lucretia Thrip: Osgood's nosy-parker of a wife
Dalbo Dall: The village wanderer *(doll-bow dahl)*
Nurse Pym: Local healer and midwife
Bedminster Shoe: The village scribe
Mr. Timmo: The metalsmith
Bosco, Dumpus & Porge: Village lads *(bah-scō, poor-gă)*

At the Hanging Stoat

Mr. Mungo: Owner and barkeep at the Hanging Stoat
Bing Rumple: A good-for-nothing sot
Farroot Rumple: Bing's brother *(fuh-root)*
Bill Thistle: An acquaintance of Farroot
Farmer Edythe: A nearby farmer *(edith)*
Freda: A barmaid

In the Great Wood

Toldir: Leader of a band of elvish hunters *(toll-deer)*
Baldar: A young elf and expert knife-thrower *(băl-darr)*
Parahir: An elf with culinary skills *(pair-uh-hear)*

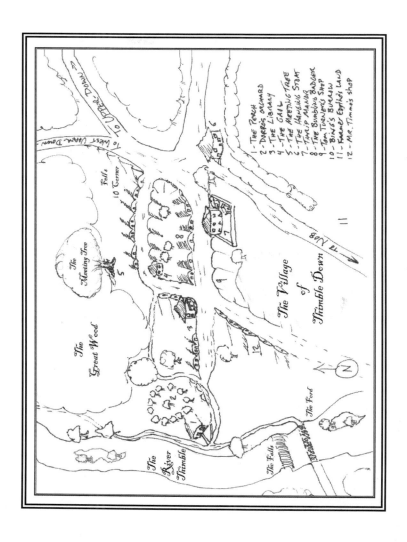

1 - THE FOREST
2 - DOBBS ORCHARD
3 - THE LIBRARY
4 - THE GAOL
5 - THE MEETING TREE
6 - THE HANGING STONE
7 - TULIP MANOR
8 - THE BUMBLINGS BADGER
9 - TOM TINKERS SHOP
10 - BIRDS BURROW
11 - FARMER EPHIE'S LAND
12 - MR. TIMMS SHOP

To UPPER DOWN

To WEST UPPER DOWN

Falls

10 Corner

The Meeting Tree

The Great Wood

The Village of Thimble Down

To NW DOB

N

The River Thimble

The Falls

The Ford

The Preface: Who is Dorro?

*I*t is now well into Autumn and many of us scribes and scholars have retreated into our snug, toasty libraries for the duration. Here we will spend the next few months, much of it in front of a roaring fire, ruminating on the ideas that have been brewing all summer. With winter winds howling outside, now is the moment to capture them with quill, ink, and a piece of sturdy parchment.

What shall we write? The deep thinkers among us will write grand historical treatises, while masters of analysis will craft theories pertaining to numbers and the natural sciences. Dreamers will write epic poems of heroism and romance; crafty storytellers will spin yarns for the cold nights to come. I, however, will begin what will likely become my life's work. In some regard, it shall blend facets of all the disciplines to which I've just alluded. No question, I've put it off long enough.

The spark that ignited this venture is the death of a truly unique personage, one who left us several months ago at the respectable age of one-hundred and seventeen years. His name was Dorro Fox Winderiver, and we buried him this past April in a quiet field near the Meeting Tree. We laid him amongst the daffodils, scilla, and anemones he loved so dearly. Many of us agreed he would have liked that.

"Who's this ... *errmmm* ... Winderiver fellow?" you might ask, scratching your chin.

For many folk in Thimble Down, our hamlet near the River Thimble, Dorro was merely the village bookmaster. He was a tad eccentric, with a mad love of ancient texts, flowers, and meat pies. He spent most of his spare moments fishing for trout from the river's clay banks. Nevertheless, for all his odd ways, Dorro reliably ran the village library for nigh on eighty years and was also admired for his translations of Halfling poetry from antiquity. As the village scribe, that is how I came to know Dorro, since he would hire me to translate minor texts, rewrite his poetry translations into something more legible (for a fellow of letters, he had truly lamentable handwriting), or run the library while he was gallivanting about (more on that shortly).

However, according to his former apprentice, Wyll Underfoot, Mr. Dorro had a far loftier role and, in his words, still remains most important figure in Wyll's life. "Without him," Underfoot told me in a formal interview not quite two years ago, "I could have been slaving in the back of a small, dank cheese shop or slinging ales in a fetid tavern. Worse, I could all too easily be dead."

And yet to others, Dorro Fox Winderiver was something quite apart. Within Mr. Dorro's tall, yet slightly pudgy frame lurked an uncanny mind that was equal parts precision and curiosity. It often transpired that when the local constabulary was stumped on a mystery, be it a stolen pig or ghastly murder, Mr. Dorro would be consulted for his guidance and skill at "puzzlin' out puzzles," as the local Thimble Downers might say. Yet he was no armchair detective. There were many a time when these investigations turned dangerous, putting him and his comrades directly in harm's way. As Wyll Underfoot noted in our interview, the boy was often in the thick of it, standing back to back with Mr. Dorro as they faced some deadly foe, knives drawn and blood about to be spilled.

In essence, those are the various guises of Dorro Fox Winderiver—a local scholar, quiet eccentric, friend and mentor, and a crackin' good sleuth. (In short order, I suspect that you, like many others, will regret never having met him.)

This brings me to the present day, when I am largely retired from my professional calligraphic activities and have more time to do as I please. As such, I will embark on pulling together the adventures shared by Mr. Dorro, Wyll, and others, many of them jotted down over fifty years ago. Back then, a younger version of myself would sit at one of the thick, wooden library benches in Thimble Down's library, writing up their escapades as case studies for future use by scribes, readers, and historians. Mr. Dorro cautioned me not to embellish the stories with excessive fantasy, lest it hurt the credibility of these accounts, and for that I am eternally grateful. In return, I always told the bookmaster I would eventually publish this trove. He would scoff and say, "Tut, tut, Mr. Shoe—who would honestly read such nonsense?" But I knew that Dorro was secretly pleased at my ambitions.

So without further delay, I shall finish editing and collating these case studies and bring them to publication. Collectively, they will be known, henceforth, as the *Chronicles of Dorro*. I apologize in advance for filling the narrative with a certain "creative reconstruction" of conversations and adventures. They are all based on facts and accounts that I have gathered, yet occasionally, I had to make a few educated guesses, particularly when trying to ferret out the thoughts within Mr. Dorro's own mind. If I went too far, you have my deepest remorse, but again, I felt it was all necessary to make a streamlined narrative that would entertain as well as inform.

In the following pages, I shall relay the chain of events that brought young Wyll Underfoot into Dorro's life, as well as detail one of the most infamous and heinous crimes ever to occur in the village of Thimble Down. It's rum stuff.

Yours faithfully,

Bedminster Shoe
Mr. Bedminster Shoe, scribe, Ret.

*November 11, 1772, A.B.**
(*After Borgo, first king of the halflings)

1

An Unwelcome Return

I'm surrounded by the dead ...

Sighing, Dorro sat back and lit a long, curved wooden pipe. According to his silver pocketwatch, it was just a quarter past eleven in the morning. "All I do is translate the work of dead poets," he lamented. "What an utter bore."

He picked up his quill, stabbed it in the ink jar, and resumed his work, taking scrolls of poems written in ancient *Havling* verse and deciphering them into modern Halfling, the language of his particular folk. As much he might have preferred sitting by the fire in his cozy burrow, Dorro Fox Wynderiver was nonetheless satisfied of his position as bookmaster of Thimble Down, a village near the River Thimble. Slowly swelling with pride, Dorro blew several large smoke rings over the poetry

1

scrolls on his desk and watched them sail out the window. The dark cloud of ennui passed as quickly as it had come.

Thimble Down was a typical Halfling village, one full of tall trees, tall grass, and very *short* people. At five-feet tall, Dorro was actually considered a bit on the statuesque side, even without his silver-buckled black leather shoes. He had sloppy brown hair and an oval face, wore half-moon reading specs during work hours, and had a penchant for looser, comfortable clothing, which hid a tummy that, for some inexplicable reason, was growing larger as he edged into middle age.

(Certainly, Dorro—like any self-respecting Halfling—would never consider that the traditional diet of four solid meals a day had anything to do with this phenomenon. In contrast, Thimble Downers firmly believed in the honest nutritional value of buttered pumpernickel toast with jam, sweet cakes, and all manner of ciders, lagers, and wines. And naturally, a dram or two of the old honeygrass whiskey never hurt either. *I feel like I'm getting thinner with age*, Dorro thought, squeezing himself out of his desk chair with more than a few grunts and groans.)

Deciding to take a break from the morning's translations, Dorro grabbed his scarf and walking stick. He placed a well-worn "Back after a quick nap" sign on the library door and went out for a walk in the warming sun. It was a cool, crisp day in April of 1721, *A.B.*, and Thimble Down was waking up from another snow-caked Winter. As always, it was worth the wait.

Dorro ambled down the packed-dirt trail away from the village and mentally ticked off a list of spring ephemerals coming into bloom: *There is a patch of snowdrops, the remains of the yellow winter-hazel, the dullish purples of hellebore, bright blue scilla, and—oh!—here come the first daffodil buds!* All Halflings were fond of trees and flowers, but Dorro was fairly daft about them, especially daffodils. He picked daffs by the armful throughout the month of March and April, crowding mantles and table-tops with vases and old jam jars packed with their yellow, white, cream, and orange cups. It was a fragrance to die for, he thought.

Drawing closer to the water's edge, Dorro passed several burrows and hillock-houses that belonged to his neighbors, each a comfortable, earthen dwelling built into earth with bright and sunny front windows, a grass-covered roof, and a garden in front. Then he passed his own abode, lovingly dubbed the "Perch." Of all the homes on this lane, Dorro's was among the most coveted, with its kingly view of the River Thimble, numerous bedrooms and food cupboards within, and a fine apple-tree orchard not thirty feet from the front door. Inherited from his long-deceased parents, the Perch was his pride and joy—a pride that sometimes bordered on the edge of quiet conceit, but he hoped no one noticed. Dorro lived alone, but saw plenty of the village folk at the library, and, on rare occasion, would have a neighbor or two over for herbal tea, apple-bread, and discussion of poetry or some other piece of Halfling literature. His was not a life of wild adventure, but that's the way he preferred it.

However, there was one eccentric passion that fascinated Dorro.

While Thimble Down was a tranquil village, from time to time, nefarious acts occurred within it fair borders, or in other towns in the Halfling counties, such as Water-Down, Upper-Down, and Nob. These crimes would often happen where you'd expect—in taverns or banking establishments, or out in the deep woodlands where uncouth rogues would hold up wagons traveling between settlements. Yet sometimes, mortal crime happened closer to home.

When these misdeeds turned to something worse—even murder most foul—Dorro would be called upon by the portly county cop, Sheriff Forgo. While Forgo didn't like the general populace to know he asked for help from the bookmaster of Thimble Down, he realized that Dorro had a sharp mind for "puzzlin' out puzzles." In fact, Dorro had helped him track down more than a few thieves, liars, forgers, and gambling cheats over the years, as well as ruthless murderers. But the fewer folk who knew about that, the better, Forgo always thought.

✡ ✡ ✡

Dorro arrived at the river's edge and soaked in the magnificent panorama. The River Thimble was a wide, calm expanse that rarely flooded, though its torrent could be quick after a rainstorm. But that wasn't what the bookmaster was thinking about.

"I know you're out there, my pretties. And I'm coming to get you, and soon!" he said loudly, to no one in particular. A few feet away, the village wanderer Dalbo Dall stirred from his nap against a giant sycamore tree and briefly regarded Dorro speaking to the wind. Dalbo considered asking Dorro whom he was talking to, but decided he would prefer more sleep and promptly nodded off again, dreaming of tankards full of ale with thick, frothy tops.

Of course, Dorro's lone oratory would have sounded odd to Dalbo, but the bookmaster knew exactly whom he was addressing—fish! In just a few weeks, as the sun warmed the river more, the people of Thimble Down would know that the sign "Back after a quick nap" meant that Dorro would be down at the river, taking his rest with hook 'n' line in the water. The River Thimble was simply brimming with fat, wriggling brown trout, bass, and perch, and Dorro wanted to catch them all. Well, perhaps not all, but he was an avid fisherman, and tossing a line in the water was, to him, among the finest pleasures a Halfling gent of leisure could enjoy. (And of course, you now understand why his burrow was named the Perch, both for its panoramic view of the river and for the delicious, yellow-striped fish that resided within its waters. It was a pun that made Dorro giggle on occasion).

"I'll be back, my scaly foes," he exclaimed and turned to walk back to the library and finish his translations of ancient—and quite dead—Halfling poets.

☆ ☆ ☆

On the same afternoon that Dorro ambled down to the river and dreamt of fish jumping on the end of his line, Bing Rumple turned up in front of the Hanging Stoat, one of Thimble Down's popular taverns, accompanied by two others, his brother Farroot and their acquaintance, a large, well-muscled brute named Bill Thistle, who sported a jagged scar down his left eyelid and cheek.

Bing Rumple was among Thimble Down's least savory creatures. In fact, some thought the words "sniveling," "sneaky," and "lazy" had actually been invented just to describe this poor excuse for a Halfling. Bing spent most of his time at the tavern, gambling, swearing, and groveling for coins so he could buy more ale and honeygrass whiskey. Some thought he was even behind the petty thefts that had occurred in this and surrounding villages. The purloined purse, the rifled coat pocket, the missing pot pie left on a windowsill—all had the faint whiff of Bing Rumple about them. Yet no one—not even

Sheriff Forgo—had been able to catch Bing in the act and, thus, he remained innocent in the eyes of the law.

Last summer Bing had disappeared, and many residents of Thimble Down thought that he simply moved on to a new hamlet where he could continue to sneak, steal, and drink. Or even better, maybe he went off and politely died somewhere, sparing them the expense of a funeral or the bother of digging a hole. But everyone in Thimble Down was wrong.

Flinging the Hanging Stoat's door open with a crash, Bing and his cronies strode into the room. All within fell silent.

"Thought I was dead, did'ja? Well, I *ain't!*"

Bing then laughed out loud in his raspy voice and ambled up to the bar. "Gimme a pint for me and my mates, you fat oaf," he said, staring menacingly at the rather porcine barkeep, Mr. Mungo, who was also the tavern's owner.

Mungo eyed him suspiciously. "Do you have any coin this time, Bing?"

"How's this, you lumbering goat-herd?" And with that, Bing slapped down two silver tuppers on the countertop. Mungo grabbed them and held them close to his face, testing their weight in his hand.

"Seems real enough," he replied disapprovingly and began to draw a few milk stouts for Bing, Farroot, and Bill and set them on the bar. "Where ya been, Bing? Some folk hereabouts thought you had moved on, permanently."

"You *wish*." Bing scratched his closely shorn head and stared around the room balefully, recalling a history of gambling games gone wrong, debts owed, and far too many ales in his belly. "In fact, I have made my fortune and...," raising his voice so everyone could hear, "... I don't care who knows about it!"

"It's time for Bing Rumple to get a little respect from this motley crowd," he continued loudly. Snickers broke out around the room, as fellow Thimble Downers recalled Bing's spotty past. Casually reaching across the bar top, Bing grabbed his earthen mug of milk stout and heaved it across the room, shattering it on a far wall and sending bits of beer and crockery in every direction.

"You will change your attitudes, useless little maggots—and mind your tongues, too." There were far fewer snickers this time.

At that, Bing unstrung his cape's clasp and let his brother and Bill remove it from his shoulders, rather dramatically, as if they were in a theatrical production. Many in the Hanging Stoat gasped, for on Bing's left breast was a gleaming gem, one so bright it looked like a star in the tavern's dim light. Bing also had a fine sword strapped to his belt and, indeed, in contrast to his crooked posture of the past, he now stood tall and proud. Clearly, this was not the cowering Bing Rumple of yesterday.

Intrigued, a few of the tavern's guests warmed up to the "new" Bing and came over to ogle at his gem pin and sword. "What is it?" they asked.

"It's an Elvish brooch and it's *mine*," he sneered, taking a gulp of freshly poured milk stout. "It was my reward for deeds of bravery and valor!" They peered closer at the pin. It was an intricately crafted arrangement of silver leaves, each one finely wrought and covered with tiny, clear gems. Few in Thimble Down had ever seen such a jewel at all, and none of this fineness.

Bing then regaled the Hanging Stoat's denizens with tales of his adventures, especially how he, Farroot, and Bill had traveled eastward in search of new opportunities and become ensconced in a border war between elves and goblins in the vast, dark forests of the realm. Bing was short on specifics, but thanks to the ale and the otherwise dull conversation on this evening, most folks were enraptured. He rambled on about joining a band of elfin hunters who were defending their lands from invading goblins. He spun tales of battles and ambushes, with himself as the hero who saved the elves from disaster. As a reward for his bravery, the elves gave Bing this ancient brooch, along with a sword and a generous bag of coins. Mungo the barman remained suspicious, but the rest of the barroom crowd had become neatly spun around Bing's finger.

Thimble Down had a new celebrity.

News of Bing's return spread through the hamlet the next day. In a small, sleepy Halfling village like this, any news was big news, and this story quickly became a phenomenon. His legend grew overnight.

"Did you hear that Bing Rumple slew fifty goblins ... all by himself!"

"Bing saved the King of the Woodland Elves and was given a fortune in gold and jewels as a reward."

"The villagers want to make him our new Mayor, and he deserves it!"

Certainly, the real Mayor of Thimble Down was not pleased with this latest rumor. "Over my dead body!" the Mayor roared as he slunk down the lane, but noticed that no one was listening. In a snit, he returned to the official Mayor's Burrow to stew over this latest state of affairs.

Over in the library, word of Bing's return had also reached the ears of Dorro Fox Winderiver, who was taking delivery of fresh books from the bookmaster in the nearby village of Nob. *"Didja* hear, Mr. Dorro, sir," said Cheeryup Tunbridge, a village girl who helped stack books, re-roll scrolls, and sweep the floor. "They say Bing fought off a hundred mountain goblins, saved all the Woodland elves, and returned home with a vast fortune to his name. It's very romantic."

"Bah, young Cheeryup!" replied Dorro with an imperious air. "How could a useless sack of oats like Bing Rumple do anything more than crawl inside a glass of ale? Must be more of the drunken fool's imaginings."

Yet throughout the day, Halflings kept coming in and out of the library, claiming that it was true and that Bing Rumple would soon become the King of all the Halflings.

"Rubbish ... *and poo*," snorted Dorro, to no one in particular.

2
The Apple Thief

At half past five in the afternoon, precisely, Mr. Dorro sent Cheeryup on her way home, after first pressing five copper pennies into her hand for half-a-day's work, and proceeded to lock up the library. He had forgotten about the annoying stories involving Bing Rumple he'd heard that day and was looking forward to a quiet evening at the Perch.

As it was very early Spring and getting brighter in the evenings, he felt it was time to inspect his apple orchard and decide which trees needed pruning for the growing season ahead. Apple trees require good ventilation, without any crossed branches or suckers, which is why a hard pruning near the last frost is always a fine idea. This would be as good a time as any to start, figured the bookmaster. Along the way, Dorro was also going to check on his winter stores of apples from last fall, which he kept in the food cellar adjacent to his garden shed. Furthermore, he thought, he might as well "test" the hard cider he'd fermented in October, just to make sure it was aging well. Downing a mug or two of the ol' cider in the cellar—for purely scientific reasons, of course—would be a prudent thing to do, he decided. Dorro was a man of principle.

Dinner was also on the agenda. Mrs. Fowl, from three burrows over, was a superlative cook and was only too happy to sell her vittles to appreciative customers. Dorro particularly favored her meat pies and pureed root vegetables, which she mashed with lots of fresh herbs and homemade butter. Even as Dorro walked down the lane toward his burrow, he was already imagining the lamb pie and mashed rosemary turnips sitting in his larder, both waiting to be popped into the oven for an hour or so. Just the thought of it made his heart skip a beat. (If you haven't guessed by now, Mr. Dorro liked his supper. And every other meal, too.)

Stepping through the portal of his warm and cozy burrow, Dorro took off his scarf—there was still a nip in the Spring evening—and rekindled this morning's fire to warm his dinner. Puttering around the kitchen, he was happy as he could be. His home was built for light and comfort; there was a sitting room in the front, just to the right as you enter the front door, with large windows to capture the sunlight. This is where he'd entertain guests on occasion, though normally, this was Dorro's reading and writing room. A long wooden settee with a thick cushion on top was the site of many, many naps, particularly in winter, when the sun was shining through the windows. There, he'd often curl up like a cat for a toasty half-hour's rest.

To the left of the Perch's entrance was his kitchen, where he proceeded at once. With the fire alit, he carefully placed the lamb pie and root vegetables in the oven, whereupon Dorro put his scarf on again and went outside to inspect his orchard. Upon exiting, he took in the grand vista of the river in front of him and climbed up behind his burrow, toward the spot where his orchard was meticulously laid out. Many decades ago, his grandfather Lorro had planted the trees, twelve apple saplings in a perfect circle with one in the middle—a baker's dozen. Each tree was a different variety and all their apples were simply delicious. And while it was only April, Dorro was already imagining the fall harvest: apple pies, apple crisp, pork dumplings with apple slices, apple sauce, apple jelly, and in fact, apple everything. "Thank you, Grandfather!" he quietly acknowledged.

For a moment, the bookmaster felt woozy from this veritable apple-drunkenness, but finally regained his composure. Now, off to a brief bit of work. First, he would stop in the garden shed and food cellar, where he'd "test" the hard cider and pick out a few tools to use for his pruning. *That's odd*, he thought, approaching his shed. *Who left the door open? Must be Mrs. Fowl's cat again, chasing a mouse in the night. Bother!* But upon entering his garden shed, Dorro noticed some of his tools askew and, the adjacent door to his food cellar was also open. *This can't be good*, he thought. And he was right.

Dorro grabbed a lantern from inside the door and lit it, using the box of wooden matches he kept there at all times. With the lamp's faint glow ahead of him, he descended the dark stairs into the cool, dry cellar, hoping that a wild animal hadn't made its way in and gobbled up all his good apples, cheese, and dried meats, or worse, made its nest there. *There's nothing less pleasant*, he mused, *than trying to evict a grumpy mother badger or hedgehog, especially if she is protecting her newborns.* "Not pleasant at all!" he said out loud, to no one in particular.

Upon reaching the bottom stair, Dorro confirmed that things were definitely out of order. A basket of his favorite Flitwyck apples was tipped over and strewn across the floor, and there were a few green Candleberry apples mixed into the wrong pails. The cheese wedges looked like they'd been meddled with, too. "Sweet King Borgo!" Dorro exclaimed, wringing his hands together, "This will not do, not do at all! There's clearly a thieving hand at work here." At least it wasn't a cross badger, he figured, but no one likes a break-in, especially to one's larder.

Unfortunately for the apple thief, this was the cellar of Mr. Dorro Fox Wynderiver, chief bookmaster and amateur sleuth. Moreover, no one messed with a Halfling's beloved pantry! The next time the villain visited, a nasty trap would be awaiting him. Dorro rushed up the stairs to his garden shed, where he found a nice selection of rope, buckets, and tomato cages. Walking up to his potting bench, he quickly sketched out a diagram on a scrap of paper. Then Dorro giggled. And he giggled again as he brought his supplies down the stairs and began to assemble a little surprise in the food cellar. "I hope you like my apples and cheese, cunning sneak-thief," he chortled deviously. "And please come back for more; there's plenty here!"

Dorro was having so much fun, he even started to whistle a happy jig.

☆ ☆ ☆

The next morning, Bing Rumple was in full stride. He'd been walking in and out of shops, a chop house, pony stables, and many of the other burrows and houses that composed the center of Thimble Down, bragging about his exploits in the east. With his brother Farroot and Bill Thistle following him like a pair of leering weasels, Bing was enjoying his moment in the sun.

"How do you kill a ferocious goblin?" A youngling had just asked him this very question, and now he was preparing a grandly entertaining response. "Why, you can do it many ways, my boy-o," he said in a tough voice, but trying to stifle a grin. "You can stick him in the throat with an arrow at fifty paces, or sneak up from behind and garrote the bugger with a sturdy piece of rope. Me,

I generally just cut 'em to pieces with this elvish saber. Look!" he said, drawing the glimmering blade out of his scabbard, "you can even see bits of dried, black goblin blood, and burnt flesh in the crevices." At this, the Halfling children screamed with a mix of fright and glee and ran off to tell their horrified mothers. Bing and his pals roared with laughter.

As he expected, most people in Thimble Down had never even seen a goblin or troll up close. "What do they look like? Do they have bloody fangs?" asked young Tom Talbo, quivering with delight. Bing seemed to think for a moment before replying, "Oh course they do, young sir. And they have large bulbous eyes, thick grey-green or black skin covered with festering sores, long muscled arms, and meaty hands with claws on the end. They are fearsome to be sure, and if you get too close, they can shred yer intestines in a mere flash." Bing embellished his tale each time someone asked. He'd never been a celebrity before, and he rather liked it.

"The worst of it was when me 'n' the lads were trapped with an elfin hunting party, pinned down by about a hundred and fifty goblins that outnumbered us mightily," he rambled on. "We were on the top of a small bluff with goblins and trolls all around us. The elves fought valiantly, but we saved the day. Let me tell you the whole story."

"Ya see, goblins hate fire, and by a stroke of fortune, the top of the bluff was covered with dry, dead brambles and bushes. So I braved a rain of goblin arrows and ran over to the elf chieftain. I said, 'Toldir'—that was his name—'go ask yer men to gather all the brush and big rocks possible, and arrange them on rim,' I says. Of course, Toldir got pretty steamed at me for calling his warriors *Men*, because of course, elves ain't Men and Men ain't elves, if you reckon my meaning. But in the heat o' battle, these things happen. Anyway, the elves did as I asked, and soon the entire edge of our bluff was ringed with brush and big boulders. I'll hand it to them elves—they are strong and can move quick-like, especially in a pinch."

"As a further stroke of luck, the elfin hunters had leatherskin bags filled with deer and musk oil from their recent kills, which we used to drench the brush. At Toldir's command, the oil was lit afire, creating a massive inferno around the perimeter. I gave a shout of '*Heave-ho!*' and we used sticks and logs to push the big rocks and flaming brush over the lip and down onto the enemy, who were stricken with terror. Those goblins that weren't killed outright by the boulders and stones were hit with the flaming brambles and verily burst into flames. And any demons that escaped this hell were soundly stuck with deadly elvish arrows or, might I modestly say, by the edge of my sword as we charged down the hill to destroy the enemy. With the goblins either dead or in complete disarray, our troop was able to escape and rejoin the larger elf forces to fight another day."

"*Huzzah!* Hurrah for Bing!" applauded his audience. Bing, Farroot, and Bill tossed handfuls of pennies into the crowd to curry their favor even more, driving the children mad with joy. Still, some of the older Halflings at the edge of the crowd couldn't put the image of the sniveling Bing Rumple of yester-year out of their minds. "How could that miserable excuse for a Halfling be such a hero?" they thought. But in general, the village folk were greatly entertained, and this was a great boon to local merchants who hadn't seen crowds this big since the harvest festival of the previous year. Up and down the hard-packed dirt lanes in Thimble Down, sellers were bringing their wares into the open air, especially pies, cakes, and any variety of dried, candied meats on a stick, which only cost a penny or two and were gobbled down rapturously.

Many in the crowd were also ogling the gem-encrusted brooch pinned on Bing's left breast. Indeed, more than a few secretly began to covet it. Among them was one Halfling who decided—at that very moment—to steal it.

Even if it meant someone had to die.

3
Pandemonium

*D*orro was in a peevish mood the next day. The Perch had been violated and that rattled the Halfling immensely. His leisurely walk to the library the next morning, however, proved therapeutic, and, with the April wind blowing through his mop of hair and Spring flowers blossoming more abundantly each day, his spirits began to rise. Today, he mused, he would be translating the works of the ancient scribe Bodurdo into the modern Halfling tongue. While Bodurdo—a noted poet from the 2nd century, *B.B.* (BEFORE KING BORGO)—wrote in a dense, rambling style that defied most translators, Dorro felt more confident about the task with each step. He blurted out, to no one in particular, "Watch out, Bodurdo—today, you're *mine.*"

Up in a nearby maple tree, just off the path, a sparrow looked at the strange little creature talking to himself. It cocked its head (the avian equivalent of rolling its eyes) and quickly flew away in search of a nice wormy breakfast.

Soon, Dorro arrived at his place of occupation. The library itself was a typical freestanding building in Thimble Down. It had a circular footprint, timbered construction and off-white plaster walls. Accenting the light exterior color were dark wood-framed windows and timbers poking through every few feet, demarcating the floor and roof lines. It had two full floors, packed with books, and a few large windows, giving Dorro the sunlight he loved, but still providing enough shade in the rest of the building to protect the books and scrolls. And like all Halfling burrows, the library had a grass-covered roof, crowded with sedums and dwarf grasses planted in a thick cushion over its timbers. The plants and moss absorbed the rains and let them drain off slowly, preventing leaks and negating the need for any gutters or drains. It was a time-honored method of Halfling construction.

As he approached the building, however, Dorro felt a sudden chill. *Something is not right*, he thought.

The front door of the library was locked, so Dorro began walking around the perimeter of the building. All seemed fine until ... *there!* He noticed a second-story window slightly ajar in the rear. "Drat, darn, and confoundment!" he shouted.

"Mr. Dorro?" he heard from the other side of the building. It was Cheeryup Tunbridge, arriving to help open the library and finish re-shelving the books read by yesterday's patrons.

Dorro quickly turned the corner and said, "I'm sorry, Cheeryup, but it looks like there's been a break-in. Stay here while I investigate." The girl blanched.

The bookmaster unlocked the door and poked his head through. He suddenly wished he hadn't pretended to be so brave and left Cheeryup outside. While Dorro was a Halfling of above-average intelligence, courage was not his strong suit. "Um, my dear, maybe you should come with me, in case there are, err, damaged books." The lass was more than willing to venture into the building, showing far more boldness and confidence than the librarian.

With Dorro in the lead (but only just slightly), the pair entered. Instantly, the bookmaster felt two things—first, there was no one else in building, but worse, something was very wrong. They searched the stacks on the first floor and all was fine. Then Dorro put his foot on the first rung of the ladder up to the restricted galleries on the second level. Above him, there was an open, circular gallery in the middle of the second floor, and along its edge was a walkway with bookshelves that extended all the way around the building. This was where they kept all manner of ancient scrolls, leather-clad tomes, and other dusty artifacts.

As he ascended, Dorro felt a growing apprehension with each rung. Finally, he peered over the top of the gallery and screamed. *"AHHHHHH!"* If he hadn't grabbed the ladder at the last second, the bookmaster would have fallen to his doom. There, staring him in the face, was the earnest visage of a small brown dormouse, which apparently wasn't at all afraid of this panic-stricken Halfling.

"Is everything okay, Mr. Dorro?" Cheeryup called from below.

"Uh, yes, yes, my dear, all is well," Dorro blustered, still trembling like a leaf inside, a bead of sweat trickling down his temple. "I was just trying to scare the intruder, in case he was still in the building."

Starting to believe his own tiny lie, Dorro clambered up into the walkway and gazed around the gallery. The dormouse, in the interim, scarpered off, realizing this giant was no threat to him nor his hunt for breakfast. Dorro tiptoed around the perimeter, seeing no sign of disarray. But as he got to one corner of the gallery, he noticed something. There was an opening in this section of shelve, behind which he stored scrolls he was translating for quick retrieval. But as he peered behind, he saw a few scrolls pushed aside into a heap. On the floor, instead, were bunched-up blankets and, more damningly, some apple cores and cheese bits. Dorro grabbed the edge of a bookshelf to steady himself.

He had found the lair of his apple thief.

✼ ✼ ✼

Later that day, Bing Rumple headed toward the tavern, where he was to meet up with brother Farroot and Bill Thistle, who had sneaky errands of their own to run. Along the road to the Hanging Stoat, Bing ran into Sheriff Forgo, who was ambling around the county on his worn, haggard pony, Tom. The Sheriff and Bing had a long history, most of it with the former's hand firmly on the latter's collar and leading him to gaol.

In short, they despised each other.

"Well, well, if it isn't Bing, the famous goblin slayer," laughed the tubby Sheriff from atop his pony. Rumple stopped in his tracks and glared balefully at the lawman.

"I hear you're the talk of the town. But let me remind you, Mr. Rumple, this is *my* town and I'm watching every move you make. You may have convinced half of Thimble Down that you're some sort of dandy, but I know better. You're a lowly maggot who deserves a good whack from my cudgel." For theatrical effect, the Sheriff pulled a heavy stick from his saddle and tapped it on his palm.

"I haven't done anything wrong, *your lordship*," Bing replied spitefully, "So save your threats for truant school-children or runaway sheep dogs. I could have your job with a wave of my hand. Don't tempt me!"

Forgo laughed again, adding, "Oh yes, I've heard that you're pretty free with the silver these days. You can try to buy influence, but the Mayor and I have already spoken about you and your rat-faced brother. We're watching you and counting the days until you leave again. But the

Mayor is delighted that your grand stories are drawing villagers into the burrow shops of Thimble Down. He asked me to personally thank you."

Forgo gave Tom a kick and the pony began trodding toward the nearby village of West-Down, where a hot dinner and a bucket of sweet oats were waiting for them. Rumple disliked the Sheriff's mockery, but held his tongue.

"Be careful, your *lordship*," Bing muttered under his breath, gripping his sword hilt with white knuckles. "Someone might stick you like a pig, just to hear you squeal."

☆ ☆ ☆

Nearly an hour later, just past supper time, the door of the Hanging Stoat banged open and, once again, Bing Rumple appeared. But instead of proudly strutting into the tavern, he took three unsteady steps and collapsed onto the floor.

"He's been murdered! *MURDER!*" screamed Freda the barmaid, who promptly fainted herself.

The tavern exploded into pandemonium.

4
The Trap

he patrons at the Hanging Stoat were running in every direction and shouting, while others scurried over to see what was going on. "Murder! Mayhem! Get the Sheriff!" they yelled. Mr. Mungo echoed the refrain himself: "Murder? In the Hanging Stoat? *Again?*" (It wouldn't be the first time, nor the last, Mungo thought to himself.)

Farmer Edythe, who was in for her twice-weekly wheat ale and stuffed beef chop, jumped up and rushed over to the stricken figure. She rolled Bing over and suddenly raised a hand. "'Old on, 'old on! Bing's breathing, though t'aint much. Get Nurse Pym and be quick about it!" Freda the barmaid was starting to come around herself and wondering what all the commotion was about.

Within a few minutes, they had carried Bing into a back room, placing him on a crude cot amid ale casks, cider barrels, and crates of food. They cleaned him up as best they could, but he had a honey of a bruise on his forehead and might have also lost a tooth or two. Nurse Pym, the village healer and midwife (and, for all intents and purposes, its doctor), showed up a second later and began to look over the patient, who was gradually coming back to consciousness. Pym was a rather round, stern-faced Halfling in her late-middle years, and she'd been caring for the people of Thimble Down for nearly thirty years. In that time, she'd had seen many cases, from drunken assaults to hideous farming accidents to the odd corpse found floating in the river. Bing looked bad, but she'd seen worse.

"I dinna think you'll need to call the Sheriff," Nurse Pym offered in her thick Low Country accent. "Mr. Bing has been banged up pretty well, but aye, he'll be fine I dare say, given a good night of sleep. Certainly, that's a right good bonk on that melon of his, but the skin dinna break, which is good. Pack ice in a towel and leave it on that yon bump for a few hours," she added, motioning for Mungo to get it quickly.

Bing began moaning in a state of semi-consciousness. "Forgo ... Forgo!"

"Bing, simmer down," Nurse Pym added again, gently patting him on the arm. "Whatever hooligan gave you this knock is long gone by now anyway."

"No!" Bing said, finally opening his eyes. "T'was the Sheriff who knocked me about, I know it! He threatened me a mere hour ago. He wants to me to leave Thimble Down. And like everyone else, he covets my elfin brooch, too," reaching across to his left breast for the gem. "It's gone! Thief! It's, oh yes, I remember. I took it off earlier and hid it from rapscallions and villains who want to steal it from me. Like you!"

"Yer daft, Mr. Rumple," urged Pym, a bit more force-fully this time. "You canna go 'round accusing everyone of being a thug and a thief. You have a nasty bang on the brain and I doubt yon Sheriff put it there. Anyway, by now, he's trundled off to dinner and a warm bed. It would be best for you to just lie here and rest for the night. Can he stay here, Mungo?"

"This is a tavern, not a hospital, Nurse Pym," Mungo groaned. "But yes, just this once he can stay, so long as he's not a nuisance. Do ya hear me, Bing?"

But Bing Rumple was already asleep, snoring away with a rising welt the size of a parsnip on his shorn head.

✶ ✶ ✶

It was Dorro's favorite time of day—supper! "Ooh, I can smell the potatoes 'n' parsley already," said Dorro, salivating as he cracked open the oven a hair. On top of the stove, he was heating up a stew of goose sausage and

29

a sampling of vegetables that he had jarred and stored last fall in his cellar—carrots, peas, and a few beets. All of them had been simmering for an hour or so, creating a deeply savory aroma that made Dorro weak in the knees. He added a pinch of pepper and sea salt, plus a few chives to the stew. He tasted it with a large wooden spoon and complimented himself, "Dorro, my friend, you have a true gift for the culinary arts. Well done, my boy!" (Perhaps humility was not one of Dorro's true gifts, but again, Halflings do love their dinner, almost as much as they love their children.)

Finally, with the table set, Dorro brought out his culinary masterpiece. He ladled some of the stew into a large wooden bowl and set it on a plate, to which he added a few of the buttered potatoes 'n' parsley. *Time to tuck in,* he thought happily as he sat down and reached for his fork.

CRASH!

Oh dear, Dorro thought, before he could take his first mouthful. *Well, maybe it's a raccoon making havoc outside. No matter.*

SLAM! SMASH!

"Drat! What? This ... is ... outrageous!" He slammed down his fork without even tasting his magnificent stew and grabbed his scarf: "No one interrupts my supper and gets away with it. That raccoon will pay with its life, if need be!"

Dorro stepped outside and peered around in the settling dusk. He heard nothing. Saw nothing. Mostly he just hoped the creature had fled with whatever morsel of food it discovered in his compost pile and would trouble him no more. He was about to return to his awaiting table when he heard a voice.

"HELP! HELP ME!"

It was coming from the left of the front door, near his garden shed. Truly alarmed, the bookmaster rushed back indoors and grabbed a lantern he always kept just inside the entryway. He quickly lit the wick and ventured warily toward the shed.

He noticed again that the door to his garden shed was slightly ajar. Pulling it open more, he peered into the gloom. By the flickering of his lamp, he saw another clue—the door to the food cellar was also open. Someone was down there.

"PLEASE, HELP ME!"

"Who's down there?" Dorro demanded, conjuring up as bold as voice as he could muster and hoping that whoever was down there couldn't hear it shaking with fear.

When he got no response, he ventured down the stairs of the food cellar, fairly trembling like a leaf in a strong fall storm. "Hullo? Hello down there?"

Dorro held up his lantern and jumped at what he saw, smacking his head on the low ceiling. At the bottom of the stair, illuminated in his lantern's dim glow, was a tangled miasma of rope, buckets, apples, and cheese bits. And there, wriggling vainly amidst it all, was a young lad. A most unhappy looking lad.

Dorro had caught his apple thief.

5
A Fly in the Web

"**P**LEASE, sir! Free me! Please!"

"*Whoa-ho,* my good man," said Dorro, slowly gaining a measure of bravado. "Are you my little sneak-thief? I think you are! Maybe I should leave you down here for a dozen hours and bring the Sheriff back in the morning. My dinner is cooling on the table and I am famished."

"No, sir. I meant no harm. I'm hungry and lost, and your larder has kept me from starving to death in the woods," said the wriggling boy.

"Hmmph," snorted Dorro. "Maybe that wouldn't have been a bad thing. I am vexed, my young man, very vexed indeed." Dorro hadn't eaten yet, which made him particularly cross and grumpy.

Dorro set down his tallow lamp and began fishing the boy from his trap. It also gave him a few seconds to appreciate his own handiwork. The bookmaster had hidden several trip ropes across the stairs, each one rising a little higher as they descended. This way, there was no possible way the thief could avoid them all, especially in the dark. On the lower steps, he also put metal buckets and tomato cages as the final stage of his booby-trap, and all across the bottom of the stairs, he wove a magnificent spider-web composed of the bird netting he used to protect his apple crop.

Just as Dorro had anticipated, the lad tripped on the third step with his left foot, tried to steady himself with his right foot, and put it right into a bucket. He then fell soundly into the spider-web, which wrapped itself around him. *A proverbial rat in a trap*, Dorro smiled to himself. He grabbed the newly freed miscreant and took him by the collar. "Now, what to do with you? You've ruined my food cellar, broken into my library, and who knows what other devilry you've been up to," he scolded.

By now, the young boy was on the verge of tears, causing Dorro a twinge of guilt, but he wouldn't yield to this blackmail. "First thing we should do is march you into the house and take a look at you. Then we shall decide your punishment and whether to call Sheriff Forgo or not! He's got a lovely gaol, y'know—that is, if you like rats, bedbugs, and moldy toast."

Exalting in his role as the wise, yet firm magistrate of his own fiefdom, Dorro marched the boy up the stairs, through the garden shed, away from the orchard, and into the front door of his burrow. But he had something more pressing on his mind than interrogating the prisoner.

"Finally ... supper!"

☆ ☆ ☆

Twenty minutes later, Dorro pushed away his plate and bowl, a full and satisfied Halfling. The goose sausage and potatoes 'n' parsley had been worth the wait. Not a complete cad, he had set up the thief across the table from him with a bit of leftover lamb pie and pewter cup of water. The meal had been conducted in complete silence.

Dorro studied the lad. He couldn't be more than twelve Halfling years, a mere child really. And he did look rather thin and pathetic—a mere wisp with a mop of straw-colored hair on top.

"Let's start simply—what is your name?" Dorro asked.

The boy mumbled something unintelligible.

"Speak up, boy!"

"It's Wyll," he said sulkily. "Wyll Underfoot."

"I dare say you've been quite *underfoot* tonight," Dorro chortled, amused at his own awful pun. The boy said nothing for a few seconds.

"I'm very sorry, sir, but I was hungry, and your garden shed provided me safe haven. I realized I couldn't stay there indefinitely, so I followed you to the library one day and figured out a way to break in and sleep there at nights."

"That was very naughty of you, young Mr. Underfoot," chided Dorro, resuming his role as the *wise*, yet *firm* magistrate of his own fiefdom. "I will require full compensation for the food you stole, plus the damage to the library window and the mess you made."

At this, Wyll said nothing. A few seconds passed and then, quietly, the boy began to weep. Dorro was not prepared for this—he was hoping for a little defiance so he could apply an even firmer hand, but no, he couldn't deal with crying. After all, it was just a few apples and cheese. And the window wasn't really broken.

Wyll then caught his breath, wiped a tear, and proffered more details: "I ran away from my home in Shrimpton-on-Mar after my mother died last month and I got lost in the woods after walking miles and miles. I slept one night in a tree, but growling badgers surrounded it and kept me awake all night. When I found your garden shed, I thought it was heaven—it was shelter and food. I might have died if I hadn't made it there. I can't ever repay you, sir."

Dorro suddenly felt a spark of pride. Did he really save Wyll's life? Well, of course he did—he just didn't know it. Dorro was hatching a plan in his head.

"I would pay for all the food I ate and trouble I've caused, but I haven't any money to my name," said Wyll.

"But I implore you, sir, do not send me to gaol. I do not like rats, bedbugs, and especially moldy toast!"

Dorro, of course, loved a good theatrical flourish and, sensing the moment, swelled in anticipation of delivering A Great Speech: "*Well*, my boy," he began in a deep basso voice, with grandly sweeping arm gestures. "Let it not be said that Dorro Fox Winderiver is an unkind and ungenerous Halfling. Despite your transgression, I shall deal leniently with you. A lesser being would toss you into the cold, but not, not I."

Rising to his full height, a masterly five-foot tall, he intoned, "Instead of paying for damages and stolen goods, you shall work off your debt by cleaning my house, working in the garden, running errands for me, and any other duties that I see fit. And for accommodations, you can sleep on the cot in the shed, especially now that it's getting warmer out. Do you accept this *wise*, but *firm* judgment, young sir?"

"Yes, sir! Thank you, Mr. Dorro. You are my savior." Dorro again felt the warmth of pride. He didn't know if what he just proposed was exactly legal, but as he toddled toward his middle years, he felt the need for an assistant and, if truth be told, he was sometimes a bit lonely. A little temporary companionship might help.

"Then it's settled, young Wyll. You shall remain here as my assistant and errand-boy until your debt is paid. Now, how about a nice bit of apple-cinnamon crumb pie and pot of hot lemon-tea for dessert?"

For the first time, Wyll Underfoot beamed.

6
Bing 'Fesses Up

"Oy, my head! What 'appened?"

Bing awoke in a daze, his noggin throbbing in agony. He didn't know where he was. It seemed to be a strange, dark place filled with crates of food and, judging by the aroma, barrels of beer. Bing slowly and unsteadily raised himself and walked out the door into a large empty room. After a few more clouded seconds he realized he was in the Hanging Stoat.

"How the bleeding hell did I get here?" he mumbled, stumbling out the door and shielding his eyes from the bright sunshine. But he didn't get far—Bing's groggy head got the better of him and he slumped down on the front step. At the same time, Mungo came round the corner, while down the hard-packed dirt lane walked Sheriff Forgo, the Mayor, and Mr. Osgood Thrip, Thimble

39

Down's wealthiest citizen. None of them looked very happy.

"Well Bing," said Sheriff Forgo, "You put on quite a performance last night. Had half the town thinking you'd been murdered."

"I almost was!" said Bing, reaching up to touch his bandaged head. "As if you didn't know! You were the one who left this beauty mark."

"Calm down, Rumple," snarled the Mayor. "We have it on good authority that the Sheriff was in West-Down last evening, so shut your cake-hole. I think it's time we started hearing the real story behind all your tales."

"Mr. Mayor, may I suggest that you simply run this bumpkin out of town and be done with it?" said Osgood Thrip in his snootiest voice. "He's a blot on our moral character and the fine scruples of our village and its denizens." (Of course, Thrip wasn't able to see Forgo standing behind him, rolling his eyes and making faces at such outlandish remarks. *What a buffoon*, thought the Sheriff. *Thrip is a blot of mustard with shoes on.*)

But out loud, Forgo said, "Okay Rumple, out with it or you'll be spending a few days in my gaol."

"I'm the victim here, Sheriff!" shouted Bing. "Mayor, I implore you to defend me!"

"Sorry Bing, it's time to start jabbering or I'll let the Sheriff have you in irons. You've had this village in a tizzy since you showed up."

"Awright, awright. But I'd be more amenable if yon Mungo got me a tankard of cider and a crust of bread to start my day." With that, Mr. Mungo ran to fetch Bing a little sustenance, if only for the curiosity of hearing some new gossip, real or imagined.

☆ ☆ ☆

With Sheriff Forgo, the Mayor, Osgood Thrip, and even Mungo staring at him intently, Bing Rumple was running out of options. He was chewing his bread as slowly as possible, but finally took the last bite.

"Well Bing. Take your pick—gaol or the truth?"

"Hear, hear, Mr. Mayor," said Osgood Thrip.

"Fine. Okay, I did stretch the truth a *wee* little bit," said Bing, washing down the bread with a last swig of cider. The other Halflings relaxed a hair and waited.

"The fact o' the matter is that there was an elfin hunting party and a clash with goblins, but well, me 'n' the boys didn't really fight all that much. Truth is, we were out in the bush for few months, adventuring for treasure and scavenging for food, when we met up with Toldir and his elf crew. They weren't happy to see us on elvish land, but allowed us to camp with them for a few nights, as long as we promised to clear out and return to the west quick enough.

"I'm glad we did join them, 'cause boy, those elves can track and hunt," Bing continued. "Just spending a little time with them taught us more about hunting than we'd learned our whole lives. From not leaving yer scent where game can detect you to how to properly hold a bow and take out your kill in one shot. Farroot improved his bowmanship quickly, and ol' Bill Thistle learned how to throw a knife with amazing aim, thanks to a big elf named Baldar.

"Of course, them elves are real solemn and when they bag a deer or a boar, they thank the creature for its sacrifice, and sing verses and songs over its dead body. It's beautiful in a way, but of course, pure rubbish! Those elves are an odd bunch." Unfortunately, neither Forgo, Thrip, Mungo, nor the Mayor had spent any real time with elves and were inclined to agree. They nodded and bade Bing Rumple to continue.

"The goblin attack, however, was quite real," Bing said, clearly enjoying this part of the story himself. "We were camped on a bluff when a rogue band of goblins saw our fire smoke and tracked us to the hill. It was a nasty battle and, honestly, I never been so scared in me life. And no—I won't lie—me 'n' the boys were not heroes that day. Mostly we just hid in the tents during the fighting, because the elves, they, err, didn't really need us. Them boys can fight like banshees and, despite being outnumbered, the elf warriors stuck a few goblins with enough arrows to make 'em look like dead porcupines.

"After the skirmish, it made sense for us to split up, them heading back to their homes in the eastern woods, with enough dried game for the winter, and us with our skulls intact. I guess they took a shine to me, Farroot, and

Bill because, before we parted, they, uh, gave this elf gem and sword to me. Said it was an honor to hunt with us, but it was time to move on."

Forgo, the Mayor, Thrip, and Mungo were enthralled, but suddenly Bing jumped up, "Speaking of moving on, it's time for me to skedaddle back ..."

"Good idea, Rumple," said Sheriff Forgo sharply. "You've been making up stories and whipping the village folk into a frenzy, mostly just to stoke your enormous ego. I think it's high time for you to disappear again."

The Mayor and Osgood Thrip agreed. "Yes, indeedy, Sheriff," added Thrip, "The crowds are getting unruly and this might backfire on our local merchants. We can't get people too riled up or they might get violent."

"Violent?" said the Mayor. "Oooo, that won't be good for my re-election campaign. Yes, Bing, it's time for you and your boys to move along." Mungo just stood in the background, slack-jawed and nodding in agreement with everyone. Despite the brisk sale of ale in the past few days, a world without Bing Rumple was a far calmer and pleasant one at the Hanging Stoat.

"You'll get no argument from me, gentlemen," said a solicitous Bing. "If you just give me and my colleagues a day to gather our belongings, we shall move on to fairer grounds." In truth, Bing had been sensing that his Thimble Down admirers were becoming tired of his tales, and he was having trouble embellishing them more and more each day. Time to move to another place, such as Upper-Down or Nob, where they could ensnare some fresh rubes and enjoy all the free beer and chops they would lavish on the seedy trio.

With his head still throbbing, Bing stood up, shook each of the Halflings' hands (even Mungo's), and started walking toward the burrow he shared with his brother Farroot. It was time to clear out. And all the more so since whoever bashed him on the bean last night was still out there. And might do it again.

✻ ✻ ✻

As Sheriff Forgo, the Mayor and Osgood Thrip headed back down the main packed-dirt road through Thimble Down, they conversed among themselves.

"What do you think, Sheriff?"

"Well, Bing Rumple is a useless sack of oats, not to mention a drunkard and a thief, but I don't think he was lying. He may know more than he's telling us, but the better news is that he's leaving. We can't ask for anything more."

"I humbly agree," offered Thrip. "He's a rogue and a scallywag. And becoming bad for my business!" He held a handkerchief to his nose, pretending to be offended. Forgo thought about his heavy wooden cudgel and how he'd like to whack Osgood with it, but not with the Mayor present.

As they passed between the baker's house and the seamstress's burrow, a figure stepped out of the shadows and lunged toward the three Halflings. "Sirs!" The trio jumped about a foot in the air.

"Dalbo, you blithering idiot!" yelled the Sheriff, still flustered and puffing, "What in King Borgo's name are you doing? I could run you in for being disorderly! Especially since I can already assume yer drunk."

Dalbo Dall was, unofficially, the village wanderer of Thimble Down. He had no real home or address, but was a kindly sop beloved by all. He lived on the pennies and handouts his fellow citizens bestowed upon him, sometimes in return for a small favor or odd-job in the yard. After years living out of doors, the tiny old Halfling had a brown, wizened face full of wrinkles and an unkempt appearance, to say the least.

Dalbo looked at the threesome and said in the grandest voice he could muster, "Sirs, apologies for my abrupt greeting, but I must speak with ye. Further, I am quite lucid, at least fer the moment. As you know, I have made my abode in the beautiful woodlands, alleyways, and refuse piles of our fair village and, well, I do see much. I must inform you, however, that there be strange doings in the woods."

"Really?" said Forgo. "And how many tankards have you drained this fine morning, Dalbo?"

"Why sir, I am most offended," the vagabond retorted. "I am sober as the Mayor himself" (causing the

Mayor to flush and feel glad he didn't take a wee nip this morning before coming over.)

"Suffice to say," continued Dalbo, "two nights back, I was camping behind the baker's hillock-house and was quite comfortable in the tall grass. But around two in the morning, I awoke to strange whisperings. I slowly sat up and spied some dark figures moving under the tree line. I couldn't hear what they were saying, but did hear the name 'Rumple' clear as a bell.

"And last night I saw dark shadows crossing Farmer Edythe's field, where I was lounging amidst the early Spring peas. They're quite good, by the way—she'll have a fine crop this year. I like to munch on them raw, of course, but I really prefer them lightly sautéed with a little butter and tarragon ..."

Forgo jumped in, "Dalbo! I could run you in right now if it wasn't getting toward lunch. You'd better stop these ridiculous stories or else."

"Sheriff, lying is against my better nature. I truly saw the things I did. Mark my words, Bing Rumple should watch out for himself. Something—or someone—is out to get him."

"For criminy's sake." Forgo fished in his pocket and counted out three copper pennies into Dalbo's brown, wrinkly hand. "Clear out, Dalbo, you're being a public nuisance," at which the itinerant gent happily ambled off, followed shortly by the Mayor and Osgood Thrip, both of whom felt that most of the morning had been wasted.

But Sheriff Forgo wasn't so sure. He walked up to his lamentable pony and clambered on top. He took a last look around Thimble Down before noontime luncheon and got an uneasy feeling in his gut. Sure, Bing and his thugs were leaving soon, but as Tom began bearing him down the lane, he had a sense something bad could happen at any moment.

A few hours later, he wished he hadn't been so right.

7
The Brooch

The morning after Wyll's unceremonious arrival in the Winderiver burrow-hold, Dorro felt things were going swimmingly. For his part, the lad spent his first night in one of the back bedrooms and found it far more comfortable than a tree surrounded by hungry badgers. Not sure of his duties, Wyll rose early, kindled a fire in the kitchen, and waited for his new master to arise. "This," thought Dorro, enjoying the warmth of the fire, "is going to work out *well.*"

"And how was your sleep, lad?"

"More than satisfactory, Mr. Dorro. May I pour you some tea?"

Inside Dorro was leaping for joy and doing cartwheels in the sun. Outwardly, he kept a straight face and said drolly, "Yes, why thank you, Wyll. When you're done with the dishes, we must slip into the village for a few errands before our work today at the library."

However, Dorro wouldn't make it to library on this day.

✵ ✵ ✵

The same morning, Sheriff Forgo was heading back into Thimble Down for a cursory patrol before finding a tree against which he could eat his second breakfast and, more importantly, grab a quick nap. It was cloudy outside, but he thought the rain would hold off for a few hours. As he got closer to the shops and other merchant burrows in the village center, he saw a crowd, and that only meant two things: "Bing, and *trouble.*"

True to form, there was Bing Rumple in the middle of the crowd, along with Farroot and Bill Thistle, looking angry and maybe a little scared. "Sheriff! Sheriff Forgo! Just the Halfling I wanted to see."

"Okay Bing, calm down," said Forgo, trying desperately not to blow his stack and throw Rumple in gaol for not leaving town."

"Calm down? Sheriff, I'm a victim! I've been robbed. Someone broke into my burrow and stole my elvish brooch. My special award for bravery—gone!"

The crowd around Bing and the Sheriff was highly entertained by these events. Nothing this exciting had

50

happened Thimble Down for years, not since that scamp Hugo Farlow stole biscuits from the bakery and was put in the stockade for three days. This was proving to be even better, some were claiming.

"Gosh, I'm sorry to hear that, Bing," said Forgo, feigning sympathy, but suddenly he raised his voice, "But I told you and your miserable posse to get out of town or else! We're tired of your shenanigans."

In the background, the Mayor, Osgood Thrip, and Thrip's formidable wife joined the fray and were making their way toward the center of the crowd. "In the name of public decency, Sheriff, throw this Halfling in gaol," said Lucretia, in a nasally voice that could peel plaster from a wall. "He's a poor role model for our village's younglings."

"Hear, hear," said her husband, who really was as afraid of his wife as everyone else in town. "You're spot on, as usual." Lucretia approved of his groveling, but gave Osgood a right dirty scowl just the same. She had to keep him in line, lest he begin to think she'd gone soft.

"Well, Bing, what's your story this time?" sighed Sheriff Forgo.

"After the assault on my fragile person yester-night and the awful way I felt during the entire day, I returned to the burrow last night to pack and make ready for our departure," said Bing. "I awoke this morning and Bill, Farroot, and I started pulling together our belongings to pack on our ponies when I went to retrieve the elf gem, which I had carefully hidden a few days ago. And it was gone! Gone from a place only I knew of. Neither Farroot nor Bill knew of my secret hidey-hole either. I've been burgled!"

At this point, Bing Rumple began blubbering like a toddler, which made the Sheriff roll his eyes, though many in crowd began to feel sympathy for their recent hero. "Poor Bing," they said, "He was always such a nice, sweet Halfling," forgetting the years of drunkenness and thievery that preceded this show of emotion. (Admittedly, the good folks of Thimble Down had rather short memories and really weren't the brightest creatures in the world. But they meant well and always loved a good sob-story. Plus, this morning's entertainment was killing the time between breakfast and lunch, which was another asset.)

"If I may," said Bing's brother Farroot, "Bill and I actually saw the thief and can identify the rapscallion."

"Go on," said the Sheriff, the Mayor, and Osgood Thrip in unison. And in the back of the Sheriff's mind, he was recollecting on Dalbo Dall's visions of strangers in the night—maybe the two incidents were related. Or maybe, he also thought, he was dealing with a bunch of idiots who should all be in gaol.

"Last night, the three of us were coming over the hill toward our burrow," continued Farroot, who spoke with a soft, oily voice. "It was in the gloaming of dusk, but as we crested the top, Bill and I saw a small figure bolting from our beloved home. It looked like a small boy, a youngling of about eleven or twelve Halfling years. But then again, then again, in the dim light, we couldn't be sure and wondered if it was our imagination. Bill and I compared our notes this morning, and now we're sure we saw a boy, especially in light of this malicious theft."

"Well Farroot, you said you and Thistle could identify the culprit. Go on."

"Indeed, we can. It's ..." At that moment, Dorro and young Wyll Underfoot came wandering down the main lane of Thimble Down, on their way to their morning's errands. "... *him!*"

"Farroot, you blithering cod-brain," said the Sheriff, clearly about to blow his lid, "Are you implying that Dorro Fox Winderiver, the flippin' bookmaster, broke into your burrow and stole the gem? Winderiver couldn't steal a cherry pie if it was sitting right in front of him!"

Dorro, of course, was completely baffled by the situation, and kept wondering why everyone was staring at him. "Did I forget to comb my hair this morning? Did I grow an extra eye in the middle of the night?" He checked his breeches quickly. "Yes, I did button my fly before leaving the burrow."

"No, not him, Sheriff. That strange lad next to the bookmaster. It was him that done it!" All eyes suddenly moved on to Wyll Underfoot. Farroot marched across the lane to where Dorro and Wyll were standing in front of the pony stable. "Here's your thief, Mr. Sheriff, sir. This pint-sized scofflaw from parts unknown."

By this time, Wyll was cowering behind Dorro, who had actually considered hiding behind Wyll. "Sheriff

Forgo, this is some mistake. This boy, Wyll Underfoot, has been in my care since last evening when I found him, err, in my food cellar."

"And what was he doing there?"

"He was, err, well, it's a bit of a misunderstanding, but he was there taking some apples and cheese, when he got caught in a trap I set for him." Dorro immediately regretted opening his mouth.

"So you admit he's a thief?" said the Sheriff, growing more interested by the second. Behind him, Farroot and Bill exchanged grins, while Bing looked frightened and, well, back to his old sniveling self.

"No, he's a boy who got lost in the woods and he, um, borrowed some food from me and broke into the library to sleep for a few nights." Now Dorro had really put his foot in it.

"I'm afraid, Mr. Winderiver, that we're going to have to take this little thief into custody."

"No! Please, Sheriff! It's all a misunderstanding," cried Dorro, "He's a good lad who just got into some trouble. I want to help him start anew."

The mob, however, wanted a real show.

"Arrest 'im, Sheriff!"

"Mr. Mayor, have the rat hauled in!"

"C'mon, Thrip—string the little thief up!"

Sensing a simmering riot, the Sheriff pulled out his cudgel and yelled, "ALL RIGHT, YOU RABBLE! CALM DOWN! THAT'S AN ORDER!" The Thimble

Downers immediately shut their collective yaps, for fear of the Sheriff's stick.

Then in a calmer voice, Forgo said, "I'm sorry, Dorro. But we have evidence—you admitted yourself that the boy is a thief and we have witnesses, albeit shaky ones." Farroot and Bill immediately looked sheepish, glancing at their feet and fingernails, anywhere but the Sheriff's intimidating gaze. "Let me take the boy to gaol for the moment. I will treat him kindly, but for his own safety—and the law's sake—we must lock him up while I investigate."

Dorro felt a big lump in his throat, while Wyll clung to his middle, softly crying. "Please, Mr. Dorro, don't let them take me. I'm ever so sorry for taking your apples. I'll never do it again!" The bookmaster was consumed with guilt, but had no other choice.

"I'm sorry, Wyll. You go with the Sheriff now. I have his word that nothing ill will befall you," he said as calmly as he could muster. And then in a louder, bolder voice, "But mark my words, Farroot Rumple, I will find your true thief and, if there isn't one, you may find yourself in gaol. I won't rest until Wyll is free again!"

Farroot and Bill both snickered. "Do as ye may, little bookmaster, do as ye may," said the former.

At that, the Sheriff edged his pony closer to where Dorro was standing and put his hand out, "Hand him up, Dorro. Let's do this quickly before there's a riot."

With tears running down his cheeks, Dorro pried Wyll's hands off his waist and lifted the youngling onto the back of Forgo's pony, Tom. "I have failed you this time, lad, but not a second time. Dorro Fox Winderiver will crack this case, and then I will crack some heads. You must trust me!"

But Wyll, clearly in shock, would not look at Dorro. The Sheriff gave Tom a little kick and they slowly trotted out of the crowd and toward Thimble Down gaol. Dorro felt like his world had just shattered.

As if on cue, a light drizzle began falling from the sky.

8

Contrition and Cogitation

Bereft of his new charge, Dorro felt lost. He eyed Farroot Rumple and Bill Thistle suspiciously and they, now feeling a bit cowardly, slunk in the direction of the tavern. More curiously, Bing Rumple followed them, looking quite different than he had previously. He seemed a smaller Halfling than just two days ago, somehow, more timid and stooped. He was afraid. But of what?

As he often did when Dorro was upset, he decided to walk along the River Thimble's banks and watch the currents. Somehow, it cleared his head and helped him order his thoughts. With the mob dispersing, Dorro decided he'd leave the library closed today—with the rain, there wouldn't be many visitors anyway and a stroll to the river's edge would do him good. Soon he began muttering to himself.

"Focus, Dorro, focus! You can't be overwhelmed by this setback or you will never get Wyll freed. Now, let's see ...," he pressed his fingertips to his temples. "I discovered Wyll in my cellar at half past 6 o'clock and he was with me continually until just now." He shuddered again, thinking back to the unfortunate events of just a half hour prior.

"Farroot claimed he saw a boy fleeing his burrow sometime between half past five o'clock and an hour later. Considering that Wyll got caught in my trap previous to half past six, it's *possible* that he was at Bing and Farroot's burrow, which is about a quarter-mile away. But it's unlikely—he would have had to steal the brooch and then high-tail it to my food cellar, where he was caught. Well, I guess it's possible. But I still don't like it. Something doesn't fit quite right. And lastly, where's the brooch?"

Dorro made a mental note to go through Wyll's belongings when he returned to the Perch, as well as search the garden shed and basement. He figured the Sheriff would plan on doing the same thing, so best he do it first—and fast. The bookmaster's brain was finally warming up, and his thoughts became more logical as he reached the edge of the River Thimble. It was still raining, but only lightly, so he edged over to his favorite oak tree, which had just leafed out and provided a little cover from the drizzle. He pulled his clay pipe out and lit the dregs of yesterday's pipeweed with a wooden match.

"Next problem—what was it about Bing's behavior today that was so troubling? Think, Dorro, think!" He scrunched his face together and scratched his chin, as he delved into this latest cogitation: "Wait—he was acting differently. For the past week, Bing has been strutting around Thimble Down like the ghost of King Borgo. Bold, brash, and cocky. And this wasn't at all like the sly, sniveling coward who left here last summer. Yet today, Bing was back to his creepy former self. What happened?"

Now Dorro stooped over to pick up a handful of small, flat rocks and began skimming them off the surface of the river. Three skips. Four skips. Five skips!

"I wonder if Bing is lying," he resumed, talking out loud to no one in particular. "Maybe no one stole the brooch and he's just hiding it. Maybe he's trying to quietly sell it, get some loot, and clear out of town. I wouldn't put it past him.

"But hold on, let's get back to the brooch itself. It is reputedly of elvish craftsmanship and, conceivably, may have some unusual properties. Far-fetched, perhaps, but the elves are a strange race and there are all sorts of tales about their abilities to enchant talismans, jewels, and weapons. Not that I believe in such things, but we can't rule it out."

Dorro filed that thought away for later retrieval. Granted, Dorro Fox Winderiver wasn't a Halfling of great bravery, but his library training meant he could mentally sort, file, and retrieve reams of information in a blink. Furthermore, he had a razor-sharp mind that could ferret out even the littlest problems. As Sheriff Forgo had noted on more than one occasion in the past, the Halfling had a gift for "puzzlin' out puzzles." Dorro took that as a fine compliment.

"Next question," the bookmaster continued, still skipping the occasional flat rock and wondering when the rain would let up. "Who would benefit from stealing the brooch? Well, really just about anyone. It's assuredly valuable, but who would buy it? Maybe that's where I need to focus my energies—who is the would-be buyer? Now *that*, my friend, is an interesting thought."

For the first time in an hour, Dorro smiled. He usually did that when he stumbled over a clue that could pay dividends later in the investigation. But now back to his burrow. He needed to gather some food and clothing, and bring them to Wyll at the gaol. His earlier blunder in the village was still weighing heavily on his conscience. "Don't get too prideful, Dorro. You still have a long way to go, my old chum," he mumbled to himself, before turning and heading up the hill to the Perch.

"Too prideful, indeed, Master Winderiver!"

"Who said that?" Dorro spun around. A disembodied voice seemed to have descended from his favorite oak tree. But then a small figure gimped into view from behind the trunk. It was Dalbo Dall.

"Oh, it's you, Dalbo. Eavesdropping, are we?"

"Not hardly, m'lord," said Dalbo sarcastically, flashing a toothless grin. "But I did hear a few of your ramblings and thought I might have some information you might find useful."

It wouldn't be the first time Dalbo Dall tried to get a few pennies off Dorro for a pint of ale. "Thirsty, are we? Well, what do you have to say, Dalbo?"

Dalbo Dall stood patiently for a few seconds until Dorro fished into the pocket of his knee breeches and came out with two copper pennies and dropped them into the hobo's brownish hand.

"Oh yes, now I remember," say Dalbo, coyly. "Just the other day, I told the Sheriff about some strange doings about the village at night. I've seen rather large creatures tracking through the woods—not Halflings, but man-sized creatures about, oh, six feet tall. They move in a pack and I can hear them whispering. But I don't know what language they're speaking. They move off quick-like when they hear me, but if I was to guess, I'd say them was lookin' for somethin'. I've seen them three times in the past week. And there's one other thing."

"Well, out with it!"

Dalbo kept quiet and started looking at his filthy fingernails. The bookmaster found another penny in his pocket and tossed it to the other Halfling.

"As I was saying," continued Dall, with a sly wink. "Even though I couldn't understand yon big creatures' tongue, they did say something I did ken—'Rumple.' I heard it clear as a bell on two occasions. Now that I think about it, seems like Bing Rumple is being tracked … like game."

Dorro slowly raised his hand to his mouth. He turned for a moment to gaze at the river and process this frightening thought. When he turned around, Dalbo Dall was gone.

He again turned the thought over in his mind, while knocking his pipe against the tree to get out the last ashes. Yes, it was possible, Dorro thought. Bing Rumple was being hunted.

✦ ✦ ✦

As he neared the Perch, Dorro noticed someone standing on his front bit of lawn. It was Cheeryup Tunbridge, who was picking dandelions and making a necklace with the stems. She was a fine girl of about twelve or so, figured Dorro, though judging by her patchy dress, her mother barely made anything as the village seamstress and her father was long dead. He tried to keep her busy at the library, putting a few extra coins into the family's coffers each month, but worried about her future nonetheless. But there were other matters pressing.

"Hullo, Cheeryup," Dorro offered, trying to sound upbeat. "I'm sorry, I forgot to tell you that the library was closed today. Something, um, came up suddenly."

"Oh Mr. Dorro, I've heard all about your misfortune with that young lad you were protecting. That was awfully brave of you!" said Cheeryup with all the enthusiasm and perk she could muster. She was well-named, Dorro mused. "I've come to offer my help. And who is the boy?"

"Whoa, my young lady—you are bundle of energy," he retorted, with a smile. "But yes, the boy—a certain Wyll Underfoot—was in my charge, though I have not done well by him. He is, or was, our little sneaky visitor in the library, though I have talked with him and found that his road has not been an easy one."

"Why is he in jail? Please say you didn't have him arrested, Mr. Dorro."

"I might as well have. No, I was hoping to turn him into my errand-boy, but we were in the wrong place at the wrong time. Those wicked Rumple brothers trumped up a charge that he stole Bing's elvish brooch, which is outlandish. With a mob behind him, Sheriff Forgo was forced to take the boy into custody, perhaps to save his life. But in gaol he is and, I fear, it's entirely my fault."

Cheeryup put her hand to chin, as if to process a deep thought. After a minute, she said firmly, "No, Mr. Dorro, I've thought about it, and you are merely a victim of circumstance. Moreover, we need to rescue young Mr. Underfoot."

Heartened by her vindication, Dorro felt a little confidence growing. "I'm not sure the Sheriff would like us to rescue him, my dear, but we can bring Wyll some food and blankets, which will have to do for now. Will you help me gather some goods?"

"Yes, Mr. Dorro, I'm ready to serve!"

With that, Dorro smiled and opened the door to his burrow. The two entered and took a quick left turn into the kitchen. "Now Cheeryup, if you head back a few paces, you'll find my first pantry, full of dried meats, nuts, and a small jar or two of honey. Please bring a nice selection." For his part, Dorro opened up the bread basket in front of him and pulled out a reasonably fresh loaf of rye bread, which he wrapped in a towel. He fished under the counter and found a willow basket, into which he placed the bread, a spoon, three Flitwyck apples, a clay jug of cider, and Cheeryup's just-delivered supplies from the pantry. Soon, the basket was overflowing with comestibles; it would keep Wyll hale for at least a day or two.

"Now dear, go grab a thick woolen blanket from the second bedroom down the hall and we'll be all set." The young girl sped back deeper into the burrow and returned like a shot with the coverlet.

"Let's away to the gaol, Cheeryup!"

And with that, the two went out the front door, turned left down the path, and headed toward the Thimble Down gaol, just as fast as their Halfling legs could take them.

9
The Trouble with Bing

---

t was mid-afternoon when Dorro and Cheeryup reached the village's small gaol, a waddle-and-daub building on the outskirts of Thimble Down. The Sheriff saw no reason to keep them from his prisoner, and in a jig they were inside the lockup with Wyll. The boy was sitting on a bed of wood and straw, looking despondent and weary. But he perked up quickly when he saw his would-be master.

"Mr. Dorro, sir!"

"Now, now, Wyll, we shall get you out of here, mark my words," said Dorro. The boy brightened. "First, however, we've brought you something to eat and a stout blanket to keep you warm tonight. And, oh dear, where are my manners? Master Wyll, may I introduce you to

Miss Cheeryup Tunbridge. She helps take care of the library, which you already know all too well."

Wyll blushed, but held out a hand that Cheeryup gently clasped. "Greetings, Master Wyll. I do agree with Mr. Dorro. I do not know you, but I trust Mr. Dorro and I believe you are innocent. We shall see you are freed."

"I agree, young people, but we have a long road to walk first. I don't think the Sheriff is as convinced as we are. We must first vindicate the boy and find the rogue who stole Bing's brooch. In the meantime, Wyll, try a crust of bread with a dab of our local honey on top. It will give you solace, at least for a few minutes."

After they had given Wyll the food and bid their farewells, Dorro and Cheeryup stepped outside the gaol. There they found the Sheriff, along with the odious Osgood Thrip and his boorish wife. "Visiting the criminal, are we, Dorro?" Lucretia sneered maliciously. "We don't like thieves in Thimble Down. P'raps he'll think twice next time if the magistrate cuts off a finger or two."

"Come, my dear," said Osgood. "It's bad enough to be at the gaol, but you don't want to be seen conversing with *the bookmaster*. People will talk."

Dorro was about to give them a piece of his mind (or, at least, a look of extreme vexation) when Farroot Rumple ran up to the group, followed by Bill Thistle. Both Halflings were out of breath.

"Sheriff! Sheriff!" gasped Farroot. "Bing's missing! We were jumped in the woods!"

"Slow down, slow down!" snapped Forgo, clearly tired of the Rumple brothers and their endless dramas. "What happened, you dunderheads?"

Catching his breath, Farroot said, "We had a few ales at the Hanging Stoat this afternoon, after the, err, the unfortunate events that transpired today." He received a stern look from the Sheriff at this remark, as if he knew who was really to blame.

"We were heading back to our burrow, cutting through the woods north of Farmer Edythe's pastures, when we were assaulted. A group of big men leapt from the bushes and knocked me and Bill to the ground. Gave us a proper clocking on the heads, they did, and as such we don't remember much."

Behind him, the thug-like Bill Thistle nodded in grave agreement as Farroot continued: "After we gathered our wits, we realized they had scuppered off and took Bing with 'em. My poor brother was kidnapped!"

"You say they were men?" Forgo asked dubiously. Men-folk rarely came to Thimble Down and, when they did, it was solely for the trade of dry goods, pipeweed, whiskey, and food.

"Well, they were big like men. Real six-footers, if you ask me." Bill nodded again and this time, actually grunted in assent.

This set the Sheriff thinking about Dalbo Dall's ominous report of strangers lurking in the woods at night. "Well, maybe you're telling the truth—or maybe not," added Forgo. "You've been a heap of trouble these past few weeks, and I'm at the end of my tether with the lot of you!" Farroot and Bill looked suddenly guilty.

"But I am the Sheriff," he proclaimed, posturing a bit for Osgood and Lucretia Thrip, who were hanging on every word, "I will organize a search gang and we will comb Thimble Down and the Great Wood for your unfortunate brother. I suggest you two help out for once and we'll see if we can find Bing."

"'Tis a waste of your time, Sheriff," advised Osgood in his most pious voice. "You know, we help pay your salary!" Lucretia merely stuck her nose in the air, as if there was a smelly bit of cheese on her upper lip.

Ignoring both of them, Sheriff Forgo threw back his shoulders, thrust out his ample gut, and walked over to Tom, who already knew it would be hours until he got a fresh bucket of oats and sweet straw to lie on. The lawman heaved his portly self onto the pony and headed back toward the Hanging Stoat to gather a few, likely half-drunk, Halflings who would aid him in the search. However, he'd promise to buy them a round of honeygrass whiskey at the end of the hunt, which was sure to bring on a few takers. No matter what, it would be a long night, Forgo knew.

Dorro thought the same thing, but he wouldn't be spending the evening looking for Bing Rumple. Instead, he grabbed Cheeryup's elbow and gently urged her toward her home. Then he'd retreat to his burrow for a few hours to meditate on recent events. He would also reflect on the dire warning he received from Dalbo Dall. The hobo's words echoed in his head: "I've seen rather large creatures tracking through the woods—not Halflings, but man-sized creatures about, oh, six feet tall. I couldn't understand their tongue, but they did say something I did understand: 'Rumple.'"

After depositing Cheeryup on her doorstep, Dorro scratched his head. *Who are these dangerous giants in the forest?* he wondered. *And, of all the Halflings in Thimble Down, why would they kidnap an imbecile like Bing Rumple?*

10
Surprise Visitors

---

heriff Forgo was exhausted. It was 8 o'clock in the morning and he was standing in front of the Mayor's official burrow-hold, mentally preparing a report on the night's fruitless search for Bing Rumple. There was no sign of him anywhere in Thimble Down. His search gang worked until about six hours prior, when they all retreated to the Hanging Stoat for that promised jigger of honeygrass whiskey before calling it a night. Forgo headed for the gaol, where he plopped his hefty carcass in the cell next to Wyll Underfoot's and grabbed a few hours of fitful sleep.

After his nap, he rapped on the Mayor's door. A few moments later, a housekeeper answered the door and said that Thimble Down's first citizen would meet him outside in a minute. *Wonderful*, thought Forgo sarcastically, rubbing his belly. *I've spent most of the night in the cold, wet woods keeping our village safe, but the Mayor wants to finish his soft-boiled eggs before he has time to meet with me. Oh joy!*

Just then, a commotion down the lane took his mind off his annoyance with the Mayor. Forgo heard shouting and running, and the sound of many feet. A minute later, he could barely believe his eyes. "G-g-g-giants!" was all he managed to say.

As Halflings scrambled out of the way, a troupe of extraordinarily tall creatures were walking straight down Thimble Down's main thoroughfare toward the Mayor's burrow. Straight for the Sheriff! Forgo momentarily froze and went weak in the knees before he remembered who he was. With all his effort, the lawman stood as erect as possible and thrust out his chin, just as the giants stopped in front of him. They easily stood a foot or two taller than Forgo and he quaked in their presence.

"W-w-w-who are you and why have you invaded our p-p-p-peaceful village?" was all the Sheriff could summon from his vocal cords. The giants said nothing. Forgo looked them over, up and down. They were fierce warriors, tall and lean with thin faces, high cheek bones, and long straight hair of yellow, brown, and black. None of these creatures were, what you might say, well-muscled, but each was nonetheless taut and powerful. Forgo knew any one of them could snap his neck in a second. That is, if they didn't draw the deadly swords or bows slung over their shoulders and belts.

"We demand to speak to the leader of this encampment," said the giant in front, a yellow-haired behemoth with a hawk-like visage and piercing blue eyes. At that very moment, the door behind Forgo opened and out stepped the Mayor with a little blot of egg yolk on his chin.

"Well Sheriff, tell me the news about...*GREAT GOBLINS!*"

The Mayor nearly fainted, jumped, and choked all at once. He leapt behind the Sheriff and grabbed the lawman's shoulders. Inwardly, Forgo rolled his eyes and thought it was time he got a raise for protecting this blubbering fool of a politician.

"Mr. Man-Giant, kind sir, this is the Mayor of our village, err, standing right behind me. It is he you want." The large creature before him glowered at being called a "man-giant."

The Mayor squeezed Forgo's shoulders even tighter and cowered as low as he could.

"However," Forgo continued, his head craning upward at a steep angle, "I am Sheriff Forgo, the Mayor's official representative, and am empowered to parlay with you. Again, what brings you to Thimble Down? We are a peaceful settlement, yet we will defend ourselves vigorously. We are ferocious in battle."

"Have peace now, little one, and pray keep your hand off your sword. We have no intention of starting a war. But a piece of advice—dare not call us 'man-giants' again. It is a grave insult."

"My apologies," Forgo choked, "Then, what are ye?"

"My name is Toldir and I am leader of this elven band. We are hunters from the Woodland tribes of the east. And we are neither giants nor, thankfully, foul stinking men. In simpler terms, we are elf-folk."

"Elves!" said Forgo and the Mayor simultaneously, jaws agape—right along with the dozens of Halflings standing behind them and those gawking out burrow windows. Indeed, virtually no one in Thimble Down had ever seen a real, live elf before. They were beings straight out of fairy tales.

"We mean you no harm. However, we want it back— that which was stolen from us by a thief in the night?

"And, what would that be?" ventured the Sheriff, almost afraid to ask.

"Do not play games with us, Halfling," said Toldir, fixing an expression that held no humor. "I want the gem of Telstar back. It is an heirloom of our people and the sacred emblem of our hunting party. It was stolen from us by a Halfling like you." Behind their leader, the other elves were looking equally grim and all were intent on Forgo's answer.

Alas, the only sound that emerged from the Sheriff's throat was a rather pathetic gurgling sound. He had no idea what these elvish warriors were talking about and, if he could have crawled under a mossy rock, he would have. But instead Forgo forced out, "What, pray tell, does this famous gem look like?"

"Do not toy with us, my chubby friend. But just to humor you, I will describe it. It's is the brightest star in the evening sky, pure sunlight caught in a gem. In your language, it might be called a 'pin' or a 'brooch'. And it was stolen by a Halfling named Rumple."

Forgo gulped, because suddenly he knew all too well what they were speaking of. "Mr. Toldir, I believe I do know what gem you speak of. But it is not here. At least not at the moment and, in fact, we are looking for it."

In his own mind, Sheriff Forgo's speech went more like this: "Drat and curse that complete moron, Bing Rumple! He stole a valuable treasure not from just any-one, but from deadly elf warriors. Only a Halfling as stupid has he could pull such a move. When I find him, I will personally wring his neck, even if it lands me in my own gaol!"

Outwardly, however, Forgo eloquently retorted, "Mr. Elf, my kind sir, I swear that we are doing all in our power to find your great gem, the Telstar. And when we do, we shall return it to you in a jig 'n' a jiffy."

"See that you do, Master Sheriff. I shall give you two days. After that, you shall feel our wrath—and our steel."

With that, the elven hunting party turned on their heels and marched out of Thimble Down, presumably back to their encampment in the woodlands beyond. Sheriff Forgo had never seen an elf before, but he knew a serious threat when he heard one and had no doubt that Toldir would slit his flabby throat from side to side if the brooch wasn't returned.

"Well, Mr. Mayor, wasn't that something? I mean...." Forgo turned around, but he didn't see the Mayor anywhere in sight. Then he looked down, where he found him quick enough: the first citizen of Thimble Down was laying on the ground, unconscious in an utter dead faint, a blot of egg yolk still on his chin.

"What a hero," sneered the Sheriff.

11
A Beam of Hope

---

t the same time Forgo was being confronted by elves, Dorro was at the Perch and felt very alone. Twenty-four hours earlier, his new errand-boy had warmed up his kitchen on a chilly morning and offered him tea when he arose. Now, the room was cold and his table sat empty. *Dorro, you silly, old fool. What have you done this time?* he thought, with much exasperation and shame.

But out loud he said, "Nothing to be done about it now, save rectify one's misdoings. Now first …"

He trailed off, and began exploring the larder for a quick breakfast. No time for anything hot, so he grabbed a leftover cream scone from the bread drawer and smeared it with a dab of butter and delicious raspberry jam—this had been jarred by Farmer Edythe herself on the other side of Thimble Down. Dorro washed it all down with a draught of cool spring water from his kitchen pump—one of his true guilty pleasures. (In fact, there weren't many burrows in Thimble Down with running water and interior plumbing at all. It was another reason why the Perch was among the most coveted residences in the village.)

"Now, time to do some digging." Dorro knew he didn't have too long, so he wrapped a scarf around his neck and shot out to the garden shed where Wyll Underfoot had slunk around and stolen some food. He had to prove that Wyll didn't steal Bing Rumple's gem. He explored the area for any sign of the brooch, but found nothing. Dorro grabbed the lantern and sprung down the stairs to the food cellar where he had ensnared Wyll in that fiendishly clever trap. The Halfling fished around the various apple buckets and shelves of cheeses and jarred fruits, vegetables, and jams, and still found nothing.

"Thank goodness," Dorro sighed. He knew, however, that the Sheriff would be along eventually to search these exact same spots, looking for evidence that could implicate his prisoner. His next stop was the library, where he had the advantage over Sheriff Forgo—only he and Cheeryup knew that Wyll had broken in and stayed a few nights there.

He scuttled back up the stairs, closed the door to the Perch and head off to the library. After a brisk ten-minute walk, he arrived and, sure enough, there on the step was faithful Cheeryup Tunbridge, awaiting him.

"Ah my dear, perfect timing!" Dorro quickly filled her in on his search back at the burrow, and the two quickly entered the library and locked it behind them. In a second, Cheeryup had ascended the ladder to the upper book gallery, while Dorro puffed along a few minutes behind her. By the time he arrived at the little nook where Wyll had illegally decamped for several days, the girl had already given it a thorough once-over.

"Nothing, Mr. Dorro. I've checked every little nook and corner."

"Could he have hidden it anywhere else in the library? It's possible, you know."

"Yes it is, sir, but on the surface, our fruitless searches are good news for Wyll. I do believe he's innocent of the charges. Don't you concur, Mr. Dorro?"

The bookmaster rubbed his cheek and looked out a nearby window. "I pray you are right, my dear. I really do."

✲ ✲ ✲

Leaving Cheeryup to run the library and help any grumpy book lovers who were wondering why the building hadn't been open the previous day ("Tell them I had a bad case of the toots!" he giggled as he ran out the door). He returned to the Perch to gather his wits and come up with a new plan of actions, but upon his arrival, none other than Sheriff Forgo was standing in front of his door, his pony munching on a bed of primroses that were just beginning to bloom.

"Tut, tut, Sheriff! Your Tom is eating my primroses. Please!"

Dorro stopped short. The Sheriff did not look well. Indeed, he looked pale and shaken, as though he'd seen a ghost or had the croup. Forgo pulled on the bridle and Tom unhappily stopped sampling the tasty spring flowers. "Look Winderiver, I've had a perfectly hellish morning and I don't need any more lip from anyone. That would include you." He proceeded to tell the bookmaster about the elf encounter.

"Well, how can I help you, my dear Sheriff?"

"You know exactly why I'm here. You were seen with young Wyll Underfoot on the morning of his arrest for theft and we assume he stayed here. Therefore, I am here to search your property."

"B-b-but!"

"I said, no lip, Winderiver. I have a letter from the Mayor himself empowering me to search and any all premises in my investigation. And I'm starting here. Still, some events this morning have made me slightly inclined to believe the boy's story." The Sheriff looked pale again and mopped his brow with a handkerchief, "Still, the law is the law. I must search your burrow." (Secretly, however, the Sheriff also wanted to nose around a bit and admire the fine furnishings and interior plumbing of the Perch. Oh, perchance to dream—a mere Sheriff living in such luxury!)

A half hour later, the Sheriff had thoroughly nosed around the house, the garden shed, and its food cellar, and had found absolutely nothing. Dorro, playing Forgo like a fiddle, had been as polite and accommodating as a pie. The bookmaster had escorted the Sheriff throughout the dwelling (Forgo taking his sweet time, of course, to admire the décor), as well as the garden shed and food cellar. Forgo peeked and pried as much as he wanted, but to no avail—he found no gem, nor any evidence of mis-doing.

"All right, Winderiver, this site looks look clean—for the moment, I'm feeling favorably predisposed toward your young assistant. If the day improves, and it couldn't have started any worse, we could conceivably release the boy around suppertime."

Inwardly, Dorro was leaping for joy, but instead said solemnly, "Thank you, Sheriff. You are a fair and just lawman." He was plucking the fiddle one last time for good effect.

"My next move is to head back into town to check with my deputy about his search of Bing Rumple's burrow. We're hoping to find evidence there, too."

"Your deputy?" Dorro asked gingerly.

"Yes, I've deputized Mr. Mungo in this time of special emergency. Thimble Down needs all the capable Halflings it can get during this precarious time."

Again, Dorro said nothing. Mungo was the owner of the Hanging Stoat and an affable, if slow-witted, gent, but the thought of him as a deputy made him want to giggle. Fortunately, he was able to suppress the reflex and instead nodded his head grimly. "Sounds like a wise decision, Sheriff." *Plink*, went the fiddle again.

"Tell you what, Winderiver," puffed the Sheriff, his large belly beginning to groan as it got closer to lunch. "Why don't you accompany me back into the village? I'll check in with Mungo on the state of Bing's burrow and, if all seems in order, maybe we can release your lad after lunch."

Enthusiastically, Dorro closed up the Perch and began walking back into Thimble Down, as the Sheriff rode his depressed-looking pony. The two Halflings didn't speak much, but it was becoming another glorious spring day, with the daffodils beginning to leaf-out in mass, along with azure punctuation marks of anemones and scilla flowers. The fields and lanes of Thimble Down looked like an oil painting to the bookmaster. Out of the blue, the world seemed very hopeful to Dorro.

It was a feeling that wouldn't last long.

12
Death in the Downs

---

*T*he Sheriff and village bookmaster ambled back into the village just before luncheon, Forgo taking the opportunity to tell Dorro about his episode with the elves that morning. Yet on the whole, both were feeling rather more cheery than either of them felt earlier in the day. For the Sheriff, the investigation was proceeding apace; eventually, he'd bring Bing in for some tough questioning, break his nerve, and recover the lost elf brooch. As for bookmaster's helper, young Mr. Underfoot, he was probably in the wrong place at the wrong time and could be released.

Forgo would also have a stern talking-to with Farroot Rumple and Bill Thistle about the evils of false accusations, especially the part about how the accusers themselves can end up in gaol. Forgo smiled to himself—yes, he would look forward to that conversation, especially if he could make those rats squirm a little. *It's little things like this that make being a lawman so rewarding,* he thought.

As for Dorro, he was beaming with the thought that Wyll would be free soon and they could return to the Perch for a good dinner and a new start tomorrow. Certainly, he was curious about the missing brooch, but Bing Rumple and his no-good brother were undoubtedly up to something. Maybe he could assist the Sheriff in puzzlin' out this puzzle.

As it turned out, neither Forgo nor Dorro would get their wishes. For just as they were in amidst the shops, passersby, and general hustle 'n' bustle of Thimble Down, Forgo saw Mungo rushing toward him from the opposite direction. And the expression on the barkeep-turned-deputy's face was even stranger—it was one of pure terror. To add insult to injury, Mungo was accompanied by Farroot Rumple and the weasel-faced Bill Thistle. "Goblin poo," whispered the Sheriff under his breath.

The trio rushed up the Forgo and Dorro, completely winded and frantic. "Okay boys, what's the problem this time?"

"Well, your Sheriffness-ness," panted Mungo awkwardly. "I did what you told me to do. I went to the Hanging Stoat to find Bing and tell him you wanted him to meet you at the gaol for a 'nice talk about the weather,' just like you told me. Well, he weren't there, but these two gents were, so they graciously accompanied me back to Bing's burrow-hold, where they said he was resting after such a stressful morning."

So the three of us ambled over, but when we got there, something was awfully awry, Mr. Sheriff," added Mungo, still not getting the hang of official protocol. "It looked like there was a break-in. The door appeared to be kicked in, and the jamb and frame were in splinters. We peeked in the door and almost every bit of furniture in Bing's burrow was smashed to bits. Shards of crockery everywhere. We weren't sure if the culprits behind this crime were still on the premises, so we, err, decided to come get you, since you're the sheriff and all."

Inwardly, Forgo thought Mungo was a blinking idiot and probably the last Halfling he should have deputized, but the damage was done. He looked at Farroot and Bill, and noted that they were giving each other strange looks. This was not good.

"Let's move, you three bumpkins! Bing could be in trouble and here we are having a tea party in the lane. Winderiver, you can come or stay—it's your decision."

And with shocking agility for a Halfling that size, Forgo swung up on his pony Tom and urged him into a cantor toward Bing's burrow on the far side of Thimble Down. Behind him, the motley gang of Mungo, Dorro, Farroot, and Bill Thistle ran in his wake, huffing and panting, the barman bringing up the rear. Within a few minutes, they had arrived at site of the alleged break-in. Bing and Farroot lived on the wrong side of the village in a shabby conglomeration of hillock-houses and lean-tos near the road that ran north to Upper-Down and West Upper-Down. It was called Fell's Corner. For many in this neighborhood, the general squalor of their homes was balanced by the fact that it wasn't far from the Hanging Stoat—indeed, many were among Mungo's best customers.

As they drew up to the front door, Sheriff Forgo could indeed see that something was amiss. The door was swinging on its hinges, the breeze causing it to creak evilly. One of Bing's windows was also broken, but Forgo didn't know if that was new or something the Halfling never got around to fixing. "You three," he said, gesturing at Farroot, Bill, and Dorro, "stay here and keep quiet. As for you, Mungo, you're my deputy, so watch my back as I enter. I'll go first. If there's trouble and I go down, you'll need to jump the wrong-doers and tie 'em up."

Of course, the look on Mungo's face told a completely different story. If there was going to be trouble, he'd promptly high-tail it out of Bing's burrow and back to the Hanging Stoat, just as fast as his short, stubby legs would carry him. He was beginning to deeply regret this deputy nonsense. What was he thinking? But for the sake of his feeble pride, he'd follow the Sheriff through the entrance.

The two Halflings entered into the burrow, while the three others waited outdoors. Dorro had nothing to say to Farroot and Bill, both of whom he figured were miscreants in one way or another, so he just looked up in the air. They, meanwhile, regarded the bookmaster as a snob who could use a good beating one of these days. In some ways, they were both right. But suddenly the tense quiet was broken by a scream. The door flung open and deputy Mungo ran out the door, sweating and gibbering about something. *"Buh...gasp...evil...knife...DEAD!"* And then the deputy of Thimble Down promptly fainted in a heap of blubber.

A half second later, Sheriff Forgo emerged from the gloom, and casually eyed his unconscious, and soon-to-be-fired, deputy. "It's a bad business. Mr. Farroot. It's my sad duty to inform you that your brother is dead." Both Farroot and Bill Thistle looked genuinely shocked and pale.

"Bing is lying in one of your back bedrooms, face-down on the floor. His head is all stoved in. And I found this sticking out of his back." Forgo opened his hand and showed the three Halflings a small knife about seven inches long. It was ornately decorated on its bone haft, while the silvery blade was crusted with something thick and oozing. Remnants of Bing's blood and tissue.

"I don't suppose any of you know what these letters and artsy things mean," said the Sheriff, eying the unimpressive trio in front of him.

Dorro, however, responded instantly. "Indeed, I do recognize these figures—I'm not the village bookmaster for nothing, my dear Sheriff."

Forgo merely grunted a *harumph*, but Dorro puffed out his chest for a brief lecture. "These letters are composed in a type of calligraphy that is quite unique. They are runes, which by themselves aren't particularly unique to us scholars of the ancient world, but when combined with this kind of imagery," He pointed to the finely etched trees, stars, and flowers on the bone haft, "there can be only one explanation."

"Well?"

"This isn't a Halfling creation. It's from a forge in the east." Forgo and two others behind him still looked befuddled.

"Sheriff—this is an elf's blade."

☆ ☆ ☆

For a moment, Sheriff Forgo just stared at Dorro, his mouth hanging open as he processed the information. "I guess we shouldn't be surprised. Only a fool would try to pull one over on an elf. An elf warrior, no less. Bing was crazy to think he'd get away with it. And now ..." He trailed off.

There was a sound behind them. Mungo sat up, "Wot 'appened?"

"Get up, you buffoon!" snarled the Sheriff. "Run as fast as you can and fetch Nurse Pym, or find yourself back at your crummy tavern, a lowly bar keep." While that thought actually sounded wonderful to Mungo, he figured he'd keep Forgo happy for another few hours before returning to his beloved Hanging Stoat.

"Yessir!" Mungo jumped up and toddled off toward the center of the village, where Nurse Pym practiced. Not more than twenty minutes later, deputy Mungo returned with the healer of Thimble Down. Actually, Pym arrived on the scene first, with Mungo laboring up the lane after her.

"What is yon problem, Sheriff?"

"Didn't Mungo explain the situation?"

"No, he just banged on my door and then spent about a minute panting and gibbering like a troll. Then he trotted off in this direction. That could only mean trouble at Bing Rumple's burrow."

"Well," noted the Sheriff, "At least we have one intelligent Halfling in this village," shooting Mungo a baleful glance.

"Without further fanfare, Nurse Pym, I must inform you that Bing Rumple is dead and his corpus lies within this burrow-hold. As our healer, I need you to examine the body and make an official report to me and the Mayor."

Nurse Pym stood there with a blank look on her face. Forgo wasn't sure if she was in shock, but added, "Of course, you'll be compensated for your time."

"Why didn't you say so? Now, where's the corpus?" When it came to death, Pym had no sentiment. She had attended hundreds of births, deaths, and everything in between, including a handful of grisly murders.

"Follow me. And you there, Winderiver, you come too. You will be the Nurse's witness."

Flustered, Dorro had little choice but to follow Sheriff Forgo and Nurse Pym into the hillock-house, leaving Farroot Rumple, Bill Thistle, and, sitting on the grass in a heap, an exhausted Mr. Mungo. A crowd was growing, too. While Fell's Corner saw its fair share of crime, this Halfling neighborhood didn't get a murder every day. It was as good an excuse as any for a public gathering and, later, the inevitable drinking party.

Dorro, however, was not enjoying the moment. A shiver ran down his neck the moment he stepped into Bing and Farroot's home. Nearly every piece of furniture, cheap and tawdry as it was, had been smashed to smithereens. Cabinets had been ripped apart and there was food and clothing tossed everywhere. To Dorro, it looked like a fire, a riot, a flood, and violent warfare had occurred all at once.

"Follow me," said Forgo, as he headed down a hallway toward the back of burrow. He stopped at the second bedroom to the right and stood aside to let Nurse Pym in. "Remember, this is a place of criminal activity. Only touch what is necessary. And for Borgo's sake, Winderiver, stop looking like you're about to wet your breeches."

With that, Dorro thrust his nose into the air and followed Pym into the room. He nearly wretched, however, as the smell of death filled his nostrils. Behind him, Forgo smiled at the bookmaster's reaction. Still, he knew how useful Dorro Fox Winderiver could be in an investigation.

Brave, he was not, but the Halfling had an eye for detail unmatched in the village, if not the entire county.

Trying to be as professional as possible, Pym noted, "Well, aye, Bing's dead." Forgo rolled his eyes and thought, *the knife hole in his back must have given it away.*

While hardly thin, the nurse was still quite agile and quickly crouched by his body. To her left, Dorro began making observations. Bing was lying face-down, as the Sheriff had noted. There were not, however, signs of a tremendous scuffle in here, nothing like the wreckage in the front parlor and kitchen. No, the bedroom was almost serene and Dorro made a mental note of this fact. The bed was unmade, but he figured that someone like Bing Rumple never made his bed. In fact, aside from the dead body on the floor, this looked like a rather typical Halfling bedroom.

Pym continued examining Bing's body. "This is a wee puzzle, Sheriff. I mean ..." she scratched the back of her substantial neck. "Rumple died from a blow to the head," she said, gesturing to the bloody, red welt on his left temple. "It was from a hard object. Heavier than a stick—more like a rock, a bar of some metal alloy or," eying the thick, eighteen-inch maple staff on Sheriff Forgo's belt, "something like yon cudgel."

The lawman blanched and issued a quick "harumph!" before Nurse Pym continued.

"In any case, Bing died instantly and, I'd guess, never knew what hit him." She then tried to move his arms and legs, but they were just beginning to stiffen. "I estimate that he's been dead a good three or four hours. But no longer, I'll warrant."

"The comical thing is" Pym chuckled to herself, much to the horror of Dorro, "this knife stuck in his back. Well, truth is, someone stabbed Bing—*after* he was dead."

"What?" The Sheriff was clearly rattled. "That's absurd."

"That's the thing, Forgo, it is absurd. The knife is almost theatrical in nature. Whoever killed Bing simply coshed him on the head. But they wanted to make a point and so thrust this silver blade into his aft ribs. Granted, it's a serious injury, but without the head wound, Bing might be in my hospice recovering, instead of staring at the floor. It's uncanny."

Bizarre, indeed, thought Dorro. *So who would want to make a point about killing Bing Rumple. Certainly the knife is very damning.*

"Him's been murdered by elves," trumpeted the Sheriff, "That's plain as day. Bing stole their brooch, so they claimed their revenge. That ferocious Toldir and his troupe hid out for him after breakfast and invaded the burrow. They smashed the joint up looking for their Telstar brooch, but when they didn't find it, they took repayment the only way they knew how, by conking him on the noggin and sticking him with this strange knife. Savage, willful murder."

"But Sheriff," chimed Dorro for the first time, "Why did the elves only destroy the front of Bing's burrow and not these rear bedrooms? Seems illogical. Why not search the entire house?"

"Uh, maybe they gave up the search and just wanted blood? I wouldn't put it past them, especially the way that giant elf Baldar threatened to slice my throat this morning."

"'Tis true, Mr. Dorro," added Nurse Pym. "I heard from three Halflings this morning, all of whom heard the big elf make this very threat. These are dangerous creatures, to be sure."

Dorro wasn't convinced. He didn't doubt that the hunters had threatened Forgo, but he didn't think of elves as bloodthirsty killers. Then again, he could be wrong. And if he was, the elves were still lingering on the edge of Thimble Down and could strike again. Especially if their brooch still hadn't been recovered. He didn't envy the Halfling who possessed this treasure. It was a trinket that could cost him—or her—their very life, just as it had cost Bing's his.

✫ ✫ ✫

Shortly thereafter, Nurse Pym finished up her examination and informed the Sheriff it would take her a day to analyze her findings. At that point, she'd made an official report to him and the Mayor.

As for Bing Rumple's body, there wouldn't be much of a funeral. Most Halflings liked to bury their dear ones in the Great Wood, as there was something about this enchanted area that provided solace to grieving families. After a few years, family members would often venture back into the woods on a Saturday and point to a young elm or oak, saying, "Hey, that's my late Uncle Ernie! He's come back as a fine sapling." Halflings were fond of thinking that death was merely the beginning of life again.

As for Bing, his funeral would be just like his life—cheap and miserable. As with most low-lifes and strangers in Thimble Down, his corpus would be covered in thick burlap by his family and his legs and arms then bound in rope. Most likely, his brother Farroot and Bill Thistle would carry the body into the woodlands and bury it as quickly as possible. Then they'd return to the Hanging Stoat and hoist a few tankards in memory of good ol' Bing. A few visitors might join them in the toast, but in general, the Rumples were not a popular family, and this particular one was the bottom of the heap. One would be hard-pressed to find any Halfling that would miss Bing Rumple.

Which, as Dorro later mused, was particularly odd.

13
Wyll's Grievous Mistake

heriff Forgo and Dorro walked back into the heart of the village after one last look around Bing's tragic burrow, both of them depressed and exhausted. Like any good Thimble Downers, both gents had only one thing on their mind at this critical juncture—lunch! It was well past the noontime luncheon, drawing closer to 2 o'clock, which was unthinkable to a Halfling of any intelligence. Half crazed with hunger and their stomachs gurgling up a storm, Forgo and Dorro slumped into Mr. Millin Parffin's family tavern on the main lane through the village, the Bumbling Badger. They didn't even peruse the chalk-drawn menu on the wall. Forgo just yelled, "Feed us! Now!"

Within a few seconds, several members of the Parffin family, including many of their eleven children, swarmed into the room, all bearing ciders, fresh seeded bread and butter, fruit, nuts, and a creamed dandelion soup as the appetizer course. For the first five minutes or so, neither Forgo nor Dorro had any clue what was happening around them. Really, there's nothing more scientifically intriguing than the feeding habits of a hungry, full-grown Halfling, especially since many of their external receptors become muted and all their intense power of concentration become focused on what's in front of them. Namely, food.

Feeling the blood lust of lunch upon him, Dorro grabbed a piece of bread, smelled its fragrant, thick hard crust, and tore off a chunk. He quickly smeared it in rich dairy butter and crammed it in his mouth. It was gone in a flash. Forgo kept pace by grabbing his tankard of golden apple cider and taking a lusty throat full. Then he ate a pear in four bites, and began guzzling the soup right out of the bowl, no spoon necessary. Dorro was about to grab his own soup when one of the Parffin children showed up bearing two cold roast chickens and laid them in front of the two eaters.

Briefly eying each other, Forgo and Dorro respectively tore into these paragons of poultry, ripping them into tasty sections and stuffing the savory meat in their mouths. They were ravenous and made enough noise to wake the dead. There were bits of meat, bone, marrow, and skin flying everywhere; off to the side of the room, Mr. Parffin knew it would take at least an hour to clean up after these two.

Twenty minutes later, it was all over. Forgo leaned his head onto the table and contentedly began to snore. His was the sleep of the happy, stuffed, and satiated. Dorro, meanwhile, decided to postpone his nap and have a leisurely smoke from his clay pipe, which he always kept in his jacket. He stuffed a wad of tobacco weed (Old Nob's Finest, his favorite variety) into the chamber, and ignited it off the candle in front of him. Dorro drew on the mouthpiece for a few seconds before getting his first mouthful of smoke. Between the bread, chicken, and this pipe, Dorro Fox Winderiver was beginning to feel like himself again. He sighed with pleasure and began fishing into his vest pocket for silver coins to pay for this heavenly feast.

This feeling of contentment wouldn't last long.

Dorro finally rose from the table, after giving Sheriff Forgo a gentle elbow to get moving. The lawman snorted loudly, realized where he was, and rose from the table as if he had never nodded off. With some relief, he noted that Dorro had paid for lunch, but threw a few pennies on the table to appear generous. (To be fair, the job of sheriff paid poorly, something both Halflings understood.)

They stepped out into the sunny afternoon sky, with the traders and villagers of Thimble Down bustling around them. It was a market day, so many folk from the outlying farms and other villages like Water-Down and Nob had streamed into town that morning to buy and sell their wares and produce. The central location of Thimble Down made it a perfect location for a farmers market and the resulting throngs were proof. There were literally hundreds of Halflings filling the streets and lanes of the village. Checking that Tom had been fed some nice dry oats and a bucket of water, Forgo grabbed the pony's reins and steered him in the direction of the gaol.

"I'm a Halfling of my word, Winderiver, and as such, we shall free your boy. I see no reason to keep him in my custody. He looked fine this morning before I headed off, but no doubt, some fresh air would do him good. Shouldn't keep a healthy lad all locked up," said Forgo, silently acknowledging the free lunch he had just received, too. The two turned the corner and headed toward the gaol, where young Wyll Underfoot was waiting in his cell. But upon getting closer to the building, the Sheriff felt some unease. This was usually the point where there'd be a mob or someone running toward him with a panicked look on their face. But this was different—the lane in front of the gaol was empty and there was no one around.

"What on earth is the matter, Sheriff? Your face looks grave."

"Somethin' ain't right, my friend. T'ain't right at all!"

Forgo reached the aging, plaster-and-timber building and stepped through the front door. There was absolute silence within. His years as a lawman had enabled him to sense when another creature was about—a hint of breathing, the slight scuffle of a foot movement. Forgo heard nothing. And when he and Dorro stepped further into the gaol, they saw something else.

The door to Wyll's cell was open. And the boy was gone.

A look of disappointment showed on the sheriff's face, while Dorro felt like crying inside. "The prisoner's escaped, Winderiver. He must have figured a way to jigger the lock with his breakfast spoon or some other implement. Indeed, young Mr. Underfoot is really in the soup now."

"Maybe he just stepped out for some fresh air," offered Dorro with a forced smile, but he knew it was a pathetic attempt. Wyll had not only escaped, but he had run away from Dorro as well. He was crushed.

"When we catch up to that scallywag, he will be put under 24-hour guard and held over for trial in front of the magistrate, the Mayor," said Forgo. "And if I have my way, he'll be found guilty."

"But Sheriff, he clearly didn't kill Bing Rumple. He was in gaol at the time!"

"I'm well aware of that, Winderiver. I checked your boy after breakfast, by which time Bing was already a corpus. But his escape is proof of another crime. No two ways about it—he stole the elves' brooch, the Telstar. And now that he's fled, he's gone to where he hid it and will be far down the road by now. My guess is that we'll never see that youngling again."

Dorro was shattered. He had so believed in Wyll Underfoot's story. Had he really been that gullible? The bookmaster had trusted Wyll's tale and was hopeful this could have been a new chapter in both their lives. But it wasn't to be—the lad was gone and the evidence was grim. Dorro realized that he'd been played for a fool.

A few hours earlier, Dorro felt that he'd played the sheriff like a fiddle and was neatly engineering Wyll's release. But now the last string on the fiddle broke and, standing next to the sheriff, he quietly began to cry.

You're nothing but an old fool, Dorro, he scolded himself. *You should be ashamed!*

✲ ✲ ✲

Outside the gaol, the sun was busy warming the earth, and spring flowers of yellow, pink, and periwinkle-blue were popping all over the lanes and fields of Thimble Down. Robins, catbirds, and chickadees could be heard chattering overhead, while the oak, maple, and crabapple trees were begin to leaf out for the long Summer ahead. It couldn't have been a more perfect Spring day.

And yet, Dorro Fox Winderiver couldn't have been more miserable.

He stepped out of the gaol and headed for home. Maybe while puttering around the Perch a flash of inspiration would strike him, a way to figure out this debacle. But then again, he realized, Wyll was probably miles away by now. Furthermore, the boy was a thief and now an escaped prisoner—there wasn't much Dorro could do for him anymore. Even with his best thinking, Wyll had broken many laws and was in great trouble.

Fifteen minutes later he arrived at his hillock, and stood in his front garden, looking at the immense view of the River Thimble and waiting for something, anything to come to him. "Think, Dorro!" he cried out loud, "Think of something. You've never frozen up before. Come on, man, think!"

He stared blankly at the river. "Mr. Dorro!" It was a loud whisper, coming from his left. He peered around and saw nothing.

"Mr. Dorro, *please!*"

The bookmaster knew that voice. "Wyll! Wyll, boy—where are you?" Dorro turned toward his garden shed when the door flung suddenly flew open and out ran the youngling, straight into his arms.

The two hugged and cried for several long minutes. "I knew it! I knew they were wrong about you!" said the bookmaster, finally looking at Wyll and tousling his messy yellow hair. The boy smiled. "But you are also a scamp and in some real trouble. Why did you run away? The Sheriff was just about to release you when we discovered you had fled."

"I'm sorry, but I was scared. I can't catch a break, so I thought it was best for me to go back on the road and fend for myself," said Wyll. "I didn't know you were coming—I thought you had given me up!"

"Yes, that was my fault and I apologize. But now we must go back and tell the Sheriff you were scared and confused, and receive your just lumps."

"No, sir, please, NO! I can't go back!"

Dorro looked at the boy sternly. "There's one other idea, but it's not a very good one. You can continue to hide in the shed for a day or two, while I work on the murder of Bing Rumple."

"Who? And what murder?"

"Nevermind boy; it has nothing to do with you. But can you swear to me you didn't steal anything from someone named Bing Rumple?"

"Who? I mean, I only ever stole your apples and cheese, Mr. Dorro, and only because I was starving. I swear it, I do!" pleaded Wyll.

Dorro exhaled loudly, as if a huge burden had been lifted from his shoulders. "I knew it, lad—I knew it all along."

Just then, Dorro heard a squeal behind and saw a flurry of yellow hair and smiling teeth flying at him and the boy. It was Cheeryup. "You found him, Mr. Dorro! You found him! Hurrah!" She squeezed the both of them and shed a tear or two herself. It was a moment of great joy.

"Listen children, especially you, Cheeryup. It is imperative that we keep Wyll's hiding place a secret. If he is found, we could all find ourselves in gaol, and no amount of pleading to Sheriff Forgo would do anything about that. Do you hear me, girl?"

"Yes, Mr. Dorro, I promise not a word. And I will bring Wyll food every day."

"If anyone asks, say you're helping me plant rows of peas, lettuce, spinach, and kale, as I'm so busy these days," said Dorro. "That will take you in and out of the garden shed many times without anyone asking questions. And, of course, while you're there, I'd appreciate it if you really would help me plant my seeds. I'm awfully busy these days!"

He smiled. "And of course, I will pay you for your labors, my dear."

"Agreed," said Cheeryup in her most solemn, lady-of-business voice, shaking Dorro's hand. Then they all began giggling and ran to the shed to put their plan into action.

14
The Pot Begins to Boil

*W*hile the three conspirators were still at the Perch and hatching their plans, things were heating up in the village. No question, the peaceful, quiet streets, market and shops of Thimble Down were becoming explosive. Word of Bing Rumple's murder spread up and down the lanes like a pack of ravenous Halflings at an open buffet. By four o'clock, everyone in the village knew of the tragedy and many had come outside to gossip with their neighbors about it.

"Bing was murdered by the elf warriors! They've gone on a murderous rampage, and we're next!"

"No, you dashed fool. 'Twas that boy who stole the brooch. The little rat stabbed poor Bing right in the back when he wasn't looking."

"I 'eard it was neither. There were strangers in the woods—probably goblins—and they bashed Rumple's bean in with rocks and clubs!"

The crowd gasped with horror, and began spinning ever wilder and more ridiculous stories. By the time Sheriff Forgo arrived in the center of the market, along with the Mayor and Osgood Thrip, Thimble Down was on the verge of sheer pandemonium.

"CALM DOWN, THAT'S AN ORDER!" roared Forgo, waving his cudgel high in the air. His face was beet red and his commendable belly was shaking all over the place. "WE WILL HAVE PEACE OR I'LL ARREST THE LOT OF YOU!"

Most citizens in the town did a quick calculation and realized that if they were arrested, they'd probably miss supper and thus simmered down instantly. A quiet gripped the mob, aside from the sound of someone's stomach rumbling at the thought of missing dinner.

Forgo put his foot in the stirrup and hoisted his bulk onto Tom's back. The creature almost visibly grimaced. "Now if the lot of you shut up, I'll give you the latest news."

The Halflings of Thimble Down stared at Forgo in rapt attention.

"It is true, Bing Rumple is dead." There was a gasp from the crowd and hushed whisperings from all around the Sheriff.

"Ah, Bing was a good lad. Everyone liked him and he was cheerful to the end."

"Poor boy—such a helpful fellow and always a kind word on his lips."

"Mr. Rumple was a model citizen. Never had a drink or a vice in 'is whole life!"

Forgo rolled his eyes, comparing what he was hearing to the mean, drunken sot that Bing Rumple was in true life. While he loved his fellow Thimble Downers, truly, they were as dumb as sheep. (Which, he further realized, was a gross insult to sheep everywhere.)

"Simmer down, folks! Let me continue." The crowd shut up yet again. "At eleven o'clock this morning, a search party consisting of myself, deputy Mungo, and Dorro the bookmaster, as well as the victim's brother and friend, descended on the Rumple hillock-house. There, we found the domicile to be in almost complete ruination. And in a rear bedroom, we found the lifeless corpus of Mr. Bing Rumple." More gasps from the crowd ensued.

"After a thorough examination by Nurse Pym a short while later, we determined that Bing had been murdered by Halfling, or Halflings, unknown."

"What about them elves?" shouted someone in the crowd.

Not wishing to start a riot, the Sheriff replied, "We are examining all possibilities, Bosco—I'd know your troublemaking voice anywhere, so keep it shut!"

"Go get 'em, Bosco, me boy-o!" laughed someone in the crowd.

"Oy Bosco—give 'em 'ell!" giggled another.

Forgo closed his eyes for a minute, trying to keep himself from bashing someone's head in. "But right now, this public assembly is at an end. By order of the Mayor, I hereby order this mob to disperse. And if you don't, I may start crackin' heads!" The crowd grumbled loudly, but few made any attempts to leave. Always fast on his feet, the Sheriff continued, "And by further order of the Mayor, all pubs and taverns may open early tonight. And by early, I mean right now!"

There was huge cheer from the people and suddenly the Thimble Downers broke off in a dozen different directions, heading for their favorite pub and a pint of beer, cider, or perhaps a small glass of mead or honeygrass whiskey. Forgo, meanwhile, rubbed his hands together at another job well done, while the Mayor and Osgood Thrip tried to look innocuous, knowing full-well that Forgo had just saved their skins. Again.

✲ ✲ ✲

The following morning, Sheriff Forgo returned to the gaol, a little worse for wear after a few long days and few too many glasses of the honeygrass himself last night. Certainly, he deserved it, but was hoping for a quiet morning as he gathered his thoughts for the investigation into Bing Rumple's death. As he turned the lane leading to gaol, however, he saw his first problem of the day. As it turned out, it would be the first of many.

There, standing in front of the gaol and clearly inspecting the shrubbery (of which he no doubt had an opinion), was Dorro Fox Winderiver. Honestly, the Sheriff felt he'd seen enough of the bookmaster in the past day or two. No, he didn't dislike the Halfling, but Winderiver was a different sort from himself—a prickly, smarty-pants, loner type. Not the sort Forgo would like to sit in a tavern and share a pint and a bawdy joke with. Winderiver was the sort who liked to sip tea while staring at trees and thinking way too much about everything. At least the oddball enjoyed fishing—now that was something the two had in common.

They also had another thing in common—murder.

They had worked on a few cases together, thefts and even the odd floating body in the river (usually a trader from up north who'd lost his footing on a raft), but the death of Bing Rumple was in a whole new league. This was cold-hearted murder, and the culprit was either someone who lived in Thimble Down or, worse, one of those elves, any one of whom could skewer the Sheriff for breakfast. As for the Halfling in front of him, Forgo didn't need Winderiver's help, he boasted to himself, but yes, he could admit that at the times the bookmaster could be extremely useful. *Navigate this carefully, Forgo, me boy*, he chided inwardly. *Get Winderiver to use his brain cells to help crack this caper, but make sure he reports directly to you and you only.*

"Why, Dorro, me ol' mate," said Sheriff Forgo, a bit too cheerfully. "Errr, what brings you to our fair gaol on this lovely morning?"

The bookmaster looked up at the increasingly cloudy sky and cocked an eyebrow—the Sheriff never called him "Dorro." Ever. *What was the Sheriff up to?* he wondered. "My dear Sheriff, we have unfinished business. I know that you're still cross at young Wyll Underfoot's escape, but I truly feel there's more to this story and that the boy is innocent. Furthermore, we have the Rumple matter to attend to ..."

"Well now, Dorro, me pal," Forgo interrupted. "Let's not worry about the lad. He's twenty miles away by now and hiding in someone's barn loft. Trust me, we'll never see his likes again—I've seen a hundred younglings like him before. Eventually, he'll find a little village and a nice girl, and calm down. Who knows? Maybe he'll even find work and lead a respectable life after all. It's happened before."

"But Sheriff..."

Forgo jumped in again, "Now as to the murder of Bing, that's a trickier fish. You've been very useful to me in the past and, naturally, the Mayor and good people of Thimble Down appreciate it 'n' all. I'm closing in on the culprit myself, but if you have a few minutes, we could use a little of your inestimable help."

Of course, the Sheriff had no idea who the murderer was, but no point letting Winderiver know that.

"Well, Sheriff, if you could use my modest talents, you shall have them, of course. What would you like me to do?"

Thinking fast, Forgo spouted, "We need you to interview some of the suspects. I'd start with Farroot Rumple and his strange compatriot, Mr. Bill Thistle. Also poke around the Hanging Stoat for information. You might also talk to Dalbo Dall—he's crazy as a canary, but he hears lots of things. However, it's important that you bring all the information to me, so I can use it to build the larger investigation."

To Dorro, it sounded like Forgo wanted him to do most of the legwork, while he sat on his duff at the gaol and smoked his pipe. In other words, the way things usually worked. But as usual, Dorro also had plans of his own and certainly would not inform the Sheriff of these machinations.

"Why certainly, Sheriff Forgo, I'll only be too delighted to assist you in any way I can. I can speak for everyone in Thimble Down in saying that we know we're in your good hands and that you'll find the devil who killed Bing in jig time."

"And you'll report with any information you gather?"

"Of course, Sheriff. I'll report in daily, per your instructions."

With that, the Halflings exchanged stiff, affected smiles and bid each other a good day. Both, however, realized something else: *The investigation had just begun.*

15
Fishing for Answers

<hr />

s usual, when Dorro had thinking to do, he headed for the river. Somehow, watching the currents and eddies of the River Thimble calmed his mind and opened up fresh avenues for thought and inquiry. This time, he made a brief stop at the Perch and grabbed his fishing pole. Dorro often did his best thinking with a line in the water.

He scrambled down to one of his favorite spots, near a huge willow tree whose roots loved being in the deep, dark, wet earth by the river. This was Dorro's first time fishing this Spring and he hoped the trout might already be moving to the warmer water along the river's edge to start breeding. And with the skies still cloudy, it was prime fishing weather, whatever the season.

"I'm baaack, my pretties!" Dorro chimed as he made his first cast, using a long bamboo pole with a simple, but effective reel crafted by the village metalsmith, Mr. Timmo. It held a very thin twine that was waxed to prevent tangles and allowed him make accurate casts of thirty feet or more. It was easily the finest fishing pole and tackle in all of Thimble Down and was worth every piece of silver he paid for it.

Dorro put a worm on the end of the hook and attached a cork bobber that allowed the line to float quietly about twenty feet off the river bank. Every few seconds he gave the line a minute jiggle, making the worm appear to be a small wounded fish, one that would attract a bigger fish.

"Now there's a thought," he said out loud. "If some-one killed Bing because he had a small treasure, could I catch the culprit if the murderer thought I had a bigger treasure?"

Almost on cue, Dorro's bobber disappeared from the surface and he felt a mighty tug on his pole. "Fish on!" shouted the angler, as he began to battle with his silver, shimmering adversary. The fish tried a variety of tricks to rid himself of the hook—it dived, swerved, and even tried to tangle up the line around a dead tree branch under the water's surface. But still, Dorro held on, slowly coaxing the fish to shore. Finally the creature broke the surface with a mighty jump. It was a giant rainbow trout, fighting for its freedom.

Inch by inch, Dorro brought in his catch, until, its energy spent, the fish resigned itself to its fate and gave up.

The bookmaster-turned-angler lifted the beautiful trout from the water and admired its colors, lines, and fiery spirit. Yet he had captured the trout and now held its life in his very hands.

"As much as I'd like to see you on my dinner plate tonight, my fishy foe, I have too many appointments today and not enough time to prepare you for the frying pan," said Dorro to the gasping trout in his hands. He reached into its mouth and quickly popped the hook out. Then he gently put the fish back in the water and stroked its body while the water's current refilled its gills and lungs. In a flash, the trout bolted and disappeared back into the cool depths of the River Thimble. Dorro smiled.

"Enjoy your freedom, Mr. Trout. But there's someone else I'd like to catch on a hook, and when I do, he won't get away so easily," said Dorro aloud, gazing out over the river. "Thank you for the lesson, my scaly friend."

"Now all I need is a big, juicy worm."

✵ ✵ ✵

Newly energized, Dorro sprung up the hill to the Perch and tossed his fishing pole into a corner of the shed. He felt ready to launch his own investigation into Bing Rumple's death, but needed a little help first, and for that, he returned to the library. In truth, Dorro had neglected his place of employment for several days now and felt that he needed to check in.

Thankfully, among Thimble Down's residents was a scribe-for-hire, one whom Dorro would periodically hire to run the library while he was off on an "adventure." A slight, somewhat stooped fellow, the Halfling's name was Bedminster Shoe, and he was a capable-enough fellow of letters. He was quite able to manage the building, its collection, and the needs of its users. Shoe was also terribly fascinated with Dorro's investigations, which flattered the bookmaster to no end. In fact, the scribe often rambled on about publishing a work about his detecting work, which seemed patently absurd. But no matter, figured Dorro—Bedminster Shoe was both reliable and eager for a few coins to make his time worthwhile. It was a perfectly serviceable arrangement.

When Dorro arrived at the library some fifteen minutes later, he strolled through the front door and, sure enough, there was Shoe, helping Mrs. Flim find the perfect book to help improve her garden yields this Summer. (Apparently, she had run out of jarred string beans and beets in mid-February, and had still not forgiven herself for this grievous transgression.)

"G'day, Mr. Dorro, sir," said Bedminster Shoe, as Mrs. Flim trotted off to the stack containing all books, pamphlets, and scrolls related to raising string beans and beets. "Are you back for good or do you need my services a while longer?"

"Ah, Mr. Shoe, if I could prevail on you for a few more days, that would be most helpful," said Dorro, counting out a few coins on the countertop. "My, um, business activities will take me elsewhere for a while."

"Oh, are we detecting, Mr. Dorro? If so, may I prevail to interview you and the principals in this case once it's completed? I'd sincerely like to document it for my ongoing research."

As much as Dorro appreciated Bedminster Shoe's library help, he didn't know quite what to make of his "research" and inquisitive nature. But no matter, the bookmaster thought, I don't have time for re-shelving this week's books, and Mr. Shoe is more than willing to keep the place going for a few days. But Bedminster wasn't the Halfling he was looking for.

"Of course you may interview me down the road. But say, Mr. Shoe, is Cheeryup here today? I have some special duties for her."

Not fooled a jot, Bedminster replied, "Of course, Mr. Dorro, she's up in the gallery, cleaning up a mess behind one of the racks." Shoe knew all too well that Dorro was on a new case. He'd keep his ears and eyes open for details to use in his inevitable case study.

Dorro, meanwhile climbed the wide oak ladder—almost stairs really—into the gallery, the same ones where just a few days ago he'd come face-to-face with a rather terrifying dormouse. But the fewer people who knew about that, the better. "Cheeryup? Cheeryup—are you here?"

"Yessir, Mr. Dorro!"

She had quietly approached him from the other side of the gallery and thus he had not seen her. And once again, Dorro had a terrible fright at the top of the ladder, almost as bad as the dormouse! (Maybe we need proper stairs, he thought briefly, and more mousetraps!)

"Ah, girl, glad to find you. Have you, ahem, 'weeded my garden' today?" Dorro asked, winking clumsily. "I'm sure it will need an even bigger weeding tomorrow."

"Why of course, sir. I spent a good hour up there this morning, weeding and *feeding* your new plant. It won't be hungry for a good while yet."

"Capital news, Cheeryup! I'm glad you're nourishing my garden regularly. Do you, perchance, have time for additional duties? I am delving into the matter of the unfortunate Mr. Rumple and may well have need for another set of hands. Naturally, there is remuneration involved, to cover your time and expenses."

"Oh yes, Mr. Dorro, I shall report for duty when summoned!"

"Good to hear, he noted, lowering his voice to a whisper, "For the moment, however, please continue feeding my garden and helping Mr. Shoe run the library. But I feel that I shall be needing your help sooner rather than later."

With that, Dorro descended from the gallery and left the library, thanking Bedminster Shoe on the way out for his time and efforts. *A good scribe and scholar*, he mused, *though a tad eccentric*. Which, of course, was the pot calling the kettle black.

☆ ☆ ☆

Dorro's next stop was the Hanging Stoat, where he hoped he could catch up with Farroot and Bill Thistle and ask them about their activities over the previous few days. Naturally, he'd buy them a few stouts or ales as a courtesy. There were few regulars at the tavern that would turn down a pint for a bit of light conversation.

As it turned out, when Dorro was getting toward the middle of Thimble Down, once again a mob was brewing. In their midst stood several tall, fierce-looking creatures. The elves were back and they did not look happy. And the big one in the front was having a tense conversation with Sheriff Forgo.

"So the thief would stole our brooch is dead, you say," said Toldir gravely, without any trace of remorse or pity.

"Mr. Rumple was murdered yesterday," replied Sheriff Forgo. "Whether he was a thief or not remains unproven."

"He was a thief and deserved to die."

"So you admit you murdered him."

Toldir bent over and pulled his face as close to Forgo's as one would wish and stared him straight in the eyes. "We are Woodland elves, hunters, and soldiers of honor. Perhaps your miserable Halfling race stoops to the shame of murder, but not elves. However, if you ever deign to accuse me of murder again, I might make an exception—especially if my victim was a dim-witted Halfling like *you*. Do you understand me, friend?"

"Err, why of course, Mr. Toldir," said Forgo, trying to look anywhere but into Toldir's blazing blue eyes. "I must have misunderstood you there for a moment."

Suddenly, another voice was heard in the rising din. It was from Baldar, a big, younger elf in the pack. "... he deserved to die, this Ring Bumple. I do not regret his death."

Forgo was now thoroughly confused. Was *this* elf admitting to the murder? But he remembered Toldir's threat and wasn't about to accuse another elf. Things were getting heated.

"Sheriff, you need to tell the elf what you found at the crime scene," yapped Osgood Thrip, who always seemed to be lingering on the edge of trouble spots. "Tell him now!"

Forgo grimaced and looked sideways at Thrip, quietly wishing he could punch Thimble Down's wealthiest citizen right in the nose.

"Mr. Thrip has a point there, Toldir. In actuality, we did find something interesting at the crime scene. Sticking out of victim's back was, in fact, a blade. It was a silver knife with a bone handle." Forgo noticed that the elf's eyes were becoming wider as he pulled the blade from his pocket.

"We brought it to our learned bookmaster, who examined the ornamentation, specifically the carved flowers, trees, and stars on this beautiful handle."

"My knife! It has been missing for months," fumed Baldar, the younger elf.

"Therein lies the problem, Toldir. We found your kinsman's knife in Bing Rumple's back."

Suddenly the crowd swelled around Forgo and the elves, and broke into an uproar.

"There's yer murderers, Sheriff! Arrest 'em!

"How could they kill poor, sweet Mr. Rumple?"

"Only a cold-hearted elf could commit an atrocity like this in Thimble Down."

At this, both Toldir and Baldar rose to their full heights, well over six feet tall, as did their elvish companions. More, they each clasped their weapons, slightly drawing swords from their scabbards or gently pulling an arrow from its quiver and fitting it to the bowstring. The elves knew when violence was about to happen and how to get in proper fighting position. Unfortunately, the Halflings of Thimble Down did *not*, and figured that their ranks could easily overpower a half dozen elves, which was patently untrue. In fact, this mob had no idea how close they were coming to a bloody and tragic encounter.

"Sheriff Forgo," said Toldir under his breath, but firmly, "I would advise you to disperse this mob. My hunters are deadly fighters. Even a horde of goblins this many wouldn't stand much of a chance against six of our best Woodland fighters. And just to be clear—this is not a threat. It's a simple fact."

Forgo knew how perilous this situation was becoming. To make it worse, just next to him, Osgood Thrip was yelling, "Arrest them, Sheriff! Have you no courage? Maybe we need a new sheriff in Thimble Down!" How dearly would Forgo have liked the elf warriors to rain their fury down on that idiot, Thrip.

He looked back at the elves—Toldir was standing like a statue, but clearly this younger fellow, Baldar, was itching for a fight. You could see it in his eyes. Forgo put his hands on his hips and turned to face the mob.

"SIMMER DOWN, YOU BUNCH OF NITWITS!" bellowed the Sheriff in his loudest voice. Indeed, Forgo's voice had always proved one of the most effective tools in his arsenal. "Now, this is what we're going to do. You're going to go back to your business, while I deal with these here elves. That is, unless you want an elvish arrow in your eye or one of your arms hacked off. Well deary-me, that might ruin your whole day. And it's almost luncheon time. Who wants to eat lunch with an arrow stuck in their eye. Do you Bosco? How about you, Mrs. Pumble?"

Bosco, Mrs. Pumble, and the rest of the Thimble Downers instantly calmed down, at least enough to reconsider subduing six elf warriors. Many realized the Sheriff was quite right—a skirmish right now might certainly affect their enjoyment of lunch and a good nap afterwards. *No*, they collectively thought, *Luncheon with a hacked-off limb would not be enjoyable at all*.

En masse, the once-rowdy crowd ceased their clamoring and heckling and proceeded to back off, quietly slinking off to consider more important matters, such as lunch and the ongoing retention of their limbs. Even the churlish Osgood Thrip slinked off to a dark hole somewhere and, of course, the cowardly Mayor of Thimble Down hadn't even shown up. The crisis passed, but still, many of the Halflings still believed that Toldir or one of his elves had killed Bing Rumple. However, it was the Sheriff's job to deal with that matter—that's what he was paid for.

While the crowd disappeared into the alleys of Thimble Down, Forgo and the elves remained standing in the lane. There was still unfinished business. "Well Sheriff, I am impressed," said Toldir. "On the surface, you seem puny to us, but that was very brave of you, taking on a large mob like that. I suspect that you yourself are a man of honor. Clearly, the Halflings of this village respect you."

Forgo had never considered this before. He'd always just considered himself a common lawman and accepted his lot in life. There were few compliments, no awards, and the pay was lousy; Forgo just figured this is the way it was. Yet here, a strange elf captain had just praised him and the Sheriff felt his heart swell with pride. It was something he'd never felt before.

"Well, err, thank you, Mr. Toldir. Just doing my duty and all that. Nothing to fuss about," said Forgo, almost blushing.

"However, Sheriff, we still have two problems—the Telstar brooch is still missing. And you have Baldar's prized hunting knife. And we won't leave your village until we have them back, no matter the cost."

Forgo thought for a moment and said, "Mr. Elf, sir, give me a few days. By that time, we will have fully conducted our investigation and, in the interim, you can at least have your knife back. As for the brooch, we will continue hunting for it. But it may have been taken many miles away by now and quickly sold for some silver coins and gold."

"For the sake of you and your Halfings, my good Sheriff, let's hope not. Woodland elves are not to be trifled with. We shall return in three days, and when we do, we will search for the brooch, using any means necessary," said Toldir forcefully, leading his band out of the village toward their encampment in the Great Wood.

Forgo gulped. Maybe Toldir hadn't murdered Bing Rumple, but he wondered if Baldar had. And if he did, just how was he going to arrest a deadly elf hunter like that? He gulped again and went off in search of some cold cider and a bit of mutton to quell his queasy stomach.

16
Dorro Investigates

aving witnessed Sheriff Forgo's entire encounter with the rather intimidating elves—
safely hidden, of course, behind a gutter
spout—Dorro finally ventured forth after the mob and
hunters had cleared out. The Sheriff was left standing in
the middle of the lane looking very alone. The bookmaster considered talking to him and praising him on his deft
actions, but quickly changed his mind and shot down a
side alley. He would report back to Forgo later; for now,
he had more important matters to attend to.

Dorro sped southward, away from the center of
Thimble Down and veering toward the western side
of town. He was heading for the Hanging Stoat, where
certain villagers would be gathering for lunch and a beer
before a quiet afternoon at work or, more likely, napping

against a mossy tree. More to the point, he was hoping to catch a few particular folk in the tavern and, for the price of a few pints and perhaps a nice piece of tender, slow-cooked beef brisket, might entice them to share a few secrets. Hopefully, the beverages would suffice, he thought, checking his pocket for coins.

Within five minutes, he had arrived at the Hanging Stoat, and saw its owner Mr. Mungo in his customary position behind the bar. Mungo was a congenial sort who was happiest while pulling brews for the locals and sharing a story or a laugh. Of course, he also moonlighted as Sheriff Forgo's deputy, but as everyone was learning, Mungo was pretty dismal at the job. Though both he and Dorro had been at the scene of Bing's murder just a day or two earlier, for the most part, they just ignored that episode and carried on as normal. Dorro opened the door of the tavern and spied the barkeep right off, "Ah, Mr. Mungo, and how are we today?"

"Much better to be back at the Stoat, doin' what I do best," said the barman cheerfully. "And what can I help you with today, Mr. Dorro? I don't reckon that you come to the Hanging Stoat all too often. If you're hungry, I've been cooking some lamb 'n' turnip stew all morning—it's a keeper!"

"Well yes, I may take you up on that. But I'm just looking for..." Dorro trailed off while scanning the tavern and its patrons. "Yes, that's who I'm looking for. Give me a few minutes, Mungo, and then send Freda over to take our order, if I'm still here."

The bookmaster cautiously wended his way around thickly hewn tables, benches, chairs, many of them filled with the Hanging Stoat's none-too-distinguished clientele. Fortunately, the dim light made many of them hard to recognize and vice-versa, as it wouldn't be too seemly for the bookmaster of Thimble Down to be caught frequenting this particular tavern. Dorro had standards to maintain.

Finally reaching his destination on the far side of the room, Dorro stepped into a shadowy alcove, lit by just a few candles. "A-hem," he coughed. "Good day gentlemen. We meet again."

The two Halflings at the table stopped the quiet conversation and slowly looked up. "Oh, it's you—our very own dandy bookmaster," snorted Farroot Rumple. "Looking for overdue books." At this, his greasy companion Bill Thistle snorted with a suppressed laugh.

"Actually, Farroot, I want to talk about your dead brother."

Both Halflings immediately froze and fixed evil glares on Dorro. "What did you say?"

"You heard me, Farroot. I'm not one to mince words. However, I feel it would be far more pleasant if you allowed me to buy you and your colleague a tasty brown stout or cold cider to slake our thirsts and facilitate the conversation."

Neither Farroot nor Bill had ever turned down a free drink, even from a pesky toad like Dorro Fox Winderiver. Farroot eyeballed Dorro. *He's tall for a Halfling*, thought the surviving Rumple brother, *but he'd go down with just one punch. And I might thoroughly enjoy that.* Bill was thinking the exact same thing.

Thankfully for Dorro, Freda turned up at that very second and took their orders. The barmaid also recited the day's lunch special and, regrettably for Dorro's purse, both Farroot and Bill enthusiastically ordered big bowls of lamb 'n' turnip stew. In this own head, however, Dorro thought to himself, *Eat up, friends. For as they say, there's no such thing as a free lunch. Especially when I'm paying.*

In short order, Freda set a pair of brown ales on the table, a fine example of Mungo's latest batch that he brewed in the back room. It was a thick, malty drink, with deep amber coloring, a hint of hops and herbs, and good frothy head. Both Farroot and Bill took deep gulps and sighed with contentment, which pleased Dorro to no end. He, meanwhile, ordered a small glass of mead for himself—he wanted to keep his head during this conversation.

"Again, Mr. Farroot, I want to express my sympathies on the untimely demise of your brother. I know you were very fond of him. And I want to help catch his murderer."

"Err, thank you. Bing was a good lad. He was younger than me by a few years, but a shrewd 'n' crafty fellow nonetheless," said Farroot, knocking back more of his ale. "I know he had a bad reputation and all, but Bing was good at heart. He just had a fondness for the drink and that addled his judgment at times. I'm sure you understand."

"Of course I do," lied Dorro. "Can you elaborate more on your travels with the elves in the past months?"

Farroot and Bill exchanged quick looks before the former carried on: "Well, the three of us—Bing, Bill 'n' me—were feeling bored and restless last summer, so we decided to seek our fortunes elsewhere. I mean, Thimble Down is a fine-enough village but Halflings of adventure like us seek greater excitement in our lives."

Inwardly, Dorro groaned. To him, the three were less *Halflings of adventure* than *no-good, drunken louts*.

"Pray continue," he said, politely.

"We considered going west, but there are just more Halfling villages that way before you get to the sea. And north brings you to country full of strange, odd folk, not to mention the coming cold weather—didn't want to get trapped up there for a long winter. And the south is full of those accursed, greedy Men, so that was out of the question. Instead, we struck out east, where the lands are less charted. Granted, we knew there were elves, goblins, and gnomes that way, even the odd dwarf or two, but we sought gold and treasure, and would fight if we had, too.

"A'course, Bing was reluctant to go. He loved the Hanging Stoat—it was a second home to him—and he wasn't as much an adventurer as Bill 'n' me, but we talked him into it. So late last summer, we packed up some provisions and slunk out of town in the dead o' night. We walked and camped for weeks, always heading west and using the sun and stars for direction. Eventually, the Halfling villages began to disappear and we found ourselves in wild country where there was no law or rules. And in fact, we kinda liked it there—at least Bill 'n' me did. Bing missed his old table here in the Stoat, but truth be told, he was a coward at heart."

Freda showed up with two steaming bowls of stew for Farroot and Bill, and Dorro quickly winked at her to keep the brown ales coming. By the light of single candle on the table, he noted that Farroot was enjoying his own storytelling and the bookmaster wanted him to keep going, lest he confess to something. To his left, Bill Thistle said nothing, just nodding periodically and tucking into his ale and stew. Dorro trusted that one about as far as he could throw him.

"So, where was I? Oh yes, out in the wild lands to the east. One night, after several days of drenching rain, we were sitting around a fire, roasting a hare to delicate perfection, when we suddenly realized there were a handful of arrows pointed at our noggins. Unbeknownst to us, a party of elves had silently crept up and got the jump on us. We were in a hair's breadth of being stuck like pincussions!"

"This, as you might have guessed, was Toldir and his boys. We dropped our knives and simply raised our hands—there was no way we could overcome them elves. Then Toldir asks why we're trespassing in the hunting lands of the Woodland elves and how we'd like to die— by arrow or being roasted over an open fire like the hare!

Naturally, we said we'd rather keep our skins, thank you very much, and that we were simply lost. I'm not sure he believed us, but figuring that we looked like three soggy Halflings, I don't think he saw much sport in flaying us to bits."

"So we got to talking about this 'n' that—hunting, fishing, trading, and such—and finally Mr. Toldir says we can stay with his pack of hunters for a few days until we got fattened up again. After that, he'd steer us back out west and out of elvish country. For me 'n' Bill's part, we saw this as an opportunity to learn more about the folk in these lands and what opportunities may lay there. Plus just watching them elven boys hunt was a priceless lesson in itself—they could stalk a deer or a wild goat like it was a statue. They were incredibly quiet in the woods, especially this younger elf named Baldar. He was a gifted hunter with a facility for knives. While most hunters use stone- or metal-tipped arrows to bring down their prey, Baldar liked the challenge of throwing knives at his quarry. And swear to goodness, I saw him bring down a full-size muledeer with knife thrown from forty paces. Bill learned quite a bit from him, in fact."

Bill was nodding furiously by now, not saying a word, but supporting the narrative with his theatrical head movements. Farroot took a short break to get his fill of lamb stew before resuming. "And that's about the whole of it, aside from the goblin attack that Bing told just everyone in the village about. I won't bore you with that again. But in all, the three of us spent a week or so with the Woodland elves and then we parted company."

"Then why," Dorro interjected with a smile, "did Toldir call Bing 'a thief'?"

"Of that, I'm not sure," countered Farroot slyly. "After that big battle with the goblins, the elves did confer upon us some treasure, including some silver coins, some fine knives and swords and, a'course, the famous brooch that Toldir gave to Bing for being such a good companion. Or should I say, the *infamous* brooch. Then, laden with our treasure, we began working out way back west, which took several months, since it was winter and we were traveling through hard country. And here we are."

"It's odd, y'know—we could have been killed any time in our adventures, either by illness, robbery, a charging buck, or from a goblin's axe. Yet we made it through all that muck, only to have Bing killed in his own Thimble Down burrow. There's a sick irony to that," said Farroot, faintly smiling, but looking quite sad instead. "I wish we'd never gone adventuring in the first place."

And with that, Farroot Rumple began weeping and blubbering to himself. *Oh dear*, thought Dorro. *I guess he's had enough ale already*. In a minute, however, Farroot had simply nodded off to sleep and, upon seeing that, Bill Thistle decided it was nap time, too.

Dorro left a few coins on the table and quietly excused himself. He had learned a lot from that conversation, but found no answers. "Let's see," he muttered aloud, having left the Hanging Stoat and heading back toward the library to check in. "According to Farroot, the three of them spent a week with Toldir's band and parted in good company. Toldir's comments, however, seemed to dispute that thought—in the elf chief's mind, Bing was a thief and another of them said he deserved to die. That young one, *um*, Baldar, yes, that's it! Baldar said that. He was also the one Farroot noted was an expert with knives and could fell a deer at forty paces. If true, taking down an addled Halfling like Bing Rumple would be mere child's play. Still, he seemed sincere that his knife had been lost some months earlier. This is not adding up!"

Dorro was becoming frustrated by his own logic. And again, why was Bing acting so strange when he wore that brooch. He knew that one way or another, he had to find the elves and speak with Toldir and Baldar. Granted, he could be shot by an arrow—or a flying knife—by even trying such a reckless act, but if he was going to find Bing's killer, it was a necessity. Even if one of these dangerous elves could slay, skin, and fillet him in under two minutes.

This time, it was Dorro that gulped.

17
Spying Eyes

till pondering his conversation with Farroot Rumple, much less Bill Thistle who just received a free lunch without uttering a peep, Dorro made his way across the village toward the library. It was clouding up again, but that made the daffodils seem even more radiant in the bright, diffused light. Even with the danger and chaos lurking around Thimble Down, the bookmaster couldn't resist the ephemeral charms of Spring.

He was also feeling a tad peckish, since he hadn't eaten anything—nor would he ever—at the Hanging Stoat. His discerning palate wouldn't tolerate that. Instead, he stopped back at one of his favorite eateries, the Bumbling Badger, run by Millin Parffin and his delightful wife, Nutylla. The place was always bristling with laughter and little feet, as the Parffins had innumerable children. After ordering a baked cheese 'n' chive pie with a cold mug of cider, Dorro sat at a high bar stool and looked at the scampering younglings. He liked to quiz himself and see if he could remember all their names: "Hullo, Paschtoo! Hi, Bagoon and Magoo. Hey, Bean, Flopper, and Gardy! Don't drop that tray Rowdingle—would be a quite a mess to clean up. And here are the littlest ones, Soapy, Mappy, and Chumba!" Dorro pulled some silly faces and made the toddlers giggle and run under their mother's skirt.

"Oh Mr. Dorro, you're always a delight," said the ever-cheerful Nutylla, serving up his hot pie. "The children so love having you here." The bookmaster smiled and nodded, tucking into his late lunch. He truly enjoyed the Bumbling Badger and its rag-tag collection of happy children; it was so different from his quiet, occasionally lonely rooms at the Perch. Instantly, his mind conjured up an image of Wyll. He hoped that the plan he hatched with Cheeryup was working out. If it wasn't, the results would be dire for all involved. At that, Dorro grabbed his walking stick and headed back out into the cool Spring day, after dropping a few extra coins on the counter.

Upon entering the library, slightly breathless from his quick walk, Dorro realized that everything seemed normal. There were about fifteen patrons wandering the stacks or sitting at the thick, wooden tables with benches throughout the first level. Bedminster Shoe, his bookmaster-for-hire, was sitting at the front desk, monitoring the flow while stacking various books and scrolls for re-shelving. In the upper gallery, he espied Cheeryup Tunbridge putting away more books. Indeed, thought Dorro, he could get used to having regular help in the library. It would leave more time for fishing.

He nodded to Bedminster who was talking to a villager who was looking for information about grafting fruit trees, so Dorro went to the stair-ladder and ascended, meaning to have a quiet conversation with Cheeryup. He realized how much he was coming to depend on her. *I must give her a raise one of these days*, figured Dorro.

The young girl peeked out from behind one of the shelves. "Hi, Mr. Dorro. Back here!" Dorro scuttled down the length of the open, oval-shaped gallery overlooking the rest of the library and ducked behind one of the stacks. "Hullo young lady. Anything to report?" he whispered.

"I went up to the Perch to feed your favorite plant about an hour ago. It's doing fine, but is rather bored and lonely. I think your flowers would like to run around outside for a while and go play in the woods."

"No, no! Not a good idea," urged Dorro, lowering his voice even further. "If Wyll is seen, our goose will be cooked and so will his!"

"I'll make one more run this afternoon, Mr. Dorro, just to make sure the garden is all settled for the night."

"Good, you do that. I'll be home by supper and can check the garden myself at that point. And here," he pulled his last handful of coins out of his pocket and pushed them into Cheeryup's hand.

"Mr. Dorro, this is far too much."

"Sorry my dear, I'm afraid this is the new rate for library assistants. At least those who do expert detective work on the side. Trust me, you've earned it."

Cheeryup was grinning ear-to-ear by this time, "My mother won't know what to do with all this money. She'll scream with joy."

"She'll figure out something. And you buy yourself something new, too. But now I must be off. I need to find another figure in our little puzzle and have a word with him. And again, be stealthy in your ventures!"

"I shall, Mr. Dorro."

At that, Dorro went back down the ladder-stairs, gave a wave to Bedminster Shoe and shot out the door on his next errand. Up in the gallery, Cheeryup dropped the coins in her skirt pocket; she just had a few more books to put away before she'd go finish her "gardening work" at the Perch.

Across the library, however, a patron quickly closed a book and slipped it back onto the shelf. The Halfling had been watching Dorro and the Tunbridge girl in the gallery above and clearly knew something was afoot. There were laws being broken, most likely, or even worse. Now, it was time to wait and then follow the girl when she left the library.

The patron muttered, "Dorro won't get away with his mischief this time!"

✫ ✫ ✫

Dorro headed back into the village, in search of a very officious-looking burrow. Finally, he saw it and rapped on the door, using an elegant silver knocker shaped like a bull. The door cracked up and a small, old servant woman with white hair and stooped posture opened the door.

"Is your master at home, my good lady? If I so, please say that Dorro Fox Winderiver would like a brief interview."

"He's busy," she replied and slammed the door.

While not a Halfling of great courage or strength, Dorro was nonetheless persistent, even to the point of annoyance. He didn't mind annoying folk if he got his way in the end.

BANG! BANG! BANG!

The servant again opened the door and gave Dorro an evil stare. "Be off or I'll call the dogs!"

"I know full well, my good lady, that Osgood Thrip doesn't own any dogs," said Dorro with a rather smug smile. "So if you'll be so kind, please tell him I'm here and won't be leaving until he gives me a few minutes of his precious time."

"Wait here," she snarled and slammed the door again. Dorro chuckled. He had been musing on the notion that Osgood did not have any vicious creatures on the premises—that is, except his wife Lucretia. By now, Dorro was giggling out loud, amused by his own silliness. Truth be told, Dorro and Lucretia had despised each other since their school days—she, the pushy princess and he, the fussy egghead, forever arguing over blocks and games in the schoolyard. But that's a story for another day.

Finally, the door opened again and Dorro was silently ushered into the Thrip manse. It was a grand burrow, much fancier than the Perch, but not as well sited, thought the bookmaster. While he was on the far end of Thimble Down with a view of the river, the Thrip household was right in the middle of the village, amidst the hustle 'n' bustle of everyday life. Since Osgood had numerous business interests all over the hamlet, this was advantageous to him and also reminded everyone that he was wealthy and powerful. And not a Halfling to be trifled with.

Dorro was directed into a small parlor in the front of the burrow-hold. It was richly appointed with a settee and several cushioned seats—a rarity in Thimble Down. There was a fine writing desk in the corner and a brick fireplace whose oaken mantle depicted great scenes in Halfling history, carved by an excellent artist and, no doubt, lavishly expensive. The servant left Dorro there, not offering him any tea or refreshment. Clearly, this wouldn't be an easy interview.

Briskly, Osgood Thrip walked into the room. He was shorter than Dorro, and quite a bit stouter, but he was built like a bull and had a fierce scowl on his face. This was an advantage during business negotiations when Thrip would fix on his fiercest gaze and slam his fist on the table to make a point or demand a better price.

Considering the usually congenial nature of Halflings, he often got his way.

"What is this about, Winderiver?" barked Osgood. "And why are you wasting my time? I'm in the middle of some delicate trade negotiations and am waiting for a courier with news of a big sale any minute." No one exactly knew what Osgood Thrip's business was, but clearly, he was good at it. Dorro had doubts that it was entirely legal as well.

"My sincerest pardons, Osgood, but we must speak about the Bing Rumple matter. I'm working with Sheriff Forgo and would kindly like your valuable insights into the affair."

"Oh, I see," said Thrip, taking the bait. "Martha! Martha! Bring us some tea and biscuits, at once!" The white-haired servant popped her head in the parlor door and was out again in a heartbeat. She was well trained, though sadly, had probably lived a miserable life tending to the whims of the Thrip family. Dorro felt for her.

"Osgood, we're at a crossroads in the investigation and ..."

"Why are you here and not the Sheriff," Osgood interrupted, scratching his increasingly bald pate. "Oh yes, I recall—you dabble in detection, I've heard. The library a bit too boring for you? I do understand. Well, if that lunkhead of a sheriff wants you as a deputy, I won't argue, as long as we get to the bottom of this business. It's not good for my bottom line, or that of any other merchant in Thimble Down."

"As I said, I'd like your insights, Osgood. We have two lines of inquiry so far and they're quite disparate. First, we have Farroot Rumple and his sidekick, Bill Thistle, who claim that they were indeed companions of the Woodland elves and were given the brooch, as well as a variety of knives, swords, and gold. But let's consider the source—neither Halfling is the most reputable or savory character in the village."

"No, indeedily," said Thrip, nodding to the beleaguered Martha as she set down the polished silver tea set and poured out two cups. Taking up his own, he continued, "Certainly, the Rumple brothers were bad business and had a long, unfortunate history in this village. But I can't see Farroot harming his own brother. As I recall, they were fond of each other and Farroot always looked after his younger brother, who, of course, had his problems. As for Mr. Thistle, I can't say. I only know him a little. He might be a Halfling of violence—certainly has that look in his eyes. Wild. Dangerous. I wouldn't want to sit across the table from him in a delicate negotiation. Thistle could be your villain."

Dorro had to be careful that Osgood wasn't leading him down the path of his choice. Maybe he wanted Dorro to take his attention off Farroot. Interesting, that.

"Then there are the elves," said Dorro. "These Woodland folk are very powerful and, as we've seen, very jealous, but they want the brooch back. Enough to kill for it? It's possible. Toldir is formidable enough, but then there's the young one, Baldar. Do you know what his particular talent is?"

Osgood shook his head.

"Knives. In particular, he's an expert at throwing knives and, in a hunt, can easily bring down a large boar or deer with one. Baldar can reputedly throw it with such accuracy that he can pierce an animal's heart with one throw."

"Well then!" said Thrip, rubbing his hands together like they'd just sealed a deal. "He's our murderer then. Obviously, the elves wanted their treasure back and would do anything to get it. Eliminating a relative weakling like Bing Rumple would only be too easy for beings of their strength."

"I'm not sure I totally agree, Osgood, but it's a potential solution. But if so, there are two problems. One, if they ransacked Bing's burrow, why didn't they recover the brooch? In fact, they claimed this morning that they didn't have it and were angrily demanding it back. Worse, who's going to arrest a full-grown elf warrior? Sheriff Forgo? I don't think we could apprehend any of those elves without the aid of a hundred well-armed Halflings."

"You do have a point there, Winderiver. If it comes to be that Baldar is our assailant, there might not be much we can do about it. We might just have to let it go, for the sake of the community and its safety. But there you have it—my money is on the elves. They had the motive, they had the intent, and they clearly have the skill and means to kill a Halfling at the bat of an eye. They're a dangerous lot; I just wish they'd clear out of the Great Wood and leave us alone. Bad for business, you know."

"One last question, Osgood—what did you think of Bing's behavior over the past few weeks? Bing was a sniveling groveler last year, but came back from his adventuring as a bold, brash man of the world. Yet in the last week, Bing swiftly became meek again. I find that curious."

Suddenly growing angry, Thrip growled, "Bing Rumple was a blight upon Thimble Down! I tried to help him at various times over the years, and he always squandered my advice—and my money. In fact, he owed me a great deal of silver and told me just the other day that he had no intention of paying it back. Why that lying, sneaky little weasel—he *deserved to* ..." Osgood realized what he was saying and stopped instantly.

With that Thrip took a final gulp of tea and stood up coldly, indicating to Dorro that the interview was over. "There you have it, Winderiver. Take it as you may. If you need any more of my advice, please call any time. Or preferably, don't. Good day and, be a kind fellow and see yourself out. Martha has enough to do right now."

Osgood exited the room, leaving Dorro on the settee without even taking one sip of his tea. He downed half of it to be polite and strode out the front door with walking stick in hand. Pacing back through the village, Dorro pulled out his pipe and lit it with a match. "Hmm, that was most interesting. I went in there with two potential murderers in mind. But now, I have three."

✵ ✵ ✵

At five o'clock, Bedminster Shoe made ready to close the library and kindly informed the few patrons still there that it was time to check out their books and leave. Cheeryup dashed down the stair-ladder and helped Bedminster make the final preparations for closing, locking all the windows and making sure the place was tidy for the following Monday, as tomorrow was Sunday and the library would be closed. Finally, the last of the readers exited the building. Bedminster and the young girl extinguished the last remaining candles and headed for the front door, whereupon Shoe locked it and put the key in his front pocket.

"Good evening, Miss Cheeryup. I suppose I shall see you on Monday. I have to catch up on my own work to-night and tomorrow, copying several deeds and contracts for local merchants. But I am sure Mr. Dorro will need me again, as he appears rather busy these days." The girl didn't know why Mr. Shoe appeared so happy that Mr. Dorro was out so much—maybe he liked working in the library, but also, he appeared to take a great interest in Mr. Dorro's detective work.

"G'night, Mr. Shoe—see you soon!" Cheeryup verily leapt off the library porch and dashed off in the direction of the river and Dorro's home. Bedminster meanwhile turned left toward the village where he'd grab a quick supper and then get his quill in some ink before too long. The library was quiet and deserted. Then, from behind a tree, a shadowy figure moved, quietly tailing the girl.

Cheeryup was being followed.

18
Pigtails

_____

The following morning, Dorro rose early, as he knew it was going to be a long day. He splashed some cold water on his face and walked into the kitchen. He assumed that his "garden"— that is, Wyll Underfoot—was still soundly asleep on his cot in the shed. This gave Dorro a few minutes to fix his own breakfast and get some provisions together for the lad, who would spend another long day in hiding.

He tried stoking the fire in his stove, but it had burnt out during the night, so it was time to start over. A small flame would be all he needed, so he opened a small door in the wall and pulled out some twigs and small logs. This door was connected to another outdoor shed where Dorro kept all his logs—this access chute made it easier to fetch wood without having to go outdoors, which was a life-saver in the depths of winter.

Lighting the twigs that sat on a bed of thin, dried birch bark, a small flame began licking the wood and soon a crisp little fire was underway. Dorro had a craving for eggs that morning, so he put an iron skillet on the stove's surface and let it heat up. After about five minutes, it was feeling toasty as he held his hand a few inches from the pan and dropped a slab of butter into it. While it had been heating, he'd scrambled two eggs in a ceramic bowl and chopped herbs on the cutting board. With the butter beginning to fizzle, he dumped the gooey eggs into the pan and let them begin to cook. In a flash he added the herbs—chives, parsley, and dill—and began folding the eggs over top each other with a thin, flat spoon. Dorro had also put a slab of thick oat bread on another warm part of the stove, so it could quickly toast up. Within two minutes seconds, it was all over—he'd slid the scrambled eggs onto a waiting plate, buttered up the toast and cut it in half, and poured himself a cup of cider. *Breakfast is here!* he thought rapturously and began to tuck in.

His stomach full, Dorro then prepared more eggs for Wyll, who should be waking soon. Even though the boy was in hiding, he still needed to be vigilant—any loud snores might attract the attention of passersby, and then the jig would be up. He put the next round of eggs and toast on a plate, along with an apple, covered it all with a towel, and made his way out to the shed. Granted, anyone walking by might think it odd to see the burrow-owner taking his breakfast out to a rough shed, but Dorro was a well-known eccentric in Thimble Down and most would consider it normal behavior for him.

Dorro lifted the latch with his free hand and entered the dark shed. There was a small window on the wall that let a little light in, but otherwise, it was a regular garden shed. There were tools hanging on the right wall (on either side of the door leading down to the infamous food cellar) and a potting bench on the left. Underneath were the accoutrements of the typical gardener—empty terra cotta pots, a burlap bag containing last year's compost, and some small hand tools. Along the back wall was a cot covered in heavy blankets and a quilt and, underneath it all, was Wyll Underfoot.

"Wyll, boy, time to rise!" urged Dorro in a loud whisper. The pile of blankets began to move and suddenly a head popped out of one end.

"Huh? Oh, hullo, Mr. Dorro." In a jiffy, Wyll sat up and eagerly eyed the tray in Dorro's hands. He knew that the bookmaster was mighty handy in the kitchen and never turned down any of victuals that were offered to him.

"I'm afraid, Wyll, that it will be another lengthy day in the shed for you," said Dorro. "Hopefully, this plate of eggs will at least make the morning a bit easier. And Cheeryup will be along later with lunch and can perhaps give you a little company to make the time pass more quickly."

Wyll accepted the tray gratefully, but protested, "Please, Mr. Dorro, can't I go outside a little today? I'm so bored and cooped up in here. I want to feel the wind in my hair and climb a tree!"

"I know, boy, Cheeryup told me you were feeling confined. But I fear that letting you out will merely bring Sheriff Forgo down on your head, and you know where you'll end up. At the moment, I fear that your choices are my garden shed or Forgo's gaol."

Sulking, Wyll said nothing, but ate his breakfast anyway. He knew it was futile to argue with Dorro's logic and, furthermore, he preferred the shed to gaol anyway. Dorro also slipped his hand into his pocket and pulled out a small book of children's adventures. This he handed to Wyll, adding, "Another item to help pass the day. I wish I could provide more entertainment, but this will have to do at the moment."

"Thank you, Mr. Dorro. And I'll keep quiet all day, I promise."

"Good lad. We'll spring you from here soon. Just give us a few more days."

And with that, Dorro gave the boy a wink and quietly slipped out the front of the shed. He had much to do that day.

✧ ✧ ✧

Outside the little window on the side of the shed, there was a large pink-weigela bush. As Dorro walked back toward the Perch in the opposite direction, the shrub's branches moved a bit and a figure emerged. It quickly moved back over the hillock and toward the center of Thimble Down.

In a nearby elm tree sat a catbird, which, if it understood the language of Halflings, would have heard the figure say the following: "Well, Dorro, you think you're smarter than everyone in this village. I'm here to disprove that theory. You think you can flout the rules and live above the law. Sheriff Forgo shall hear about the escaped convict in your garden shed. So shall my husband and the Mayor. And then your goose will be cooked, my friend. Cooked, good and proper!"

With a growing smile on her face, Lucretia Thrip sped back into Thimble Down, heading straight for the gaol, and then to her home to speak with Osgood. She still had not forgiven Dorro for pulling her beautiful pigtails when they were children.

19
The Great Wood

This being Sunday morning, the village of Thimble Down was quiet and its library closed. Still, Dorro had made arrangements to meet Cheeryup Tunbridge at half past nine on the building's porch. The girl had told her mother that Mr. Dorro asked for her help on a special book-serialization project and, more importantly, would be paying her for the extra work. Her mother, the village seamstress, readily agreed, as the two needed every penny they could to get.

Of course, Cheeryup knew that there was no library project and that they'd go on some adventure to help exonerate Wyll. Moreover, Mr. Dorro had instructed her to tell no one about it and come dressed for a day outdoors. As such, she put on her heavy shoes, brought a scarf, and put a few of her mother's blueberry scones in her pocket for what might be a long day ahead.

At the appointed hours, Dorro approached the building and, right as rain, there was the girl, sitting on a bench on the library's fine covered porch. "Hullo, my girl. Are you ready for a bit of fresh air?"

"Yes, Mr. Dorro! Where are we going?"

"We're going, my dear, to talk to the elves."

At that, Cheeryup Tunbridge's jaw fell open and she stared agog at the bookmaster.

After a few seconds, the girl blinked and swallowed. "El ... el ... elves?"

"I've thought about it six ways 'til Sunday and there's nothing we can do about it. The elves are an essential part of this investigation, and if we have any interest in clearing Wyll's name, we must get them to speak. They know much, yet have told us little. In fact, I haven't spoken to them at all—I'm afraid our poor Sheriff has borne the brunt of their wrath. I admit, I am nervous about this encounter, but there's nothing for it. We must go.

"If it means that Wyll is a step closer to freedom, then count me in," trumpeted the girl.

☆ ☆ ☆

The two headed north, away from the village toward a popular section of the Great Wood, where the Woodland elves reputedly had their encampment. The Great Wood was a beloved part of Thimble Down, a forest where village folk would go for picnics, walks, parties, and more. Many buried their dead in its more remote recesses, which is testament to the almost-spiritual kinship Thimble Downers felt for the place. As for the Wood itself, it was part of a larger network of woodlands that verily ringed the village on its northern, eastern, and southern edges, while the west was bordered by the River Thimble. Over the centuries, folk in the village had suggested that the woods and river formed a protective wall around Thimble Down, but these days, most laughed at the notion and called it poppycock.

Dorro hadn't made up his mind either way; he just loved rambling through trees and mossy vales, looking under rocks for salamanders and mushrooms, or spying the occasional badger or hedgehog rambling through the underbrush. Occasionally, a majestic stag would crash through the foliage on his way to better feeding grounds, and there were even small black and brown bears here and there, but they preferred to be left alone and were probably more afraid of the Halflings than the reverse. Dorro couldn't recall much trouble befalling anyone traveling in the Great Wood—it was a place of great peace and contentment, which is perhaps why the elves had camped there.

Finding Toldir and his band of hunters, however, would be easier said than done. There were hundreds of places to hunker down in the Wood, as it covered many

dozens, if not hundreds, of square miles. And them being elves, Dorro figured, they were probably fifty times
more stealthy than any Halfling, who were quite stealthy
themselves.

Dorro and Cheeryup passed under the outer leaves of
the Great Wood and began their search. He figured the
elves would likely find themselves a soft, mossy patch
near water, since that would be a more habitable place to
rest than some rocky crag up high or an exposed meadow
where they would be susceptible to discovery by some
Halfling family out for a Sunday stroll. With that in mind,
Dorro led Cheeryup toward a number of little streams and
rivulets that fed the River Thimble—it seemed as good a
place as any to start.

Without speaking much, the pair strode deeper into
the woods, treading downwards toward lower ground
where the streams ran. They walked for a good two hours
until Cheeryup sighed loudly, indicating to Dorro that it
was time for a break.

"Are you feeling hungry, girl? If so, let's find a place
to rest our tails and have a quick snack." She nodded
agreeably and they quickly found a great mossy boulder
near a stream that could accommodate the two easily.
Cheeryup pulled one of the scones from her pocket and
quickly began nibbling. "Ymmmm" was all she said as
she munched on the baked treat, laden with blueberries
she and her mother had picked and jarred last summer,
and had been saving all winter in their cool cellar. Dorro,
meanwhile, put down his walking stick and reached into

a satchel for a sandwich of cold roast beef slices, laid on seeded oat bread with a dollop of sweet mustard on either side. He had also brought a flask of cider for them to share. The two were very happy, enjoying their food in the embracing cradle of the Great Wood."

"I do love it here, Mr. Dorro. It always feels like home. I don't know why, it just does."

"Somehow, Cheeryup, we Halflings are connected to these trees and this ground, though for the life of me, I can't explain why or how. And me, a Halfling of letters and knowledge. I should have some real, empiric facts, but I don't. It's just what you, I, and just about every other Thimble Downer feels. We're part of the woods and the woods are part of us. It may not make literal sense, but there it is ..."

The girl nodded, getting up to continue their journey, but then asked, "Mr. Dorro, how are we to find the elves? We could be here for a week and not find a squirrel, must less a band of elves."

"You speak facts, girl, and I don't have an answer for you," he said as they began walking down a new trail. "But continue we must."

Then the pair froze, for at that moment, a stout boar with large tusks bolted across the small stream near them, about eighty paces away. It stopped, looked at the pair, and then turned their away. Despite the peaceful environs of the Great Wood, there was some danger, and among its most threatening were boars. They were fast, grumpy, and had been known to charge Halflings with their fearsome tusks. And this fellow looked like he meant business.

Quietly Dorro whispered, while grasping the girl's hand. "No sudden movements, my dear. This chap could run us down in about three seconds if we panicked." Cheeryup cried out with fear and Dorro realized he shouldn't have been so frank, so quickly backtracked: "However, we will be fine. Still, we need to back away from here like mice."

Holding her hand, Dorro slowly stood up and began edging away from the distant, bristle-haired boar, as it eyed them suspiciously. The Halflings had moved off about ten paces when the boar decided they were a threat. With a huge grunt, the boar launched itself at Dorro and Cheeryup with frightening speed, its feet moving in a blur of motion, the creature dropping its head to inflict maximum damage with those razor-sharp tusks. Dorro thrust the girl behind him and prepared for the worst. His last thought was, "I'm sorry, Wyll—I've let you down, lad."

With that, Dorro prepared to die.

✲ ✲ ✲

Sheriff Forgo was hoping that it would be a nice, quiet day in Thimble Down. The events of the past week had been unlike anything he'd ever experienced—not just a murder, but one involving dangerous elves, riotous mobs, and even a threat from Osgood Thrip that he should be replaced. Usually he dealt with matters ranging from lost sheep to the odd drunk who thought it would be fun to run through the village marketplace—in broad daylight, no less—without his breeches on. That was one of the nitwit Bosco's favorite pastimes and, as proof, he'd spent many a day in the gaol sobering up.

It was mid-morning on a lovely Sunday in April and Forgo was thinking that, yes, this might be a true day of rest. As proof, he sat at his desk and slowly let his eyelids close, welcoming a post-breakfast nap.

RAP! RAP! RAP!

Forgo flew out of his chair, almost straight into the air. *"WHAAAA!"* he roared, anger flaring in his eyes. Into the gaol burst one of his least favorite Halflings, Osgood's wife, that black cloud with shoes on—Lucretia Thrip—who had banged on the gaol door with her pale, bony knuckles.

"Sheriff, I have a crime to report!"

Forgo slapped his big, meaty hand on his forehead and groaned. His quiet, relaxing snooze evaporated before his eyes. "Lucretia, it's Sunday morning. Don't you have anything better to do? Like get your garden ready for spring or pull wings off helpless flies?

"I'm not amused, Sheriff Forgo," said Lucretia, her brows furrowed and stiff black ringlets of hair clinging to her forehead as if they had been ironed on. "Perhaps Osgood is correct that it's time for Thimble Down to have a new sheriff. I'm sure I could get the Mayor's ear for a few minutes to discuss the matter. Hmm, Sheriff Mungo. That has a nice ring to it."

"Mungo, that blithering idiot, why...," Forgo suddenly caught himself. This wasn't a battle he wanted to pick. "Well, my dear Mrs. Thrip, how can I help you today?" he said with an ingratiating smile.

"That's better. Now, Sheriff, I have some important news for you. I have found your escaped prisoner!"

20
Another Death

*D*orro was frozen. His arms were thrust backwards to protect Cheeryup from the charging boar, but really, there was nothing he could do. In a few moments, he'd be dead or severely mangled in vicious tangle of Halfling and beast. Hopefully, the girl would have enough wits amidst the confusion to run off and save herself.

But something else happened entirely. The speeding boar was about twenty feet away from the cringing pair when a flash of silver flew through the air and appeared to strike the beast in its neck. Suddenly, the animal tumbled forward in a ferocious crash of flesh, leaves, and earth until it came to a stop at Dorro's feet. By this time, the bookmaster was shaking like a leaf, clutching Cheeryup behind him, and on the edge of paralyzing shock.

He looked down at the muscular animal and realized it was stone dead. And protruding from its neck was … the handle of a knife!

"*What on earth!*" was all he could say before Dorro's knees gave out, and both he and Cheeryup collapsed to the ground. It had been one of the most frightening moments in Dorro's entire life. "It's f-f-fine, my dear," he stuttered, as the girl began to cry. "The beast is dead. We'll be all right." And then the bookmaster himself burst into tears.

A few minutes later, with Cheeryup's sniffling on the wane, Dorro looked up, his own eyes red and full of water. He was in for another shock, for around the pair was a ring of very tall creatures, each looking at them as if they were odd, sick, or slightly deranged. They couldn't seem to understand why anyone would be upset at killing a boar that was defending its territory from a pair of foolish Halflings, unless it was out of their shame. But their eyes also conveyed that the deed was done and they might as well make the best of it.

"Parahir, I hope you are in the mood to cook one of your fine stews," said the big one with the fiercest scowl. "This fine fellow is all muscle from tip to tail, so you'll have to slowly cook it for most of the day—or we'll be chewing tough boar meat for most of the night."

"Indeed, I am ready, Toldir, and surely, this beast will not have given his life in vain," said Parahir, a thickly set elf who seemed to be the troupe's cook. "I shall celebrate him as I tenderly braise his flesh and further thank these fine woods for creating such a mighty creature. And to-night, we shall all praise him as he nourishes us and gives us strength for another day on our long journey."

Dorro thought he was dreaming. These tall beings were the very Woodland elves he and Cheeryup had been seeking! And they were nonchalantly talking about something, though not in a tongue he understood. It was a mellifluous, gentle speech that he could have listened to for hours. Finally, he screwed up enough courage to speak.

"Ah, sirs, I first want to thank you for saving our lives. The girl and I are indebted to you."

Switching to the tongue of the Halflings, the elf called Toldir—the one Dorro had seen in the village talking sternly to Sheriff Forgo—responded, though with angry derision. "This magnificent boar is dead and you should thank him—not us—for giving his life up for your blundering. Anyone with eyes and a sense of smell could tell this is the territory of a male black boar that is searching for a new mate. He saw you as a threat and now his spirit is gone."

Dorro felt shamed and clumsy. "I *d-didn't* know," he stammered. "We were looking for you. I need to speak with you about the events that transpired in the village. It's very important."

The elves said nothing, but merely glanced at each other.

"I must ask," continued Dorro, changing the subject quickly, "how did you bring this boar down with just a knife? That kind of accuracy is unheard of. A bow and sharp, fast arrow perhaps, but not a single blade. Did I hear you say in the village that one of you has a facility with this skill?"

"You were there then," said Toldir. "We have nothing to hide. Yes, our brother Baldar is quite accomplished at throwing knives. But I don't have to speak for him."

"If you want to know how I killed the boar, little one, I shall tell you," added Baldar, who stood to the leader's left. He was younger than Toldir, but taller and more muscled. And where Toldir was pale with long, straight yellow hair, Baldar was of dark complexion and ebony-brown hair in a knot in the back. He looked quite danger-ous to Dorro.

"However, if you're trying to imply that I applied this to the death of your kinsman, Bing Rumple, I shall have nothing to do with you. Maybe I should have let the boar skewer you instead. That might have been amusing."

"No, I'm not implying anything, Mr. Baldar. I've just never seen anyone wield a blade like that before." Dorro finally stood up and helped Cheeryup stand as well. She was still shaken, but some color was beginning to return to her cheeks.

Toldir chimed in, "Baldar has been throwing blades since he was a small elfling. Over the years, his accuracy became formidable, and he is able to use it during our hunt-ing forays to bring down game large and small."

"Once he almost took off my ear," added Parahir. "And I have proof!" The elf turned his head and pulled back his hair, revealing an ear with a visible notch out of it.

"Here now, brother, that was an accident," laughed Baldar. "I truly thought you were a bear!"

At that, the elves started laughing amongst themselves and the ice seemed to be breaking, Dorro felt.

"Well sir, I'm most impressed and, despite my foolishness, I am in your debt. We owe you our lives," said Dorro, before adding quickly, "As we do to this valiant boar. To him, I offer our gratitude and deepest remorse."

The elves seemed satisfied with that answer. "Well, master Halfling, you seem genuine enough," said Toldir. "But now is neither the time nor the place to discuss the matters that are of interest to you. Further, your young charge needs to get home to recover her health and spirits. She is still shaken by the incident."

"What shall you have me do?" Dorro asked.

"Return to your village with the girl and see that she's well taken care of. Then return to these fine woods tonight and we shall speak."

"Tonight?" gulped the bookmaster.

"That is our offer—take it or not," said Toldir, resuming a stony look.

"I agree then."

"Look for us tonight after the sun sets, just under the eaves of this forest. There is an enormous elm tree not far from your village."

"The Meeting Tree? Of course, it's the site of many occasions—weddings and picnics by the score. All in Thimble Down know it well."

"Good, then it's agreed," said Toldir firmly. "Also, there is a shorter path back to your village, much quicker than the circuitous route you took to get here. Just follow this stream and you will back home in much less than one Halfling hour."

At that, Toldir nodded curtly and set off back into the woods. Parahir and another elf grabbed the legs of the fallen boar and hoisted it in the air. Before they departed, Baldar stepped up and pulled his knife from the creature's neck and patted the dead animal on its stomach. "Farewell friend," was all he said, his expression equal parts respect and remorse. The elvish hunting party then disappeared into the woods, as if they'd never been there.

Dorro blinked his eyes a few times, trying to fathom all that he'd just seen, but then remembered Cheeryup. She was still whimpering. "Come girl, we need to get you home to your mother," he said urgently.

Following Toldir's advice, the two began following the stream out of the Great Wood and toward Cheeryup's home in Thimble Down. Then Dorro would have to gather his wits for a return to the forest that night and another meeting with the Woodland elves.

He was not looking forward to it. Not one bit.

21
A Turn for the Worse

While Dorro was in the Great Wood with Cheeryup and the Woodland elves, Sheriff Forgo was back in Thimble Down making preparations. One hour earlier, he had listened in stark amazement at Lucretia Thrip's announcement that she had located the escaped boy, Wyll Underfoot, and would lead him to his hiding spot.

Even more stunning was the news that the lad was holed up in Dorro Fox Winderiver's garden shed. He hoped that the bookmaster did not know about this, but had a sneaking suspicion he did. And if so, Winderiver would be up to his neck in hot gravy.

Taking no chances, Forgo summoned Mr. Mungo from the Hanging Stoat to serve as his backup, in case the boy decided to get rough and not come along in a peaceable manner. Again deputizing that jug-head Mungo wasn't an easy decision, but better safe than sorry, he figured, especially if the tyke started biting and kicking. "Okay Mungo, this could a tricky arrest," announced the Sheriff, in his best sheriff voice. "Things may get violent, but I have complete faith in you—I know you can handle it."

Mungo was already wishing he were back at the Hanging Stoat, pulling beers and making slow-roasted pork and potatoes for his ravenous customers. *Why did I agree to be a deputy?* he cursed himself. *Mungo, you fool—you had romantic delusions of fame and adventure. You were just trying to impress ...*

He left that last thought unfinished. Re-focusing on Sheriff Forgo's still-moving mouth, he realized the lawman hadn't ceased speaking and, therefore, he should probably listen in.

"... and one more thing, Mungo—don't hurt the lad too much. You're a big fella and could squish this youngling like a beetle. So even if Mr. Underfoot decides to kick you in the shin and sink his teeth into your leg, keep your wits. We don't want the folks of Thimble Down to consider their lawmen to be bullies."

Mungo merely nodded and executed a half-hearted salute. The sooner this debacle was over, the better.

✲ ✲ ✲

Twenty minutes later, Forgo, Mungo, and Lucretia Thrip cautiously approached the Perch. To the Sheriff, the hillock-house looked quiet, but he was taking no chances. He knew if things got violent, Mungo would be next to useless and Mrs. Thrip would merely scream at him and threaten to tell the Mayor the village needed a new sheriff.

Forgo opened the gambit by quietly knocking on the door. He let a minute pass by before deciding Winderiver wasn't home. *Good*, he thought. Peering over his shoulder at Lucretia, he merely held up a hand and silently pointed toward the garden shed. The Sheriff could tell she was enjoying this. Looking at Mungo, he nodded his head toward the out building and waved the barman to follow him. Mungo froze, at least until Forgo bugged out his eyes and again nodded his head. Then the deputy began to edge toward the shed.

Forgo got there first, and being sheriff meant he was probably the one who was going to get bit and kicked first. Forgo sighed, probably louder than he should have. With Mungo quivering behind him, the Sheriff eased open the shed door and peered into the darkness within. All looked normal—flower pots, tools, a wheelbarrow, blankets, a cot, hammers—*a cot and blankets!* Forgo jumped and his heart lurched.

"Hullo in there! This is Sheriff Forgo. Come out quietly, boy." The Sheriff looked behind him again; Lucretia had a cold, stony look on her face, while Mungo looked like he was about to be physically ill. "I know you're in there, lad. Let's do this gently. We don't want to hurt you."

With that, Forgo took a step or two into the shed, motioning Mungo to follow, him looking like a sad, remorseful puppy. There was a door to the right, which, if like most Halfling homesteads, was the door to the food cellar. It would be dark down there and he wasn't looking forward to rooting around in the dark, especially with an escapee who could bring a shovel down on this head.

In a sense, Wyll Underfoot did him a favor by not hiding there. Instead, he was hiding under a pile of musty canvas tarps to the left of the door, and the Sheriff wasn't even looking in that direction. Seeing Forgo slowly crack open the cellar door and peer in, Wyll chose that precise moment to bolt for the door. With the Sheriff distracted, this would be his best chance to escape.

Of course, as these things usually go, Wyll's escape didn't happen as he had planned. He had assumed the Sheriff would be alone and was completely flummoxed when he ran into the belly of another big Halfling. In fact, Wyll also almost through the door when he literally bounced off Mungo's extensive midriff and ricocheted back into the shed. He landed in the outstretched arms of Sheriff Forgo and, within a second, Wyll was lying on the floor, staring at the ceiling. He was no match for these large Halflings, plus there was a nasty looking lady who brought up the rear.

A few days earlier, Wyll Underfoot had dutifully surrendered without incident when Mr. Dorro had given him up for gaol. This time would be different, he vowed. With the Sheriff holding him up by the armpits, Wyll chose the occasion to pull back his leg and release a mighty kick into Mungo's belly. The village barman grabbed his middle, gasped for air and doubled-over in pain.

The Sheriff, realizing that his deputy was down for the count, upped his game and prepared to take the assailant alone. He reached into his satchel and pulled out a small net and quickly tossed it in the air. Miraculously, it landed on the boy and, while it didn't cover him, it was enough of a distraction to allow Forgo to regain his vice-grip on young Master Underfoot. Wyll screamed, which got Mungo's attention and, with his belly still aching, grabbed the boy's ankles a bit harder than necessary. Squiggling like an eel, Wyll pulled back his knee again and sent a ferocious punt into Mungo's calf. The latter dropped to his other knee in agony and wailed in pain. Not finished with his act of desperation, the boy spun his head right and proceeded to bite Sheriff Forgo on the forearm with his ample incisors.

It was now Forgo's turn to scream. "Get him!" he shouted in agony, as Wyll sprang to his feet and shot toward the door, right over Mr. Mungo's sprawled body. The boy was within inches of freedom when it went horribly wrong. Wyll tripped over something hard and did a complete forward flip onto Dorro's front lawn. Lying flat on his back and again staring at sky, he looked up into the stony face of Mrs. Thrip, whose tight-lipped grin had a trace of sadism about it. It was Lucretia who had tripped

171

the boy with her bony leg and now she put her boot on Wyll's chest. That proved just long enough for the Sheriff to recover and begin binding the boy with a sturdy hemp rope.

Trussed up like a lamb to slaughter, Forgo and Mungo lifted the boy and dropped him forcefully into the back of a cart pulled by Tom. The Sheriff gave the beast a slap on its hind quarters and the pony slowly began hauling his new cargo toward the village. Wyll was soon to be reacquainted with the Thimble Down gaol.

✧ ✧ ✧

It was mid-afternoon by the time Dorro and Cheeryup returned to the Perch, deeply wearied by their day's adventure in the Great Wood. They had come face-to-face with death thanks to an angry boar, but had been saved, oddly enough, by the very Woodland elves they'd been seeking. Dorro did not like the thought of treading near the forest at night to meet Toldir at the Meeting Elm. He'd much rather stay in his cozy burrow in front of a toasty fire and read a tale about adventure and danger— someone else's!

As the two advanced up the hill toward the Perch, Dorro again got that feeling that something wasn't right. As they edged closer, the bookmaster had his suspicions proved correct, as the door to the garden shed was flapping open in the breeze. Worse, there was a noted pinned to his front door—he assumed it wasn't an invitation from a neighbor to join them for cucumber sandwiches and tea.

Dorro didn't have to look into the shed to know that Wyll wasn't there. That much was obvious. In fact, he already knew that the boy was back in gaol under the eye of Sheriff Forgo. He glanced at the note and it was as he thought—Forgo had discovered the boy, thanks to the keen observation of a fine citizen—and Dorro himself need to report instantly for questioning (and, reading between the lines, possible incarceration himself). He looked over to Cheeryup and she too seemed to already know what had happened. The tears running down her cheek made that plainly evident.

"Look my dear, we've both had a long hard day," he counseled her. "I know this is another setback, but why don't you toddle home for a rest, and I'll visit the Sheriff to see if I can sort it all out."

"But Mr. Dorro, I was as careful as can be!" she cried. "I made sure it just looked like I was gardening for you. I don't know where I slipped up."

"No use worrying about it. Let's deal with the matter at hand."

"I shan't go home, sir. I'm coming with you to the gaol, even if they imprison me!"

"Well, I've learned not to argue with you, Cheeryup. You should consider becoming a barrister when you grow up," he laughed. "You always argue circles around me, so why should I even bother?"

She didn't laugh, but seemed pleased to be allowed to accompany him. Within ten minutes, both of them had freshened up and sped off to Thimble Down to face the consequences.

No matter what happened, thought Dorro, this wasn't going to be good.

22
Upon Deaf Ears

"**W**ell, if it isn't the exalted Dorro Fox Winderiver. Our famous scholar, and aider and abettor of escaped criminals!" uttered Forgo, looking grim. He also felt betrayed. Lowering his voice, the Sheriff hissed, "I thought we were on the same side, Winderiver. Yet this is how you repay me. I've half a mind to toss you in the cell with the little rat I found hiding amidst your flower pots and dirty trowels."

"Really, Sheriff, I was only ..."

"You lied to me, bookmaster!" said the lawman, cutting Dorro off. Forgo was red with anger and breathing hard—Dorro realized this would not be an easy conversation. "I thought we were collaborating on the Rumple

175

matter, but yep, you pulled one over on ol' Forgo. Maybe you engineered the boy's escape in the first place!"

"No, that's patently untrue! But ...," Dorro took a deep breath himself and decided to come clean. "Yes, Forgo, I am at fault in many ways and, for that, I am very sorry. The boy showed up back at my burrow a day or two ago and I didn't have the heart to return him to gaol. Apparently, I have a bit of a soft spot for the lad, and it got the better of me."

Forgo's face was still hard, but Dorro felt he was on the right track, lest he himself end up behind bars. Then he wouldn't be good to anyone.

"I assumed—perhaps incorrectly—that we both felt Wyll was innocent of any matter in the theft of Bing Rumple's brooch, but I shouldn't have done what I did. I do firmly believe he is not guilty, but I should have let you decide that and not let the boy stay in my shed."

"That's a confession," snarled Forgo. "By all rights, Winderiver, I should lock you away right now. I have all the authority I need to do that."

Dorro began to grow pale, while the Sheriff continued, "Lucky for you, there are extenuating circumstances and, more than that, I *need* ... I mean, the citizens of Thimble Down need you to help settle the Rumple murder and theft. In a day or two, a gang of big, angry Woodland elves are going to descend on this town for their stolen brooch and, if they don't get it, I fear they may burn our hamlet to the ground. They're dangerous creatures and you've only made it worse."

"They're more dangerous than you think, Sheriff."

"What's that, Winderiver?"

"Um, just that I agree with you. Those elves look vicious and capable of anything!"

Dorro paused. Then he took a deep breath and spoke: "Sheriff, I was truly wrong not to have informed you about Wyll's whereabouts. You can toss me in gaol, but I don't think that will help either of us. I haven't been very good about keeping you informed as to my investigations, but I promise that will change."

"Oh really? Golly, I feel so much better now," sneered Forgo.

"To be perfectly honest, I have thus far talked to Farroot Rumple and Osgood Thrip. They haven't been terribly helpful, but I'm beginning to piece together a timeline as to the events of the Rumple brothers during their months abroad and since they returned to Thimble Down. And Thrip plays a role in this as well, though I can't tell how just yet."

"Osgood?" Sheriff Forgo scratched his chin and thought for a moment. "I'd tread carefully, my friend. Thrip is a dangerous Halfling—oh, not much to look at, but he's wealthy and powerful, and could make your life very uncomfortable. I wouldn't put anything past him, plus he has the Mayor's ear. For that matter, he could make my life very uncomfortable, too."

"I have something else to admit, Forgo."

"What?"

"I've made contact with the elves."

"GREAT GOBLINS! What in King Borgo's name were you thinking?"

"Sheriff, it was the only way. I needed to find out what their true intentions are and how deep their dealings with Bing Rumple went. They could give us a vital clue as to the murder."

"And what, my brainy friend, will you do if the elves actually did cosh Bing on the head and stab him in the back?" continued Forgo, mockingly. "Will you invite them to a tea party and gleefully lead them back to my gaol? Or is it more likely that they'll bash you on the bean next and stick a fine blade between your ribs? It would serve you right."

Dorro gulped. He hadn't thought about that before. "I'm going to see them tonight. It needs to be done."

"Winderiver—Dorro—don't be a fool. It's a trap; you could be dead by morning," implored the Sheriff, showing genuine concern in his eyes. But he saw it was no use; the bookmaster was as stubborn as his pony Tom before breakfast.

"Of course, I'd go with you, but I'd guess they wouldn't tell me anything, so it's on your shoulders," he said. "They already don't trust me. I might suggest, however, you conceal a small knife on your person. It may come in handy."

Behind the two Halflings, Cheeryup Tunbridge suddenly walked through the gaol's doorway. "Did you ask him, Mr. Dorro? Can we?"

"Can we what?" asked the Sheriff dubiously.

"The girl wants to know if we can see Wyll for a few minutes. I know I haven't done anything to earn this favor, Sheriff, but at least do it for Cheeryup. She's fond of young Underfoot and feels responsible for his recapture."

"Go ahead, girl. He's in the back—you have five minutes."

Cheeryup smiled and scampered into the back rooms of the gaol to visit her new, and lamentably imprisoned, friend.

"Tell me, Sheriff, can I at least ask how you discovered Wyll in my shed?"

As if on cue, Lucretia Thrip entered the gaol and said, "Oh, and Sheriff, I think I left my bonnet here earlier. Did you ...?" She stopped and eyed Dorro venomously. Lucretia had loathed Dorro since they were younglings in school, and nothing had softened over the years.

"Well, Sheriff, if you do find my bonnet," she continued, not taking her eyes off of Dorro for a heartbeat, "be a dear and run it over to my fine house, will you?" With that, she shot the bookmaster a look of pure hatred and left in an instant.

"I should have known," said Dorro. "Did she hire someone to follow Cheeryup to the Perch?"

"Actually, since we're *finally* being honest here, I can tell you that Lucretia did the deed herself. Apparently, she saw you and the seamstress's daughter whispering in the library and decided to follow the girl later. The rest was easy to deduce. You were about as subtle as a flying mallet."

"Damn," said Dorro, more to himself than Forgo. He'd been careless and a fool.

"And don't think this clears things between us, Winderiver. You still lied to me and I'm not one to forgive easily. But that said, we need to clear up this murder before the elves reign total war on Thimble Down and innocent blood is spilled. No question, you have your work cut out for you tonight—in some ways, the fate of village depends upon it."

"I know, Sheriff. Now, if you don't mind, I'm going to spend a few minutes with Wyll and then we'll be off. Tomorrow, I'll fill you in on the events of this evening." Forgo nodded, but said nothing, neither of them sure there would even be a tomorrow for Dorro.

The bookmaster entered the rear of the gaol, but instead of a happy reunion, he found Cheeryup sitting on a bench sobbing quietly. "Dear girl, what happened?" But she said nothing.

He continued back toward the cells and found Wyll in his own chamber, sitting on a straw-filled bed and looking black. "She betrayed me!" the boy seethed. "I thought we were friends, but she led that horrible woman and the Sheriff right to the shed. I should never have befriended her."

"Wyll, that's untrue! It was my fault. I shouldn't have laid plans with Cheeryup in the library. That's where we were spied—it all began there and it was undoubtedly my fault."

"I shall never speak to that silly little girl again."

"Boy, you're being grossly unfair. She's fond of you—you know that!"

But Wyll was unresponsive. Dorro knew the lad was angry and was unfairly venting on the poor lass. In time, he'd realize his error, but he had no time to soothe this hurt. Instead, Dorro said, perhaps a bit too crossly, "Well, suit yourself—we'll be back to see you tomorrow, when you're being a little less pig-headed. Or then again, maybe *not.*"

Wyll's face registered utter shock, but before he could respond, Dorro turned on his heels and left the cell. He grabbed Cheeryup's hand, and led her out of the gaol and toward her home. It was getting late and Dorro had a big mission tonight. He needed time to prepare for what might be the final evening of his life.

It was a hair after midnight when Wyll had decided he'd had enough. Not only was it his second time in the Thimble Down gaol within a week, but he'd been betrayed by his new benefactor, Mr. Dorro, and his newest—and formerly best—friend ever, Miss Tunbridge. If this was what the Halflings of Thimble Down were like, they could do without Wyll Underfoot in the picture. Furthermore, he had escaped from this ramshackle gaol easily a few nights earlier and he could do it again.

Later that evening, Wyll heard Sheriff Forgo snoring loudly in the front room, so it was no use going that way, he realized. But what the Sheriff didn't know was that the windows of the gaol were very old and rusty. And as Forgo and Mungo had found out the hard way, Wyll had a surprisingly hard kick. With those facts on the table, Wyll leapt off his bunk and grabbed one of the old wooden timbers lining the ceiling. It had enough of a groove along its sides for the boy to get a firm grip and hang in mid-air. And thus he got to work.

As the barred window was nearly at ceiling level, Wyll gave it a fierce kick to test its resilience. He was pleased to hear it wince in pain. There was still some iron in those bars, but as his ears told him, more than enough rust to finish the job. He kicked again. And again. And *again!* Finally, there was a deathly squeal from the metal—one of the bars was coming loose. At that, Wyll unleashed a torrent of powerful blows from his left foot, one that left him breathless. He knew he didn't have much time before he was completely winded or the Sheriff woke up and put him in a new cell.

With the last of his remaining strength, Wyll pulled back with all his force and gave the bars one last, mighty kick with both feet. Instead of knocking out one bar, the boy managed to completely dislodge the entire window assembly and all five of the bars fell outward onto the ground, frame and all. He braced himself for the Sheriff rushing in to find out what the racket was about, but nothing happened. No Sheriff, no barking dogs, no lights around the village. Just peaceful, endless quiet.

Wyll Underfoot spared no time. He had no belongings, so he scampered up the wall and straight out of the damaged window, over the mangled bars. "I'm free!" he triumphantly whispered to himself. For a brief second, he thought remorsefully of Dorro and Cheeryup, but then got the better of himself. "Goodbye, wretched village and false friends," he boasted to the night sky. "From now on, I will trust no one but myself."

With that, Wyll Underfoot raced off into the night, leaping a split-rail fence and drawing the ire of a neighborhood mutt who howled forlornly. He didn't have a destination, but Wyll didn't care—he was free and would make the most of it, even if it cost him friends, a home, and a new start in life.

"You were meant to roam, Wyll, me boy," he laughed to himself. "It's time to find adventure … not the apple cellar of a boring old book tender."

23
The Meeting Tree

*J*t was just after 9 o'clock when Dorro headed out the door of his cozy hillock-home, turned right, and headed up the River Road toward the Great Wood. He was not, as he reminded himself, a night owl and didn't enjoy the closed-in sensation of darkness, nor the shivery breezes or swaying tree branches. No, Dorro was at his best in the morning, when the sun was fresh and the shadows were few. Night was for supper, a bit of reading, and thence climbing under a pile of soft blankets for many hours of slumber.

An hour earlier, he had eaten a joyless dinner of cold meat pie, two apples, and spring water, but even with a full stomach, Dorro wasn't relishing the evening's sojourn. Within fifteen minutes, he was drawing nigh upon the Great Wood, headed specifically for its most famous landmark, the Meeting Tree. This venerable specimen was a particularly long-lived elm tree with a massive crown spanning at least one-hundred and twenty feet across. On a summer's afternoon, you'd find dozens of Halflings lazing on the grass beneath it, either chatting, napping, playing ball, picnicking, or reading a good book, all of which were well and approved pastimes for a Halfling at that time of year. Yet Dorro would be enjoying no such festivities this evening. Tonight, he was to meet the Woodland elves, and perhaps his doom as well.

Even in the moonlight, the Meeting Tree was clear to see from a quarter-mile away. Its silvery crown stood out again the dark oaks and pines behind it, a spectacle at any time of day. As he drew closer, Dorro squinted his eyes for signs of Toldir and the other elves, but saw nothing. He suddenly brightened: "Maybe they forgot and won't come," he thought cheerfully. A few minutes later, he drew up to the trunk of the Meeting Tree, still very much alone. In girth, the trunk stretched a full ten feet in diameter and its circumference was many times that number. Even as a full-grown Halfling, Dorro was dazzled every time he stood near the magnificent tree.

"*Hullo?* Hullo, my friends!" Dorro whispered as loudly as possible, hoping both to rouse the elves' attention, yet perhaps still, maybe not raise their attention so he could go home to his warm bed. He waited a few more minutes and still nothing. "Oh well," he muttered quietly, "I guess they forgot. I suppose I'll be ambling home now ..."

"Not so quickly, little one." The voice in the darkness made Dorro nearly jump out of his skin. "We still have business to attend to. And many things to discuss."

Suddenly, the Halfling realized there was a ring of dark figures around him, forming a perfect circle. The elves! They had crept up so quietly, he hadn't heard a thing. "Ah, Toldir! I was waiting for you," Dorro bluffed, his voice cracking more than he'd hoped. "Good, good, yes, we have many things to talk about. I've been looking forward to it since this morning."

Dorro wasn't a good liar and was pretty sure they both knew it.

"As you say, little one."

"Excuse me, Mr. Toldir, but I do have a name and, in fact, am not 'little' for a Halfling. Actually, I'm considered on the tall side."

Even though it was dark, Dorro was pretty sure the elf was smiling. "You have spirit, and we of the Woodland elves like that. Your village protector—Forgo—also has that Halfling spirit. We wrongly assumed that your kind merely liked to indulge in fermented grain drinks and sweet pies that make you soft in the belly and dizzy in the head. But we are wrong and pleasantly so. What is your name, if I may ask?"

"I am known as Dorro Fox Winderiver."

The elf didn't respond for a second, and Dorro noticed that they kept looked at each other in the failing light, as if to comprehend these words. "That is an interesting—and very long—name. We might have some trouble pronouncing it. '*Dohr-oh*' is a strange word for us. However, Fox is a creature we elves of the Wood know all too well. Are you quick and wily like a fox? Hmm, I'm beginning to think you are.

"However, we are very intrigued by your longish name, Wind-and-River. That is a name to be reckoned with, my friend; it has deep meaning among all elves. Wind and rivers may seem gentle and soothing on the surface, but in mere seconds, both can turn powerful and dangerous. Indeed, it rings true with your other name, Fox. Like a fox, winds and rivers are cunning and deceptive. That is a lesson for we elves. There is perhaps more to you than we think."

Dorro was surprised by this sudden compliment and didn't know what to say. The Winderivers had been a sturdy, if unremarkable, Thimble Down family for many generations. Fox, meanwhile, was a name carried down from his maternal grandmother Rose, who hailed from the nearby village of Nob. Nevertheless, Dorro was thoroughly chuffed that his name carried some weight with the elves. Unknowingly, he had put his hands on his hips and stood a little taller than just a few minutes earlier.

"Now, Wind-and-River, we should get on with our meeting. The night is already growing long and even elves have to sleep."

"I agree, Toldir. I need to ask you more about Bing Rumple and your dealings with him and his brother. And also about the elvish brooch, which you seek to recover. I would like to help you with that."

"That is good to hear. But first, let me introduce you to Parahir, the elf you met this morning during our little 'boar hunt.' You may remember him?"

Dorro nodded.

"As well as a possessing a gift for cookery, Parahir is skilled among us at the art of discourse and would have a few words with you before we commence. Do you agree?"

Dorro nodded again, though slightly confused by this elaborate ritual. He wasn't sure what this was all about—Halflings just start talking; there are no rules or rituals. For some odd reason, the thought of Sheriff Forgo's admonition about getting bashed on the noggin entered his thoughts, but he waved the idea away just as quickly as it arrived.

From the tree's shadows, the stout figure of Parahir stepped up next to Toldir, who gave the subordinate elf a quick nod of his head, as if to begin. Dorro was truly confused now. Parahir began speaking, though at first, the Halfling had no idea what he was saying. It must be an elvish dialect of some sort. "Perhaps this is a tribal blessing or some such," Dorro thought.

"Durra elleth sheebaib abee. Tul amon arra badeigh sall. Shar. Shar. Durra elleth."

Dorro realized that he still had no idea what the words meant, but decided he didn't care. Parahir spoke in a sweet, dulcet tone, one that the Halfling could listen to for hours. It was like pure music to Dorro's ears, almost like the living sound of honey. The bookmaster yawned and sat down on the grass under the Meeting Tree. "This is quite pleasant," he thought.

"Shar, abbas adee burran. Tila amon arra badeight sall."

Ah, I feel so relaxed, thought Dorro, yawning again. *Here I am with my new friends, enjoying a cool evening under the leaves and stars. I couldn't be more fulfilled. And my, Mr. Parahir here has a pleasing voice ...*

Smiling and with a sleepy look in his eyes, the Halfling laid his head on the grass and, after that, he remembered nothing more.

☆ ☆ ☆

Sometime later, Dorro began to regain consciousness. *Where am I? What's going on?* he tried to posit in his fuzzy, clouded mind. *Why can't I move my hands and feet?* With growing alarm, Dorro realized that not only were his wrists and ankles bound, but that he had been slung over the shoulder of an elf that was trotting at a quick pace through the forest.

He started to fidget and get agitated. "Help me!" he shouted, or at least, he thought he was shouting. "I'm being abducted! Forgo! Cheeryup! Wyll! Someone save me!"

But then he heard those mesmerizing words again: *"Shar, abbas adee burran. Tila amon arra badeigh sael."*

Within a few seconds, Dorro's body relaxed and again he surrendered to the voice, drifting back to sweet and utter blackness.

24
Abduction

orro opened his eyes. He was lying on his side on cold, hard ground. He blinked a few times, trying to clear his fuzzy brain. Clearly, he was in the woods. *Why wasn't he in his own bed*, Dorro wondered. Then it all flooded back: the elves, the Meeting Tree, the sound of Parahir's strangely seductive voice.

He'd been kidnapped.

Instead of figuring out how to escape and keep from getting killed by the elves, Dorro's first feeling was, oddly enough, one of embarrassment. How could he face Sheriff Forgo, who predicted something like this would happen? Dorro was a fool to have trusted the elves. Oh well, he figured—he'd be dead in a short while anyway. He brightened a little at that thought: at least he didn't have to face Forgo and admit his own stupidity.

A second later, a strong pair of hands grabbed him from behind and hoisted him into a sitting position. Bleary-eyed, Dorro surveyed his surroundings. He was in an encampment, obviously one belonging to the elves, and there was a fire about thirty feet away, with a piece of meat slowly roasting over-top on an elaborately crafted spit. He realized how profoundly hungry he was. Maybe the elves would let him have a quick snack before they garroted him or snapped his neck. Dorro hoped it would be quick.

"Good morning, Wind-and-River. I must apologize for your accommodations."

Toldir stepped into the Halfling's view. Dorro's vision was still a bit bleary, but he craned his neck up and looked Toldir in the face. He would not give his elf the satisfaction of a return "good morning" or any gracious salutation at all.

"Tell me, Mr. Toldir, are you going to kill me now, or after breakfast?"

The tall blonde elf threw back his head and laughed, "Wind-and-River, you *do* give me joy and amusement. I did not know the Halflings were such a comical race, but again, I think we've underestimated you all."

"Well, if you're not going to snap my neck just yet, perhaps you could unbind my hands and give me a little of that smoked meat first. I'm positively famished. I should like to die with a full tummy, thank you very much."

Toldir smiled again. "Of course, my friend. But two matters: do not attempt to run away. I'm sure you are fast, but only the fastest deer can outrun a Woodland elf, so you might as well as save yourself the exertion. Secondly, we are not going to kill you. Elves do not take lives needlessly and certainly not the life of one who wouldn't put up a fair fight. Do you agree?"

"Certainly. I do, however, need a few minutes to myself to take care of, um, a rather pressing need. And I shan't run away. But this is rather urgent."

Toldir nodded and some elf from behind swiftly cut the rope on his wrists and ankles. Dorro stood with a little difficulty, as his knees and legs were cramped and sore, but nature is nature, so he quickly scuttled behind the nearest tree. A few minutes later he returned, still sore, but a much-relieved Halfling.

"Thank you, Toldir. I feel much better. Now, if you aren't going to kill me, as you say, could as I ask for a small bit of food. That will put me in a much better frame of mind."

In a heartbeat, a bowl was brought to him by the honey voiced Parahir—clearly the elves' camp cook—and its savory aroma almost made Dorro swoon again. He sat cross-legged on the ground and eagerly picked up the wooden spoon that accompanied this hand-held feast. He didn't recognize everything in the bowl, but he didn't care—he was starving. The dark, succulent meat proved to be deer, which had been slowly smoked over the fire for many hours. It was delicious. Underneath was a type of cooked grain—not rice, mind you—but perhaps some-thing in the barley or cereal family and very yummy to a Halfling that had been carried roughly through the night like a sack of beans.

He also found some soft, roasted root vegetables, though nothing he'd eaten before. They were yellow and orange, and easily cut with the edge of his spoon. Dorro guessed these were the tubers of various woodland plants, but ones that only the elves knew about—you certainly wouldn't find them on any Halfling menu. And intermixed with the whole dish were green leafy herbs; to Dorro's nostrils, they were pungent like basil, but with far more fragrance. Indeed, this aromatic leaf cleared up his head instantly. In fact, he felt that this bowl of food was not only nourishing his body, but helping to restore his mind to its proper balance. Whether it was because of his immense hunger or not, Dorro would regard this as one of the finest meals he'd ever eaten in his life.

A few minutes later he placed the bowl on the ground and sighed with contentment. "Thank you all. That was heavenly. I could go back to sleep now."

"I'm afraid we have little time for that, Wind-and-River," intoned Toldir. "Further, we promised you a talk and we shall not renege on that offer. But I'm sure you wonder why you're here and why we ..."

"... kidnapped me? Yes, it did cross my mind for a second," zinged Dorro in return.

Toldir then sat on the ground in front of the Halfling, as did a half-dozen other elves. Aside from the kidnapping business, Dorro thought, this was rather pleasant.

"It is not in our nature to apologize, Wind-and-River, but in this rare case, we will: I am sorry. I won't say it was wrong for us to have taken you against your will, as we needed to protect our party and find out your true intentions. Nor were we sure you hadn't brought others with you in an attempt to attack us. In that regard, we were very wrong."

"You could have just asked. Granted, I may be 'wily like a fox,' but I don't plan ambushes, nor would I against elves who could slaughter half our village if they chose. By the way, you don't plan to slaughter half our village, do you? Sheriff Forgo is a bit concerned about that."

All the elves laughed this time. "Again, Wind-and-River, you bring us laughter and merriment. We could grow very fond you and your wit. No, I can assure you we will not slay your kinsmen, though the matter of our missing brooch is a very serious one. We will find it and woe to anyone, Halfling or otherwise, who's been hiding it. Our vengeance will be quick and furious, but do not fear—your village is safe."

"Tell me more about this brooch, your Telstar. Why is it so important? Is it worth a fortune?"

"We don't think of it in terms of your Halfling values—it's not worth gold or silver to us, though by your reckoning, we could probably buy all your lands with it. The Telstar is an ancient brooch, wrought by the elves of old. There are many songs and poems as to its beauty, but more than that, it is a symbol not only of the Woodland elves, but of our hunting party. Our group of elves has hunted together for generations, including our fathers and grandfathers before us. Even our sisters, mothers, and grandmothers are gifted hunters. But we do not kill for sport. Even elves must eat, and it is the duty of our party to hunt far and wide, and bring back ample food for the rest of the Woodland elves in our home villages.

"We're not the only ones, of course, and there are others who are gifted in the ways of growing food from the earth—you would call them gardeners and farmers. But we all have our role to play and ours is to bring in deer, boar, fowl, and more to feed our young elflings and keep us all alive throughout the winter. And to guide us, we have the Telstar, which nourishes our spirits when we've traveled through hard lands for weeks, even months at a time. It may seem like a shiny trinket to you, but to us, it's our heart and souls. And for that, we would do anything to keep it safe."

"Even kill for it?"

A hush gripped the encampment. Toldir looked for a moment like he might explode in a torrent of rage, but the storm passed quickly. "That is a fair question, Wind-and-River. Yes, we would kill for it, but only against someone who stole it from us. And that's what your Bing Rumple did. He stole that and other items of value from us, including some bone-handled knives and a wonderful sword. Yet we did not kill him—someone else had that satisfaction."

Dorro gulped, but forced himself to continue. "You know, Toldir, I think I believe you. But there is one among you who has the facility to throw a knife as was the one that killed Bing. And you yourself admit to a motive."

"You speak of Baldar." Toldir turned his head to look at the dark-haired elf to this left. "He was the one that saved you and the girl Halfling from the boar yesterday. I will not lie. He is formidable with a knife and could have easily killed Bing Rumple. But I tell you again, he did not."

Dorro very much wanted to believe him, but knew others in Thimble Down wouldn't be so easily convinced. He looked over at Baldar, whose brows were knitted and held a storm of his own within. To Dorro, he looked very dangerous. While he believed Toldir, he wasn't sure Baldar wasn't the one with a secret. *Can elves lie to each other?* he wondered.

Changing topics quickly, Dorro continued, "So you did let Bing and his brother travel with your band?"

"For a while we did," replied Toldir. "We found the Rumples, and their sneering companion, starving to death in a dale by a cold, raging river. If it hadn't been for us, they would have been dead in just a few days—clearly, they knew nothing of hunting and foraging in the wild lands. In our compassion, we took them in, nourished all three with our game, and gave them shelter. At first they seemed affable, but we quickly realized they couldn't hunt and would not bring us anything in return. So it was decided to leave them at the nearest Halfling village and be on our way."

"One night, when were encamped on a bluff not far from a settlement, we were attacked by a force of rogue goblins. Like us, the goblins send out their own hunting parties for food and, while we usually avoid each other, sometimes we clash in battle. This was a bad one. The goblins hadn't been very successful in their hunt and were starving to death themselves. They didn't want our valuables—they wanted our meat. It was a ferocious fight, but in the end, they were too weak to succeed, and many perished at the end of our swords, arrows, and axes. There was much blood spilled."

"And Bing was a hero in the battle? He said that's why you awarded him the Telstar and weapons."

"Your Rumple, like his companions, was a detestable liar. He and the two others hid in their tents during the fight, while the rest of our group fought valiantly. After the skirmish, we realized it was time for them to leave us, so we dropped them off early the next morning in some Halfling settlement. I do not know its name."

"So you didn't give them any rewards for their bravery. That's strange."

"Perhaps not strange for liars and thieves. During the goblin raid, they hid away, but also used the distraction to steal the Telstar and our other treasures. We were too busy to account for everything after the fight, but within a week we knew the brooch was gone and who took it."

"So the fact that you're hunting in the Great Wood is hardly accidental."

Toldir smiled. "You do have good hunting around this fine forest. But no, it was no accident that brought us here. We came to reclaim what's ours."

The sun was high in the sky by this time, and Dorro asked to stand and stretch his legs. "Of course, Wind-and-River, you may do as you please. You are no longer our 'guest.' However, we're not many miles from Thimble Down, so I suggest you let us escort you home. Provided you have no more questions, of course."

"Thank you, Toldir. You have told me more than I hoped. However, I will remind you that many in the village think one of your hunting party killed Bing Rumple, and it will be hard to dissuade them. I suggest you stay in the woods until we get closer to a solution."

"I will consider your advice, Fox Wind-and-River, but remember, we will get the brooch back eventually. We are not murderers, but if one of your kind is hiding the Telstar for their own selfish end, then I cannot deny that blood may be spilled. We shall be merciless at the end."

Dorro knew there was nothing else to say. Further, he was dirty and tired, and very much wanted to return to the Perch to bathe and sleep in his own comfortable bed. He had made good progress with the investigation, but there was still no clear solution. Bing's murderer was still at large and the brooch was still missing. Inwardly, Dorro wondered if he accomplished anything at all. But there was time to think about this later.

"In that case, if you don't mind, I'd very much like to go home. But first, Parahir, can I have another bowl of your extraordinary culinary creation? I seem to be happily famished again."

25
Missing and Hungry

The girl was running as fast she could. Halflings turned their heads and craned necks out windows to see what the fuss was all about. It wasn't every day that the seamstress's daughter ran down Thimble Down's main road at full tilt, and with tears running down her cheeks, no less.

A few minutes later, Cheeryup Tunbridge burst into the gaol and gasped, "Sheriff! Sheriff, please help me!"

Forgo—who had been beginning to feel he could never get a moment's peace anymore—was again startled from a little post-breakfast nap.

"*Whoa*, little one. Can't a lawman get any honest work done?" he cried, rising from his brief slumber. Really, he was more than annoyed about leaving a wonderful dream he was having, one about a quiet, peaceful village with filled with zaftig ladies who had an eye for brave men of the law, desserts after every meal, and ample trees covered with thick green moss, perfect for napping against.

Forgo sighed and stared crossly at Cheeryup. "Why are you crying and carrying on so early in the morning?"

"He's missing."

"I know he's missing. He struck out of here last night. Kicked out the window, bars 'n' all. Will cost me a pretty penny to have it fixed. If Wyll Underfoot sets foot in this gaol again, he'll feel the back of my hand!"

Now it was the girl's turn to stare. "Wyll is g-g-gone?"

"Yes, indeedy. The rat bust out of here last night; we'll likely never see him again. But, how did you know he escaped? I surely hope you and Winderiver weren't involved. If so, you might find that bookmaster behind my bars 'ere the setting of today's sun. Maybe you, too!"

"I didn't know anything about Wyll escaping," said Cheeryup, fresh tears beginning to roll down her cheeks. "This is turning into the worst day ever."

"So, who exactly is missing, young lady? Your kitty cat?" added Forgo, with more sarcasm than was necessary.

"No, it's Mr. Dorro!" she sobbed. "He didn't come home—there's no one at the Perch and his bed wasn't slept in. The elves must have abducted him in the Great Wood last night!"

At that, Sheriff Forgo leapt to his feet. The crying girl had finally gotten his attention. "Drat! I told him not to go there. Why, the fool's probably lying dead in a gully with a knife sticking in his back!"

Before Forgo could retract that statement, Cheeryup burst into fresh sobs. The lawman was instantly remorseful: "There, there, girl—I wasn't serious. Why, ol' Dorro will be ambling through Thimble Down any minute, on his way to go fishin' in the river."

The girl quieted down, but in his thoughts, Forgo wasn't so sure. He knew the elves were dangerous and had warned Dorro strenuously of this. The Sheriff paled at the thought, but knew he must face one certain fact: Dorro Winderiver might already be a corpus in the woods.

✶ ✶ ✶

Less than a mile north of the gaol, Wyll Underfoot was sitting on a fallen log, also with tears in his eyes. The boy was utterly miserable. He still felt that Cheeryup had betrayed him and he had mixed feelings for Mr. Dorro. Formerly, he thought the bookmaster the warmest, kindest Halfling he had ever known, but during their final meeting at the gaol, Dorro had been cross with him and given Wyll a good scolding. He didn't like how that felt.

"What have I done?" he wailed to himself. "I'm lost, hungry, and tired. I'd rather be in gaol with a lumpy bed and some food than out here with the flies and nothing to eat."

More than that, the village of Thimble Down had begun to grow on him, even Sheriff Forgo, who was generally fair and kind. But by escaping from gaol, he had "made his bed and now needed to sleep in it," as the old saying went.

Wyll knew that he couldn't just slumber on the hard ground and eat raw leaves, so he needed to get busy. Fortunately, he had spent several weeks sleeping in the woods en route to Thimble Down and had learned a few things. Wiping away the tears, Wyll began looking for a location to set up a temporary camp. It needed to be hidden, lest he was discovered by the Sheriff, but also have access to fresh water. He stood up and, logically, began walking downhill, hoping he would eventually find a water source.

Twenty minutes later, he found a promising spot. It was a small rise over a bubbling creek. The rise was tufted with holly bushes, which would provide sufficient protection and camouflage, at least for a few days. There was no cave for shelter, but it backed up onto a stone outcropping that should keep any rain off his head. Wyll's immediate challenge, however, was a lack of tools and fire. He began scanning the ground for useful rocks and found a stone with a relatively sharp end. *That will do*, he thought earnestly, and then looked about for a good stick. He soon spied one, about five-feet long and straight. For the next ten minutes, Wyll sat down and furiously used the rock's edge to sharpen a point. In due time, he had a basic spear that he would use to hunt and dig.

Next up, he began to gather flinty rocks, twigs, and leaves to start a fire. Wyll was aware that he actually *needed* a fire. The evenings were still cold in the forest and a Halfling boy could easily freeze to death, even in Spring. He forgot about stealing the gaol's blankets when he escaped and, in retrospect, cursed himself for the blunder.

With basic fire-making supplies in hand, Wyll next thought of food. Without anything to eat, a fire would only keep him warm—he also needed a fire in his belly to get him through the chilly night. Jumping down from his rough encampment, Wyll walked toward the creek, which was a good place to begin one's hunt for supper. He struck gold almost immediately in the form of fiddlehead ferns, which had just jutted up from the soft springtime earth along the creek's bank. Wyll knew they were edible and grabbed a few of the shoots from the ground and quickly gobbled them down. "Could use a bit of salt," he mused with an inward grin. He would double back to this location later and dig up more ferns to roast on a hot rock.

His main culinary goal, however, was fish. While he could skin a rabbit or a squirrel, the odds of him actually catching one with his primitive spear were remote and he knew it. (In his favor, Wyll was a realist and, though he didn't know it, this was a trait that would save his life many times to come.) As it was Spring, he knew that the creeks were beginning to fill up with trout that were beginning to mate for the spawning in a few weeks. That meant they'd be active and looking around the creek for a quick snack. Lamentably, Wyll didn't have a fishing line, which he was modestly handy with, but his sharp stick would have to do. Again, the thought of throwing his "spear" and actually impaling a tasty fish was remote, but he knew a few other tricks.

Wyll took off his shoes and knee stockings, and laid them on a nearby bush, quickly stepping across the muddy bank into the water. "*Oyoaiiow!*" he yelped as the icy water touched his toes. Girding himself against the chill, he began the hunt. Being careful not to slip on the slick, algae-covered rocks that lined the bottom, Wyll strode slowly into the creek until the water was midway up his calf. His best chance lay in shallow water, so that's where he headed.

There was a tiny waterfall about ten feet away, really more of a large pile of logs and stones that was backing the creek up and creating a deep pool. *This looks promising*, Wyll thought to himself. Walking slowly as not to frighten any potential quarry, he began scanning the edges of the stony pool, looking for any stray trout lurking amidst the rocks. "There!" he whispered, as a dark shadow zipped around a boulder and darted back to deep water. That was a clever trout who knew there was trouble afoot. But a few minutes later, Wyll saw another—a fat brown trout patrolling around the shallow rocks in search of floating insect larvae and other tempting treats.

Still, Wyll was acutely aware this wasn't a game. He needed to catch this fish in order to eat and live another day. Any sudden movements or noises would alarm the trout and send him back to the safety of the depths. Moving at the slowest speed possible, Wyll maneuvered himself into a place that effectively blocked the fish from escaping, unless it zipped through the boy's legs. Finally within three feet of his prey, Wyll pulled his torso back slowly and, like lightning, stabbed at the fish with his makeshift spear. The fish had already caught a glance of Wyll's reflection in the surface and blasted through the fissure by the Halfling's left foot to safety and freedom. "Drat!" Wyll cursed. This wasn't going to be easy.

With his feet growing colder by the second, Wyll grew despondent. "I shall never eat," he lamented. "Fiddleheads won't make for a full belly, not at all!"

Another dark shape flashed by his foot. This trout popped into the little rocky pool he was looming over. This looked like a good one—big and fat, and full of tender flesh. Wyll could almost imagine it slowly cooking over his fire. But before he got too far ahead of himself, he focused on the matter at hand. He had to actually capture this fine fellow or else dinner would just be a dream. Looking at his spear, he realized it wouldn't really help him in the long run. Wyll would have to land this prize another way.

He slowly followed the fish as it meandered amid the rocks. If the trout was aware of him, it made no notice. Wyll saw his chance—the fish had just swum into an even smaller pool in which there was only one way out. Knowing that his survival might depend on the next few seconds, Wyll rushed the fish, knowing it would seek to escape, but instead of letting him slip out the small exit, he herded it further into the watery rocks with his hands. With each second, the boy closed in and the fish jutted from pool to puddle and back again. Wyll was intentionally driving it toward shallower sections of the rocky bank.

Bending over, he then began scooping water behind the fish to keep it moving forward. In its frantic escape, the trout lurched forward faster and faster—until it made a fateful mistake. It made a giant leap, hoping to land back in the big, deep pool. Instead, it fell upon the creek's muddy bank. It flopped up and down, but it was too late. Wyll was upon the trout in a heartbeat, scooping it up with his bare hands. In his excitement, he hadn't accounted for its slippery scales and the trout once more flopped back to freedom. But by this time, Wyll had pushed the fish far from the water's edge and the doomed creature landed on a tuft of grass. The young angler grabbed it firmly by the gills and hoisted it in the air triumphantly. The battle was over.

Provided he could make a good, roaring fire, Wyll would soon dine on freshly roasted trout-on-a-stick, with a delicate accompaniment of grilled fiddlehead ferns. More importantly, he'd live for another day, and, for that, Wyll realized he owed the trout his deepest, most profound gratitude.

26
Cheeryup Takes Charge

heeryup Tunbridge sat just a few feet away from her mother, who was quietly mending a torn jacket sleeve back into place. The girl watched as her mother used quick, deft hands to return the frayed fabric to a wearable condition. Following her mother's needlework took her mind off more troubling matters, notably the fact that both Mr. Dorro and Wyll were gone. Cheeryup had woken a few times during the night and cried until she fell back asleep again. She had dark circles under her eyes, but otherwise, there were no outward appearances that something was wrong. Or so she thought.

"Out with it, my dear," said Mrs. Tunbridge, not making eye contact and continuing to sew with incredible agility and precision. "I know when my daughter isn't happy, and those bags under your eyes tell me I'm right."

"I'm fine, Mother, really."

"I'm waiting, Cheeryup—we can sit here all day," rejoined her mother, coolly. Her daughter said nothing.

"Okay then, I'll tell the story," said her mother. "You may think your doddering old mother only knows about triple-stitching and which print patterns will look best in the Summer sun, but give me an ear and let me tell you about my customers. You see, dear, my sewing clients are Halflings from all over this village and beyond. And they tell me things—I rarely have to leave this burrow to know what's happening around Thimble Down. I know who got drunk last night and thrown out of the Hanging Stoat, who's about to have a wee baby, and even who's making eyes at whom. And I know all about *you*."

Trying not to give anything away, Cheeryup just stared at her black leather shoes. Her dress was beginning to make her itch, but fidgeting came naturally to her anyway.

"First of all, I know all about your adventures with Mr. Dorro."

At this, the girl looked up fast and guiltily at her mother.

"Don't give me that puppy-dog face, Cheeryup. I have known Dorro Fox Winderiver since we were in school together some forty years ago, and he was a mischievous scamp even then. No, he wasn't a bad youngling, but in some ways, he was artful in his actions. Maybe not the brightest lad in our class—nor is he now—but he's extremely clever and has a gift for figuring out the strangest problems. Even back then, Dorro was a bit of a loner, always off in the woods searching for salamanders rather than playing with us. A queer one, that."

Mrs. Tunbridge laughed to herself and then added, "You know, Dorro and Lucretia Thrip were always squabbling as younglings. They fought like dogs and chickens all the time. He'd pull on her pigtails and she'd chase him across the play yard, cursing him the whole way. Actually, I think she was smitten with him and was just mad that it wasn't reciprocated. Or, well, maybe it was. But that was a long time ago."

"Suffice to say, young lady, I know that anyone who spends time with Dorro will become wrapped up in his little investigations, and I have been sure for a long time that you have become part of these machinations. 'Library assistant,' *indeed.*" she added with a wry smile.

"But I do help in the library, doing all sorts of chores for Mr. Dorro, as well as for Bedminster Shoe."

"Is Shoe in on Dorro's adventures? Doesn't seem to fit his odd personality, but who knows?"

"No, I don't think so, Mother. Mr. Shoe merely watches the library when Mr. Dorro can't be present. But yes, sometimes, I've done an errand or two for Mr. Dorro. He says I'm of great value to his investigations, especially this current one, and we can also use the extra coins. And I'm never in any danger. Well, almost never."

Cheeryup decided not to tell her mother about the elves and the fierce boar that almost ended their lives.

"Enough about Mr. Dorro, my dear. Tell me about this boy."

Again, Cheeryup stared at her mother, this time in disbelief. "How did you know?"

"I told you, girl, I have customers from all over the village and I hear things. There's a young boy, about your age, who was taken into Mr. Dorro's care until he was arrested on some silly charge. Believe me, if Sheriff Forgo had as much brains in his head as his pony Tom, I'd be amazed. He's a dolt—imprisoning a young boy on the word of numb-nuts like Osgood Thrip and Farroot Rumple."

"Wyll is innocent—I know it!" plead Cheeryup frantically. "He'd never steal anything, except if he was hungry. But he apologized to Mr. Dorro for that and they're friends now. Or at least they were. And now Wyll is gone." With that, the girl began crying again.

"I know you're fond of this boy, Cheeryup. So I have just one question for you."

"Yes, mother?" she said, stifling her tears.

"Why are you still here?"

"What do you mean?"

"If you know the boy to be innocent and he's gone off somewhere, why aren't you searching for him?

"I d-don't know ..."

"My guess is that he hasn't gone far away—in fact, there's no place to go around here, except perhaps Nob or

Water-Down. Or maybe he's camping by the river or in the Great Wood; you did say he slept in the forest before Mr. Dorro found him. So if it were me, I'm mop up those tears and pack a lunch. And put on some sturdy shoes. You're going to be walking a lot today."

With that, Cheeryup bounded across the room and threw her arms around her mother's neck. "Thank you! And I'll be back tonight, I promise!"

After a quick peck on the cheek, the girl flew into the kitchen to make a sandwich for the day's adventure. "I'll find Wyll!" she said to herself with great excitement, "I know I shall!"

27
Full of Surprises

t was a full day's journey back to Thimble Down for Dorro and his escort of Woodland elves. They spoke little, but Dorro didn't care—it was a beautiful Spring morning and he was enjoying the sight of leaves budding out, mayapples and ferns emerging from the leaf-strewn soil, and dozens of songbirds flitting from branch to branch. It wasn't lost on him, however, that he was growing hungry. Parahir had offered him some nuts and dried fruit when they arose that morning, but that was several hours ago and, indeed, the bookmaster's stomach kept its own schedule.

"Excuse me, Toldir, but might we break our fast with a little lunch?"

"I'm not familiar that Halfling word, Wind-and-River," replied the elf leader, not breaking his stride. "What is a *lonch?* And why should we break it?"

"It's pronounced '*lunch,*' said Dorro, rubbing his chin and trying to be as diplomatic as possible. Thinking quickly, he continued, "It's a daily ritual among Halflings, one where we give praise to spirits of earth that surround us. And we perform it by consuming some excellent food. By doing this, we prove ourselves to be better and truer stewards of the land, sky, and water. And it's time for me to practice today's, err, ritual."

Toldir stared at him blankly. A few seconds later, he began speaking in elvish to his comrades: "*Keebra amman doth raga. Borath.*" Around him, the rest of the hunting party began giggling to themselves. Dorro didn't know what the joke was, but he was reasonably sure that he was the punch line. Still, he didn't flinch and kept the stoic look on his face. A moment later, Parahir, the elves' most excellent cook, approached with a bemused look on his face.

"Toldir has decided to let the hunters take a short rest and give us time to discuss our future plans. In the interim, I've been instructed to find you some sustenance for the remainder of our journey. Our best huntsman, Baldar, will join us to help facilitate your *lonch* ritual." Dorro couldn't help notice that Parahir said this with small grin on his face, but chose to ignore it. Besides which, his tummy was still gurgling.

Without a word, Parahir turned and bade Dorro to follow him with a nod of his head. Baldar fell in line behind the Halfling as they headed off into the woods. The bookmaster felt uneasy about being alone with a dangerous elf like Baldar, whom he knew was a deadly marksman with knives. Then again, the two elves might whip up an excellent *lonch* for him. Now it was Dorro's turn to giggle.

After speaking with Baldar briefly, Parahir continued, "In the interest of resuming our journey swiftly, Baldar agrees that stalking game and cooking it would take far too long. However, we're near a broad stream, which should be full of fish. We shall be able to land one quickly and cook it in just a few minutes. Will that satisfy you?"

"Indeed it would, as I love fresh fish. Further, I will enjoy observing your angling methods—I might even learn something new," said Dorro.

Parahir and Baldar merely looked at the Halfling like he had three eyes, but mostly ignored him. Taking a position at the side of the stream, Baldar drew an arrow from his quiver and fitted it to his ash bow. (*Interesting*, thought Dorro. *This shall be a lesson indeed*.) A few yards away, Parahir, acting as his spotter, pointed at a dim shadow moving in the water. Baldar nodded and pulled his arrow back. In a flash, he loosed the string and the arrow disappeared into the water. Expecting a fat, impaled trout to float to the surface, Dorro was confused when nothing happened. Parahir merely shook his head. Amazingly, Baldar had missed.

Dorro chalked it up to some fluke, but ten minutes later, he wasn't so sure. Baldar had missed three fish that Parahir had located in the stream and was growing more irate and frustrated with each twang of the bow. Finally, the cook spoke, "Baldar is our deadliest warrior on land, but Woodland elves are not the best anglers. Fish are sometimes too clever for us. And we did not bring a net to trap our prey, as is our preferred method."

Coughing diplomatically, Dorro said, "You know, I do a bit of fishing back in Thimble Down and am, well, reasonably good at it. If I might be of any service ..."

At that Baldar handed the bookmaster his bow, his face contorted in suppressed rage. "No, actually, I don't know how to shoot an arrow, added Dorro, declining the offer." Still, I always keep a little fishing line in my pocket, just in case. Just wait a tick."

Reaching into a deep, inner pocket of his knee-breeches, Dorro pulled out a small, flat packet of paper and carefully unfolded it. The elves were amazed to see him remove a coil of waxed silk, with a metal hook on the end. Parahir and Baldir truly had no idea what the Halfling intended, but were strangely intrigued nonetheless. Working quickly, as his stomach was still churning, Dorro advised confidently, "Why don't one of you start the fire? We should have a fish in hand in just a few minutes. At this time of year, trout are as hungry as I am and will bite at anything."

The elves tried to stifle their grins, but the bookmaster ignored them and got busy. He looked around and grabbed a reasonably straight stick measuring about six feet long. He snapped off its side branches and tied the silk line firmly to its tip. Scouring the terrain around them, he walked over to a clump of dead, rotting leaves left over from the previous Autumn and began pushing them aside. Toward the bottom of the pile, he reached in to the soft ground and pulled out a fat, wriggling earthworm who had been napping in the cool earth. Efficiently, Dorro put the worm on his hook, stepped up to the water's edge, and cast out the line as far as he could. The worm sailed out about fifteen feet and landed with a *ker-plunk* in the middle of stream.

"We are confused, Wind-and-River," urged Parahir. "How can you expect to catch a fish on your thin spider string? It will break instantly. And I must tell you, we must be getting back to our journey soon. We don't have time to experiment, and Toldir will be growing impatient."

Dorro merely nodded and smiled. The elves became annoyed at his passivity, but a heartbeat later, they noticed his fishing line moving slowly across the water. And the Halfling still had that foolish grin on his face.

"I'm most sorry, my friend, but we really must be getting back."

From complete silence, the quiet stream suddenly exploded in a frenzy of splashing water and motion. "*FISH ON!*" cried Dorro in his best angling voice, pulling up hard on his makeshift rod. Signaling the beginning of a fight, he added, "It's a big one, too. Start that fire, Baldar!"

By this time, Parahir had a big grin on his face, while the other elf merely looked incredulous. Dorro, however, was having the time of his life—"Nothing better than wrestling a fierce wild trout in Spring!" he shouted.

Since he was without a proper reel, Dorro began pacing backwards to coax the fish toward shore, and then reached out and grabbed the silk line with his own hands. "We're going to do this the hard way, my scaly friend," he said defiantly. Dropping the rod, he grabbed a second handful of line and began reeling in the fish, hand over hand. No question, this was a hefty fish and it wasn't going to surrender easily. At one point, Parahir wondered if they were going to have to instead fish Dorro out of the water, as he lost his footing a few times and headed perilously toward the edge. But digging in, the Halfling pulled in more fistfuls of line and, suddenly, a monster trout leapt from the water and arched in midair. It was truly beautiful and the elves were entranced.

The battle ensued for another minute, but then the trout began to tire. A few minutes later, it was the elves who were staring slack-jawed at the Halfling, now standing at the stream's edge with a giant, glistening trout of at least three pounds in his hands.

With a triumphant smile, Dorro turned to them and asked, "Shall we dine, gentlemen?"

☆ ☆ ☆

Less than an hour later, Dorro and the two elves rejoined the hunting party and made ready to continue their trek.

"Did my elves help with your *lonch* ritual, Wind-and-River?" said Toldir with a smirk. "I hope you found their services satisfactory."

Baldar stalked off into the woods with a dark scowl on his face, while Parahir began laughing out loud. "You were quite right about our diminutive guest, Toldir," he said, a broad smile on his face. "There is indeed much more to the Halfling than we had guessed."

Toldir looked confused, while the cook continued. "We were not able to feed him—in fact the reverse was true. Wind-and-River fed us *lonch.* And it was delicious!"

28
Lost and Found

With a small knapsack on her shoulder packed with her lunch and some provisions for Wyll, should she find him, Cheeryup headed out the door and made a quick march to the library, which had just opened for the day.

"Good morning, Mr. Shoe," she said to the Halfling sitting at the small, dusty circulation desk near the front door.

"Hullo, Miss Cheeryup. I didn't know you were coming in to help me today."

"I'm not, actually. I need to do some research before I go out on another errand."

"Hmm, can I help you at least?" Bedminster asked quizzically, cocking an eyebrow.

"Yes, per'aps. I need to look at a map of the county."

“Those you know where to find, surely,” said Bedminster. “Say, you haven’t seen Mr. Dorro today, have you? I wish he’d let me know when and for how long he wants me to look after the library. Then again, I’m not complaining about the extra coins this puts in my pocket—it’s been a slow month for drawing up wills and contracts. Just a few birth and death notices, I’m afraid.”

Cheeryup felt a pang of sadness when she thought of Dorro. While he was, in fact, perfectly healthy and in the care of Toldir’s elves, she did not know this. For all she was aware, Dorro could be their prisoner or even worse. “I’m sure Mr. Dorro will be back soon,” she said hopefully. “But I must see the map and then dash. I promise I’ll be back tomorrow to help you!”

Bedminster Shoe smiled and returned to his work. In his mind, however, he knew that she was on another secret mission for Dorro. *Excellent!* he thought, *Another case for my archives. I shall pigeonhole Dorro in a few weeks and pump him for the entire tale.*

✲ ✲ ✲

Cheeryup dashed up the ladder and found rolled-up local maps in the upper gallery. There were various maps in the cubbyholes, some for topography, a few containing agricultural information, and others showing property lines. She grabbed a larger county map that encompassed

Thimble Down and the other surrounding hamlets, from Upper-Down south to Nob, and from the River Thimble west to the eastern foothills. And surrounding everything was the Great Wood.

The girl scanned the map, trying to figure where Wyll might have fled. If he was sensible, we would have gone to another village, where he could beg for—or steal—some food, while hiding in a barn or shed. But the more she thought about it, Cheeryup couldn't see Wyll doing that again. He would be scared, she thought, and more likely to strike out on his own. Admittedly, the boy had a streak of stubbornness and even pride—he wouldn't depend on the kindness of others for a while.

No, it was more likely he was sleeping in the woods again. She shivered at the thought of him alone in the forest, especially with terrifying elves about. It was now doubly important that Cheeryup find Wyll and bring him home. Maybe he and Mr. Dorro could mend their friendship, but that wasn't her overriding concern at the moment. In her heart, she felt that Wyll would most likely be near the river or in the Great Wood, north of the Thimble Down. That's where she'd start her search.

✣ ✣ ✣

A quarter after ten o'clock in the morning, Cheeryup departed the library and struck out toward the river.

There, she'd get on the River Road and head north toward the Meeting Tree and the sprawling forest beyond. Spring was truly starting to show its colors, she noted happily, as wild daffodils were sprouting up everywhere, their yellow, cream, and white cups waving in the soft April breeze. There were also crocuses and hyacinths galore, along with a few purple-shrouded fritillarias standing at attention. If it wasn't for her hunt for Wyll, Cheeryup would have instead preferred to walk through these meadows and lie amid their daffodil-strewn glory. Thimble Down never looked better than in these few, precious weeks of Spring.

The trek to the river did not take long. On her right, Cheeryup passed the Perch and felt a twinge of regret and sadness. So much had happened in the past few weeks and the ensuing emotions were roiling up inside her. First there was Wyll's false imprisonment, for which she was not present, but then his first escape and concealment in the garden shed. At the time, it had felt like so much fun, but in retrospect, the girl realized that they'd all been foolish. It would have been wiser to return him to Sheriff Forgo's gaol immediately and let Wyll receive a fair judgment from the Mayor. In all likelihood, he would have been quickly exonerated and none of this would have been necessary.

The more she thought about it, the more peeved Cheeryup became at Mr. Dorro for agreeing to this careless tactic—he was very much to blame for Wyll's subsequent problems, despite his good intentions. It was then that she realized that, despite his prestigious position, Mr. Dorro could be very immature at times. Yet, she also knew that he was very fond of the boy—perhaps that clouded his judgment. Worse, Mr. Dorro was missing and she wondered if she could have prevented it. Sheriff Forgo hadn't wanted Dorro to meet with the elves that night and now the worst had occurred.

What if he's dead? she thought, frantically. *And what if it's my fault? Stop it—I mustn't let these thoughts cloud my head. I need to find Wyll today. If I can do that, we can go search for Mr. Dorro soon enough.*

Cheeryup got a grip on her emotions and soldiered past the Perch and began moving northwards toward the Meeting Tree. She knew that time was short and she had lots of ground to cover. It didn't take long for her to reach the venerable old elm, with its massive crown of bright, green leaves. Again, she wanted to tarry and run around the trunk playing games, but she had to stay focused. Wyll could be anywhere in the Great Wood, she knew, but Cheeryup tried to think like him and follow that line of thought.

"Hmm, from what I know, Wyll is a practical lad, so he probably wouldn't go too deep into the forest," she mused. "And didn't he say something about fishing earlier? He might head toward water, if that's the case."

Feeling energized, Cheeryup headed past the Meeting Tree and then down the gently sloping terrain toward one of the forest's many creeks. She walked for nearly an hour, stopping once to eat an apple to keep her strength up. Eventually, she found a quiet stream running through the woods and followed it for a quarter of a mile. Finally, her instincts paid off—ahead of her, Cheeryup found footprints in its muddy shore.

"WYLL! Wyll Underfoot! Are you here?" she cried out. "Please answer me!"

There was no response. She started moving away from the stream, up a little rise, when she found her next clue—a broken branch and some tramped-down leaves. This looked very suspicious, so Cheeryup followed the trail toward a few holly bushes. She ducked around a few of them, carefully avoiding their sharp, prickly leaves, and found what she was looking for: a little flat area under a stone outcropping and—*yes!*—a small fire pit and what appeared to be the skeletal remains of a fish. Wyll had been here, she knew. But why wasn't he here now?

"HELP! Help me!"

A small voice echoed throughout the woodlands and Cheeryup knew there was danger afoot—and Wyll was in the heart of it. Thinking fast, she grabbed a long, fat stick that had been lying on the ground and rushed out of the hidden encampment. But she didn't know which way to go.

"HELP!"

The sound was coming from above her. Cheeryup rushed around and over the stone outcropping into a wider expanse of the Great Wood. There was a commotion about fifty yards in front of her, heading away from the stream and encampment. She ran toward the sound of Wyll's voice and came upon frightening scene—Wyll was a few feet off the ground, holding onto the branches of a small dogwood tree and trying to scurry up as far as he could, for on the ground was a family of angry foxes. As it turned out, Wyll had disturbed their mid-morning rest and they were quite cross with him. The mother fox was irate that this clumsy Halfling had woken her babies up, and the father fox thought he'd teach the lumbering buffoon a lesson by giving his ankles a few nasty bites.

Wyll was clearly in a panic and shimmying ever further from the foxes, but the dogwood was rather small and there wasn't room to go much further. Without a moment's hesitation, Cheeryup raised her big stick and charged into the scene, screaming "Arhhhhhh!" like a warrior huntress. The mother and father fox looked at each other and decided this wasn't worth the effort—this new Halfling looked dangerous and angry. The father fox was particularly aggrieved that he couldn't give the treed Halfling some sharp nips with his incisors, but his mate's expression clearly indicated it was time to pack up the babies and scramble out of there. With Cheeryup upon them in full fury, the fox family bounded away from tree and headed back to their comfy hole on the other side of the stream.

With the danger over, the boy fell out of the tree straight into Cheeryup's arms and both younglings collapsed onto the ground. "Wyll!" screamed the girl as she hugged him tightly. He tried to master his feelings, but instead put his head on her shoulder—Wyll needed a big hug and thus didn't object to Cheeryup's display of much-needed affection.

Slightly embarrassed, they pulled apart and smiled at each other. "*Th-thank* you for saving me," Wyll finally gasped. "It all happened so fast—one minute I was walking through the woods looking for food and the next, the foxes were chasing me and yapping at my ankles."

"I'm so glad I found you—I was so afraid you'd left us for good! But you need to come back to Thimble Down with me, so we can feed you and clear up this mess."

Suddenly, Wyll looked suspicious. "I won't go back," he snarled, impatiently. "Mr. Dorro doesn't want me anymore and I won't stay in that gaol. But I'm so hungry; I don't know what to do." He seemed on the verge of crying again.

At that, Cheeryup fished in her knapsack and pulled out her sandwich: "Here—eat it. *Now.*"

Wyll didn't have to be asked twice. He grabbed the wrapped treat, tore off the paper, and sank his teeth into the hearty cheese and pickle sandwich. A look of instant bliss spread across his face. "S'ank yoo varry mush," he mumbled in mid-chew, savoring each and every bite. Clearly, the boy was famished, despite catching that big trout the day before. This morning's fishing expedition had left him empty-handed, which prompted Wyll to leave the stream and walk up into the deeper forest for food. That's where he ran afoul of the fox family.

"I have another idea, Wyll, although I do not like it." The boy nodded, indicating he was listening to the girl, but wasn't about to stop eating his heavenly sandwich just yet.

"Although I do think you should come back with me, now that I know where you are, I can continue bringing food and blankets, at least until we decide on a better plan," said Cheeryup. "I've also been to your camp site. It will do for the moment, but you'll need better provisions."

Wyll was in amazement. He'd never met a girl who could track a Halfling's footprints through the woods, battle ferocious foxes, and then come up with a clever strategy to keep him hidden from the Sheriff. Though he wouldn't say anything, deep down, Cheeryup was his new hero. Wyll was perhaps a little smitten, too, but he couldn't admit that to himself.

"That sounds wonderful!" gushed Wyll. "Last night was simply awful—I was freezing and there were bugs nipping me in my sleep. I did catch a big trout yesterday and cooked it, but I was starving again this morning and all the fish in the stream had moved off elsewhere."

Reaching into her bag again, Cheeryup pulled out another apple, a bit of cheese, some nuts, and a crust of bread. "Here, this should hold you for a few hours. I'll return later with more food, blankets, and maybe one of Mr. Dorro's old fishing rods. That might be enough to keep you going for a while."

"Has Mr. Dorro asked about me? And why isn't he here?" said Wyll, suddenly looking dejected.

"He's, um, very busy at the library," replied Cheeryup. She didn't like lying, but didn't think Wyll could bear knowing that Mr. Dorro was missing. She'd tell him in good time. Wyll didn't look happy about it, but didn't say anything.

The two younglings sat together for another half hour, until Cheeryup felt it was time to return to Thimble Down and gather supplies. "I'll be back in a few hours, Wyll. Don't worry—the time will pass quickly."

She gave him another hug and headed back toward the Great Wood and the village. Cheeryup Tunbridge had much to do.

29
The Return

orro and the troop of Woodland elves reached the Meeting Tree at mid-afternoon on the same day that Cheeryup discovered Wyll in those very woods, barely a half-mile away (indeed, she had passed by this exact spot not one hour earlier, on her way back into the village to get Wyll more food and supplies). It was time for Dorro and the elves to part company.

"This is as far as we dare go at present, Wind-and-River," said the elf leader. "We are certainly not welcome in your village, though that is our fault as well."

"I wish things were different, Toldir, but for the moment, I still have to find Bing Rumple's murderer and recover your brooch. I'm not sure how, but I will try."

"We know you will. I hope you believe that we did not kill your Halfling. Yet you know where we stand on the Telstar—we *will* have it back."

"I know. And I do know you didn't murder Bing," replied Dorro. Yet even as the words left his mouth, his eyes darted left for a quick glimpse of Baldar. He was certain Toldir hadn't killed Bing, but as for this dark, moody elf, he wasn't as sure. Baldar had never professed his innocence.

Dorro reached out his hand and, with a humored smile, Toldir returned the handshake, which he considered a quaint Halfling ritual. "I think we shall see each other again, Wind-and-River. Let us hope it is under happier circumstances."

Dorro nodded, and with that, the elves walked back into the Great Wood and promptly disappeared. He then turned toward home. As much as he had learned over the past two days from the elves and enjoyed himself, Dorro was keen to return to the Perch. There was no other place he liked better.

✲ ✲ ✲

After a good night's sleep in his own bed, Dorro ambled into Thimble Down early the next morning feeling rested. He made straight for the gaol, where he had two duties to perform: report in to Sheriff Forgo and, more importantly, apologize to Wyll for his harsh words the other day. He was sure the boy would understand and they could begin planning their next steps. Who knows? Maybe if the Sheriff was in a good-enough mood, perhaps they could arrange for Wyll's release.

Dorro stepped through gaolhouse door, but no one was there. He walked through the small building, but saw nothing. He became greatly concerned when he went to talk to Wyll, only to find his cell empty and the barred window greatly damaged. Dorro knew that something bad had happened.

"Hullo?"

It was Forgo's voice. "Here, Sheriff!" said Dorro emerging from the back rooms.

"*Dorro!* I mean, hello Winderiver," shouted the Sheriff with more emotion than he'd intended. "So you're back. I knew you would be—had no worries about them elves at all." Forgo was a bad liar, but hoped Dorro wouldn't notice.

"I had a fine adventure, Sheriff. But first, where's the boy?" Dorro grew apprehensive—he knew this wouldn't be good.

"*Ah*, him," said Forgo, stroking his chin and avoiding eye contact with the bookmaster. "He's gone. Kicked out the window frame in the back cell and scuppered off into the woods. I told you before, Winderiver—that lad is gone and never coming back. At least not this time."

"Of course," he continued, "I will have to search your shed and property to make sure you aren't hiding him again, but—judging by the look in your eyes—I'd say you didn't know about this one."

"*Curses*," spat Dorro, more to himself than Forgo. "I shouldn't have been so mean to the youngling. I wanted to teach him a lesson, but it backfired—he's left us and it's all my fault."

"I know you were fond of the lad, Winderiver, but Master Underfoot had a wild streak in him. He wasn't going to stay here long. Surely, I don't know that many children who've broken out of the Thimble Down gaol—*twice*. That's some pluck for you, I tell ye. Sheer pluck!"

"P'raps your right, Sheriff. But I did have high hopes for him. Wyll had a good heart and manners, too. I'm sorely aggrieved."

Changing topics perhaps a bit too suddenly, Forgo drove at what he was really interested in: "Tell me, Winderiver, did you get the elves to confess? Did they kill Bing?"

"No, of course not. Well, I'm not entirely sure. But they are good folk, Sheriff. I have seen a whole different side of the Woodland elves, and they are kindly and wise. However, this Telstar gem inspires great passion in their hearts and they vow to get it back at any cost. Sheriff, it is imperative that we find it and return it them as soon as we can. If not, they will come back to town and search for it themselves. And nothing will stop them."

"Then we'll call out the militia and fight them. We can't have elf warriors razing our town and stealing whatever they want!"

"Sheriff, there are two salient points to consider. The brooch really is theirs and never was Bing's. And I meant what I said—nothing will stop them. We could meet their band of a dozen hunters with a hundred fully armed Halflings, and they would still prevail. The Woodland elves are masters of many weapons, as well as fast, strong, and deadly fighters. Such a battle would leave many Halflings lying dead on the ground."

For once, Forgo had nothing to say.

"Sheriff, you and I are the best hope for solving this mystery. I feel that the elves and I are on good-enough terms that they'll give us a few days. But eventually, either we produce the Telstar—or else. It's merely a simple point of fact."

The Sheriff knew Dorro was right. A confrontation with the elves would lead to a massacre. But he had no clue how to find the brooch. It could be anywhere in the village, or sold and taken many miles away by now. Forgo was scared and rightfully so.

"So what should we do now, Winderiver?"

"Right now, I have to circle back to the library. I haven't been there for days and need to check in. Then I suggest you and I meet up at the Hanging Stoat tonight, around 9 o'clock. We should chat up the clientele and also loosen tongues by purchasing a few rounds of beer for the house. Let's hope that someone opens their mouth and makes a mistake."

✧ ✧ ✧

Ten minutes later, Dorro strode into the Thimble Down library. He had missed the place and wondered when he would be able to get back to work full time. Thank goodness for Bedminster Shoe, he thought.

"Good afternoon, Mr. Shoe," said Dorro, strolling up to the big desk.

"Mr. Winderiver! What a pleasure it is to see you. I gather you've been out on one of your investigations with this Rumple matter. Are you back for good?"

"No, I'm afraid not. I hope you'll still be available for a few days, Bedminster. I can't tell you how grateful I am to have you fill in for me. You're a lifesaver."

"Don't think of it, sir. I'm only too happy to help out," said Bedminster, adding slyly: "You will, of course, let me interview you and the interested parties when this affair is over, won't you? You know how I like to document your work for my journals."

Dorro giggled a little, "Why certainly, Mr. Shoe, but I can't think that these tales will come to anything fruitful. Just random stories of a village bookmaster with a rather peculiar hobby. And now that I think about it, I'm not so sure this one will come to a happy conclusion. That very much remains to be seen." And Dorro meant it.

"Mr. Dorro!"

The girl's excited voice from the upper gallery rang out through the entire library. In a flash, Cheeryup slid down the ladder and ran across the floor to give Dorro a huge hug. The bookmaster flushed beet red as the other patrons stared at this emotional display, but he thoroughly enjoyed it anyway.

"I'm so happy you're back, Mr. Dorro. We were so worried!"

"Who was worried?"

Lowering her voice to a whisper so only he'd hear her, "Why, me and Sheriff Forgo. He was afraid the elves would kill you and stuff your body down a woodchuck hole in the woods!"

At this, Dorro laughed out loud and whispered back. "Well, I suppose it would have be a large woodchuck's home to fit me in there, but I'm touched that you cared. And the Sheriff, too."

"Did you learn much from the elves, sir?"

"Enough, enough—more about that later," he said, lowering his voice. "I've just heard about Wyll and am greatly troubled. I suppose you know already."

"Y-y-yes, I do," Cheeryup stammered, rather awkwardly. "I'm worried about him, as well."

Dorro eyed her suspiciously. "You don't know where he is, do you?"

"No, of course not, sir!"

But Dorro noticed that she didn't look him in the eye when she said it. "Well, there it is" he said. "Wyll is gone and there isn't much to be done about it. But there are bigger fish to fry at the moment."

"Do you need my help?" she asked, almost too eagerly.

"Not yet, girl, but soon enough. Here, I owe you some silver for your special work over the past few days, and I must settle up with Mr. Shoe as well. There's much to be done."

Dorro dropped a few coins in Cheeryup's hand before heading over to Bedminster Shoe to pay him for services rendered. *This is getting to be a pricey adventure*, thought Dorro, before he went home for a quick dinner and thence on his mission with Sheriff Forgo. The investigation was clearly grinding to a halt and he was hoping for a breakthrough at the Hanging Stoat. There was no doubt—he needed it.

However, he did reflect on one bright thought: Cheeryup knew more about Wyll than she was sharing. Dorro would wager more than a few coins on that fact.

30
Osgood's Boast

Even from a distance, it was hard to miss the Hanging Stoat. While the rest of Thimble Down had settled down for a quiet April's evening, Mungo's seedy tavern was rollicking, like it was most every night of the week. It's true, Dorro thought, that even congenial Halflings need a place to vent their reckless energy, and the Stoat was as good a place as any for them to drink beer, revel loudly and, no question, misbehave. Even a quarter mile away, he could see candles burning in every room of the circular structure and hear its loud clientele as if already inside.

Yet it was here that he might find information related to the murder of Bing Rumple. While he preferred the Bumbling Badger's cuisine and ambience, the Hanging Stoat was a goldmine of gossip, innuendo, and tantalizing tidbits. That's exactly what the bookmaster was banking on.

Dorro walked through the tavern's front door and his senses were immediately assaulted by the unspeakable volume, ungodly odors, and an ocean of Halflings talking, laughing, tossing darts, giggling, and downing pint after pint of ale (not to mention small earthen jiggers of honeygrass whiskey). In the corner, a band of musicians sawed away happily on all manner of lutes, banjos, pipes, dulcimers, flutes, and round lap drums, while singing lyrics that politely might be called "bawdy." Tonight, Dorro decided to put his low-key and, admittedly, prudish tastes to the side and indulge in the sights and sounds of the place.

"A-hoy, Mr. Dorro! He turned and saw Mr. Mungo behind the bar, waving like a loon. The bookmaster nodded and politely waved back, but decided not to go to the bar, lest he be sucked into some side conversation that would distract him from the true intent of his visit. Scanning the bristling tavern floor, he found his companion for the evening. Sheriff Forgo was sitting at a corner table, partially in the shadows. Dorro moved purposefully in that direction.

He sat down unbidden and didn't look Forgo in the eyes. "You should order a drink, Winderiver," urged the lawman. "Try—even as painful as it may seem—to blend in and enjoy yourself." The Sheriff knew Dorro all too well.

Moments later, Mungo himself toddled over to the table, "A rare treat, Mr. Dorro—I'm pleased to see you here. So what can I get you? The first one is on the house!"

"Well, I can't turn down that offer, Mr. Mungo. Hmm, I'll take a dram of your vintage 1714 honeygrass, if you don't mind. I hear that you carry the best available in Thimble Down."

The barman blushed and said, "We do try, sir, we do indeed! I'll send Freda back with a cup as fast as I can. And you, Mr. Sheriff—can I refill your pint of brown ale?"

Forgo nodded and Mungo was off like a shot. "He wants to impress us, Winderiver. Wonder what for?"

"Oh, I think he's just trying to make amends for the investigation at Bing's burrow," said Dorro just above a whisper. "Maybe if he plies us with enough complimentary beverages, we'll forget all his fainting and blubbering," he added with a mischievous grin. "But I doubt it!"

Forgo also smiled, but it vanished when the door opened and in stepped Osgood Thrip, Farroot Rumple, and Bill Thistle. "Now there's an unfortunate trio," said Forgo. The rest of the Hanging Stoat's patrons similarly noticed and there was a brief lull in the roar, though it resumed quickly enough. Worse, the three were making their way directly for Forgo and Dorro's table. "This should be interesting," Dorro muttered under his breath. He made a mental note that Osgood had previously said he only knew Bill Thistle "a little." *They look pretty chummy to me*, he noted.

"Good evening, gentlemen," drawled the Sheriff, nodding for them to sit down. Their drinks showed up, and Dorro offered to buy their new guests a round as well.

"I never figured you for a honeygrass drinker, Winderiver. I would have thought you'd prefer tea, or a cup of warm milk," quipped Osgood, always looking for an opportunity to embarrass Dorro. Next to him, Farroot and Bill Thistle snickered with derision. But Dorro merely picked up his shot of whiskey, nodded with a wink, and knocked it back in one gulp.

"Freda—please set me up with another!" he shouted across the room. Osgood looked mildly impressed.

"Well, Winderiver, there's a rumor around the village that you've been off cavorting with the elves. Can this be true? Our village book lover confronting a party of deadly elf warriors? Or are you their ally, supplying them with information and who knows what else?

"Osgood, you've been listening to foolish rumors," jumped in Forgo. "Mr. Winderiver is actually assisting me on the Bing Rumple matter and has been very useful."

"And yes, it's true, I have spoken with the elves," calmly interrupted Dorro, to the amazed stares of Osgood, Farroot, and Bill. They had heard the rumors, but laughed them off. "We needed to know if they killed Bing or not, and the only way was to confront them directly. I spent two days in their company and we discussed much."

"Two days with the elves?" chimed in the smarmy voice of Farroot Rumple. "Well, Mr. Winderiver, there's perhaps more to you than meets the eye. Even Bill was afraid of those warriors, weren't you? Trembling like a little lass, he was!" His companion shot him an evil glare, but said nothing. (In light of the fact that the Sheriff of Thimble Down was sitting across the table, Bill decided to take another gulp of ale, rather than punch Farroot square in the nose.)

"Yes, we had all manner of interesting conversation. At this point, I'm quite convinced that they didn't kill your brother, though doing so would have been a mere trifle."

"How can you be so sure?"

"Because, Farroot, they are an honorable race and don't take lives indiscriminately," continued Dorro, testing the water. "Even if they had found Bing with the gem, they wouldn't have killed him for it. Maybe roughed him up a little or given him a little scare, but never murder. That is, unless Bing had sold it for gold and then, who can predict what the elves would have done to him. Probably flayed him alive. But they're still convinced the gem is here in Thimble Down or else they would have departed. Someone here in the village did it. Of that, I'm quite sure."

The three Halflings merely glanced at each other and took gulps of their respective beverages. "All well and good, Winderiver, but our latest report is that the elves have left," said Osgood Thrip, in a cold, detached voice. "A trader entering the village said he saw them a few hours ago, heading east toward the wild hills of their homeland. And if they're leaving, they probably have the Telstar gem already in their possession. And that means your investigation is, I'm afraid, closed. Their departure is all but an admission to killing Bing Rumple."

Dorro's mind began racing. *This can't be true*, he thought. *That would mean that Toldir lied to me!"* Outwardly, however, he replied, "Osgood, you can't base your information on one uncorroborated report. What if you're wrong and the elves are still in the Great Wood? If they are and still seek the lost brooch, then they will return here and recover it by any means."

"Any, as in murder?" hissed Osgood.

Dorro was a bit rattled, but he shot back. "Clearly, Osgood, we need to verify your report. If you're correct and the elves are gone, we can simply write off Bing's murder, since no one will pursue them for justice. Hmm, the brooch is gone, the elves are gone, and the ostensible murderer is gone. How convenient."

Thrip's face remained stony and impassive as the Dorro kept talking: "Yet if you're wrong and the elves are still nearby, I hope you're not the one in possession of the Telstar. Truly, I wouldn't want that brooch for all the gold in Thimble Down, especially with a party of angry elves on my trail. I like having my head still attached to its neck."

Dorro saw Osgood gulp quickly. "You're a fool, Winderiver," Thrip sneered. "But I'll do you a favor and send out a few of my traders to scour the woods tomorrow. They'll bring hunting dogs, just to make sure. I think we'll find the elves long gone. Mark my words."

At that, Thrip and his two companions guzzled down their various drinks, and left the table, leaving Dorro and Forgo alone. "You played that well, bookmaster. I didn't know you have the nerves to play dice with Osgood Thrip. He's a crafty Halfling and not one I'd like as my enemy. You seem to revel in it."

"Oh, I knew Osgood when we were in school together. He was a miserable, spoiled brat even then and would tattle on me whenever I taunted Lucretia. But it was so much fun to make her scream and chase me. Plus it would always make Osgood jealous. I suppose I was a nasty little brute, as well." Dorro began giggling at the memory of his schoolyard antics with a younger Osgood and Lucretia. Forgo, however, couldn't imagine any of them as children. The Thrips were probably as awful then as they are now, he figured.

✷ ✷ ✷

Osgood, Farroot, and Bill Thistle found a table on the opposite side of the Hanging Stoat. "Impudent wretch," growled Thrip. He despised Dorro some forty years ago and still hated him today. *I should have soundly thrashed him when I could*, he thought privately. Aloud, however, he said, "It would be a shame if Dorro wound up with knife sticking out of his back, wouldn't it, Bill?"

Farroot and Bill grinned maliciously. Neither of them liked Dorro Fox Winderiver either and would enjoy thrashing the pompous bookmaster within an inch of his life. "Don't worry about him, Osgood," replied Farroot. "We have other business to attend to anyway. It's time we made some real silver."

"What about the murder? Do you think Winderiver will solve it?" pondered Thrip.

"It hardly matters. Without the brooch or the elves, there is no evidence and no suspects. Forgo will get bored and return to his prime vocations of eating and napping. And as much as I'll miss my dear brother, we all felt he was a thorn in our sides. Bing had the business sense of a farmer's sow—he only lived to drink, and then beg or steal to make money so he could drink some more."

"No offense, Farroot, but your brother was a waste of space. I, for one, am glad he's dead—I as good as killed him myself. If he hadn't been such a dolt, Bing might be sitting here with us tonight. But I don't miss him."

"Another Halfling might call you out, Osgood, and challenge you to a duel for saying that. But y'know, I heartily agree with you. We're all glad Bing is dead. In fact, I think I owe you another glass of honeygrass for allegedly bumping him off. Freda, drinks all around!"

At that, Osgood, Farroot, and Bill burst into loud, malevolent laughter.

✵ ✵ ✵

At the next table, Farmer Edythe couldn't believe her ears. Not that she was eavesdropping—though of course she was—but Osgood Thrip had as good as confessed to the murder of Bing Rumple. In truth, she had come to the Hanging Stoat this evening to flirt with Mr. Mungo, whom she found amusing, jolly and, like herself, happily unattached. But no, she thought—tonight was not one for romance. She had just heard the admissions of a murderer.

Despite her sturdy build, Edythe rose stealthily from her chair and dropped a few coins on the table. She'd seen Sheriff Forgo earlier in the evening and prayed he hadn't left yet. Moving quietly away from her table, Farmer Edythe wanted a few precious minutes of his time.

31
Siobhán

An hour after leaving the Hanging Stoat, Dorro was sitting in his study at the Perch. He was growing increasingly confounded by the investigation. He knew he was close to finding Bing's murderer, but didn't have any evidence to prove it. Pulling a piece of parchment out of a drawer, he dipped a quill into the ink jar and started making notes, working by the light of a few candles on his ancient oak desk. It had been in the Winderiver family for at least a hundred years and was among Dorro's most treasured possessions.

He was quite sure that the trio of Osgood, Farroot, and the mysterious Bill Thistle were surely involved in some way. But how could he prove it? He couldn't see Osgood killing Bing—he wouldn't want to get his hands dirty—and surely Farroot wouldn't kill his own brother.

But he knew little or nothing about Bill Thistle. That Halfling was filthy and loutish. He may well have been the one who killed Farroot and stole the Telstar brooch, though perhaps on Osgood's orders.

On the other hand, maybe Bill merely stole the brooch and the murder was committed by the elves. In particular, he was thinking of Baldar, who like Bill, said very little yet had an air of simmering violence about him. And goodness knew, he was deadly with a hand-thrown knife. While that boar almost killed Cheeryup and himself in the Great Wood, truly, it never had a chance with Baldar in the vicinity. The elf was a cool, lethal assassin. And if he had located Bing and found that he'd already sold the brooch, then his execution would only have been a trifle to him. It would also explain why his burrow was trashed from top to bottom. The elf may have ransacked the place looking for the Telstar.

As much as he didn't want this to be the truth, it made perfect sense. Part of him wanted to see Osgood, Farroot, and Bill tossed in gaol and charged with murder and theft, but Baldar seemed like a more fitting suspect. After all, the knife in Bing's back was Baldar's own blade. That was fairly damning evidence. Dorro scrawled some more notes on the parchment, writing quickly to capture his revelations.

Now, the bookmaster came to his third line of inquiry and, honestly, he didn't want to go there. "Dorro, my friend, you must proceed," he spoke quietly to himself.

"If you are truly an investigator of integrity, you are required to explore everything. *Everything.*"

With that, he let his mind begin sifting through some thoughts and facts about—he took a big gasp of air and wrote on the page—Wyll Underfoot. At least, he admitted, Wyll was in Sheriff Forgo's gaol when Bing Rumple was murdered. However, the fact of the matter remained that the glistening, bewitching Telstar was still missing. Strangely, it hadn't turned up, neither in the flesh, nor as gossip within the active Thimble Down grapevine. If it had been sold or even offered for sale, word of it would have likely spread throughout the village quickly. No, whoever stole the brooch either still possessed it or smuggled it out of town. Or worse, perhaps the thief broke out of gaol and ran away with the Telstar in his pocket.

"Wyll, why weren't you truthful with me?" Dorro lamented again. "I thought you were a good, honest lad—I was even willing to give you a home. I'm so disappointed."

All the clues were there: Wyll had already proved himself a thief by stealing his food and breaking into in the library. Possibly he had further played on Dorro's kinder instincts to set up a home base from which to steal bigger and better prizes. Meanwhile, Bing Rumple had been showing the elvish brooch around Thimble Down like the donkey's back-end he was, thus it was sure to catch the eye of a young thief with quick hands. Inconceivable as it might have seemed a few days ago, it's possible that Wyll snuck out one night and bashed

Bing on the head that first time. And while Bing was unconscious in the back room of the Hanging Stoat, Wyll had ample time to go exploring around Rumple's burrow. I do recall Forgo reporting that Bing said neither Farroot nor Bill knew where the brooch was hidden. So who knows—maybe Wyll simply got lucky and found it.

It would explain much, figured Dorro. If Wyll took the brooch and hid it, then that would explain the actions of Baldar, who may have broken into the burrow and exploded into violence when Bing told him it was gone. The pieces were beginning to come together, as much as Dorro wished they weren't.

Worse, there might not be any closure to this crime— if the Woodland elves had truly left the area and Wyll fled to parts unknown, there would never be a conclusion to this puzzling case. And, of course, it would be far worse if the elves haven't left. They'd still want the brooch back and wouldn't accept the idea that a young thief had stolen it and bolted town. Surely, one couldn't see Toldir accepting that ridiculous explanation over a nice pot of tea, saying, "Oh well, these things happen," and peacefully leaving Thimble Down. No, instead, he would storm the village to find the thief. And Dorro felt it would be partially his fault.

He let his head hang down and let out an exasperated sigh. This was a crime without a solution and the results could be dire. He felt like he was letting everyone down.

Before going to bed, Dorro felt compelled to do one more task. Though his head was muddled from the spider web of innuendo and conjecture, the Halfling soldiered on, albeit sleepily. Dorro had already searched the garden shed for any signs of the brooch, but he recalled that Wyll had spent his first—and only—night in the Perch in one of his back bedrooms. Maybe the lad left a clue or two in there.

As the sole inhabitant of his home, Dorro did not often go into his back rooms—they were just there in case he needed them for guests, which was rarely. He picked up a lantern and proceeded into the dark recesses of his hillock-house. He entered the small room in the very back, where he had put Wyll up not even a week earlier. Dorro was incredulous that it was that short a span. It felt like a grueling six months had passed.

He set the lantern on a side table and started fishing around the bed linens. There was nothing to be found anywhere, so he peeked underneath. Again, nothing there, but...*"Whoa ho, what's this?"* Dorro exclaimed.

He pulled out a small knapsack that had been stuck well under the bed and was nearly invisible. "Must be his dirty laundry," he said, turning it in his hands. Dorro undid the floppy top and opened the bag. Sure enough, there was clothing inside, most of it smelling of mildew, harkening to the weeks Wyll had survived in the woods alone. Against his better judgment, he reached toward the bottom of the bag, surely to find more wet clothes or an angry mouse that was about to nip his finger. Instead, his fingers closed upon a piece of oil cloth.

"Now, that's curious," Dorro remarked, unwrapping the cloth in the dim candlelight. Within, he found a piece of parchment. It was too dark for him to read, so he grabbed the lantern and walked back to his venerable desk in the front study. Slipping half-moon reading glasses on the end of his nose, the Halfling concentrated on the faded ink inscribed on the page. It was a letter from someone he thought he'd never hear from again.

December the 13th, 1720, A.B.

Shrimpton-on-Mar

Dearest Brother Dorro,

Has it really been twenty years? Yes, I suppose it has. I know I haven't been a very good sister, but I do live so far away and the mail coaches here in the outer villages are lamentably unreliable. Further, I don't have your gift for words, thus the idea of writing a letter is rather strange to me. I'd rather sit with you and converse for hours, but alas, we haven't had that luxury in many years. Too many.

I'm sure things are going well for you in Thimble Down, despite the desperate cold of this Winter. Knowing you, you are curled up in front of a fireplace reading a good novel or sketching a picture of Springtime flowers. Or else, you're at the library that is your second home or daydreaming about catching trout in the River Thimble. I have little doubt of this, younger brother—you were always rather predictable. But I always loved that about you.

You may be wondering why, after two decades, I've chosen to write. You may also be wondering who the lad standing on your doorstep is and how he came to bear this letter. First, let us step back in Time.

I know Mother and Papa never forgave me for running off. Yours may be the world of facts and ideas, all lodged within books covered in tooled leather—we all knew of your passion. Yet while you reveled in your interior world of the mind, my passion was in the heart ... and on the stage. You may—or may not—know that when I left Thimble Down at the age of eighteen, I joined a band of traveling thespians. I have spent many exciting years with them, traveling among Halfling villages, and performing the greatest works of Halfling theatre on enchanting, candlelit stages. Mother and Papa would never have approved, but now I can understand the fears they had for their eldest, and only, daughter. It was my path and I had to follow it.

Eventually, a young actor—a certain Mr. Underfoot—joined our troupe and I promptly fell in love with him. We were a magical pair onstage and offstage, too. Suffice to say, these were the happiest years of my life. It was not to last, however. One night, after performing in a distant hamlet called Pumbleton, our caravan caught fire and, while I barely escaped, my beloved Samual died amidst the smoke and debris. I won't tarry here—it's all too painful to remember. But he did leave me one gift: a son, born several months later. This lovely blonde-haired boy looks just like his father and has brought me joy every day, even though life in a troupe of traveling actors is anything but gentle.

Which brings me to the present. Brother, I need you to do me a favor—the greatest favor a sibling can ask. And I only ask it because I am dying. I have the coughing sickness that has killed two in our theatrical troupe and many in the towns we've visited. My time is growing short. (My life of rebellion and, dare I say, unconventionality has finally caught up with me. I'm sure some of the local busybodies in Thimble Down would wag their fingers at me and say, "Serves 'er right!" Even so, I do miss that pretty village of our younger days. But I digress and have not yet finished my tale.)

The favor, as you may have deduced already, is to take in the blonde-headed boy on your doorstep—your nephew—and care for him until he can fend for himself. As I said at the outset of this letter, I have no illusion that I have been a good sister, nor that you owe me any courtesies. If I had been, I would have written or visited more often, but the theatre consumed my life, as did the child standing before you. Even so, I ask—no, I beg you, to make this final promise to me.

In my final weeks, I can only think of you and the cozy burrow of our childhood, where I presume you still live. Dorro, you are a good Halfling, and I have the fondest memories of us playing together as younglings. I do know you like your solitude and quiet hobbies, but still, the boy needs a home and he's walked countless miles to stand on your doorstep. If you're curious, his name is Wyll Underfoot and he is the final love of my life. Please Dorro—you cannot fail me.

With profound love, your sister,

Siobhán (Winderiver Underfoot)

✡ ✡ ✡

By this time, the tears were freely running down Dorro's face. His throat was choked up and he could barely breathe. Finally, he gasped, "But sister, I have failed you! I had Wyll right here in this very burrow and hoped to make it his home. Yet I have lost him and now my nephew is gone forever. Dearest sister, *please forgive me!*"

At that, Dorro Fox Winderiver wept as he never had before.

32
Sewing the Threads Together

$\mathcal{T}$he next morning was a perfect Spring morning in Thimble Down, sunny and warm with only the very slightest of breezes. The maples, oaks, and elms were leafing out with bright, green shoots, while the flowering saucer magnolia, apple, and cherry trees were blooming in profusion. Underneath the canopy lay a carpet of soft, swaying bluebells, punctuated in wooded, shadier spots by yellow trout lilies and white trillium by the score.

Dorro greeted this day as a true fresh start, especially after the shock he had received the previous night. His long-lost sister was dead, yet incredible as it seemed, he had a nephew who had been right under his nose. He still couldn't quite wrap his mind around these wild facts—especially that Wyll Underfoot hadn't unveiled his true identity to him. *Why?* he wondered over and over.

Dorro knew that he was still obliged to check in with Sheriff Forgo and dutifully prepared to venture into Thimble Down. After a quick breakfast of oatmeal sprinkled with nuts, dried cranberries, and brown sugar, Dorro grabbed his walking stick and pipe, and headed out the door. The weather was so fine he didn't need a scarf—the first time he'd gone without months.

At this point in the game, the bookmaster's mind was a morass of ideas and intricate threads. In addition to the investigations of Osgood, Farroot, and Bill, he was simultaneously questioning the actions of the elves and Wyll. All this, while processing the idea that, incredulously, the strange boy was actually his nephew. He stopped on the road into Thimble Down to take a deep breath and feel the sun warm his face. Dorro had too much tumbling around in his brain at the moment, but he knew eventually he would sort them into their appropriate compartments and make sense of the whole. He just needed time. He stopped to light some Old Nob pipeweed and began to walk again.

Ten minutes later, he poked his head into the library, only to find the inestimable Bedminster Shoe handling things with ease. "He's a marvel," Dorro muttered to himself as he stepped off the library's porch on his way back out. "When this matter is all settled, Mr. Shoe will find a nice little bonus in his pay purse."

It was only another few minutes until he was at the gaol. Surprisingly, Sheriff Forgo was already outside, surrounded by a small group of Halflings, the Mayor, and Osgood Thrip. Dorro ambled up to the group and stood quietly, trying to hear what the Sheriff was saying. "... and with that, I officially make you deputies of the village of Thimble Down, reporting directly to me."

Dorro looked around the group—they were young fellows he'd seen around the village, some of them farm hands, others working in the trades. Each carried a cudgel and were giving Sheriff Forgo their utmost attention (interestingly, Mr. Mungo was not among them. He had apparently resigned.)

"To continue, gentlemen, we may be dealing with some elusive and potentially dangerous characters. Someone killed Bing Rumple and that villain is obviously capable of incredible violence, judging by the state of Bing's burrow. And if that person was an elf, well then my friends, we will be dealing with a force unlike anything we've ever dealt with before. Woodland elves are fearsome warriors and can probably kill a Halfling like some of us might swat a fly." Dorro saw a few of the new deputies gulp. He didn't blame them.

"There is a possibility, however remote, that the elves who were in the village a few days ago may return and, if they do, they will be here to retrieve an item they believe belongs to them," added the Sheriff. "This has to be considered an unlawful act and therefore, we will arrest the elves on sight. We can't have wild creatures invading our peaceful village and imposing their will on us. It is the only way to preserve our laws. And if things get ugly, I hereby give you permission to use deadly force. It may be our only option."

The bookmaster could see Osgood Thrip standing behind the Sheriff, nodding vigorously. Dorro suspected Osgood was the puppet master pulling poor Forgo's strings. He probably threatened to have the Sheriff fired—that was his usual trick to ensure the latter's co-operation. In Dorro's mind, there was no need to hire a posse of deputies, but Osgood Thrip was politically astute and knew this paltry show of force would play well to the citizens of Thimble Down and help the Mayor—his own personal puppet—get reelected, thus ensuring the status quo. With his wealth and bulldog persona, Osgood was able to buy influence throughout the village, even in the Mayor's office. He meddled in everyone's affairs, though Dorro had successfully blocked him out of the library, thanks to his own not-inconsiderable wealth, which he had inherited from his parents. The difference was merely that Osgood flaunted his money, while Dorro used his to live his life as he saw fit, as well as to help the library prosper. That was his gift to Thimble Down and, indeed, he protected that venerable institution jealously.

"Then there's the matter of the missing elf brooch, the so-called Telstar," Forgo continued dryly. "Someone stole it from Bing Rumble and that person—be it Halfling or elf—may also be dangerous. When we get the report from Mr. Thrip's traders on whether the elves are still in the vicinity or not, we'll know better what we're dealing with. It's also conceivable that the thief is one Wyll Underfoot, a Halfling lad who is wily, if not dangerous. He's broken out of the gaol twice and that alone speaks volumes about his character. He's a known thief, as well as an escapee. Underfoot should also be arrested on sight."

At this, Dorro could no longer be silent. "Sheriff, I must protest!" he cried. "Wyll Underfoot is a misunderstood youngling. I can vouch for him and there's no need for violent intercession. I will pay all his fines and for the repair of your gaol."

Forgo raised his eyebrows in surprise at this and was about to speak when Osgood Thrip cut him off: "That's all well and good, Winderiver, but considering that you aided and abetted the criminal yourself, your word isn't very valuable to us. Sheriff, continue."

Forgo was about to speak up, when Dorro cut him off again: "Lies! Well, mostly. But Wyll Underfoot has been a victim of circumstance and he needs to have his day before the magistrate, that being our Mayor. I beg all of you gentlemen not to use force if you apprehend him."

"Sorry Winderiver, but the law is the law!" sneered Osgood.

Dorro looked like he was going to blow hot steam out of his ears, but instead said, "I will pay two gold coins to whoever brings Wyll Underfoot *safely* to Thimble Down and delivers him directly to Sheriff Forgo. And I mean, safe and unharmed!"

There was an audible *oooh!* from the new cadre of deputies, clearly trumping anything Osgood was about to say or offer. Two gold coins was a vast sum of money for any Halfling, particularly if you were a farm hand, drover, or shop clerk, and accordingly, Dorro had their rapt attention. But it was Forgo who spoke next: "Well, gentlemen, Mr. Winderiver has made a generous pledge here. While my instructions remain firm, his bounty on the return of the boy Underfoot is legal and valid. We are adjourned for the moment. You'll need to stick to the schedule I gave you earlier and make regular patrols around the village. And we'll check in each morning at 9 o'clock at this location. Dismissed!"

The Halfling deputies began to filter off, each one daydreaming about how they'd bring the boy in and spend Dorro's prize. Forgo was impressed with the bookmaster's ingenuity, but Osgood was clearly peeved and, after a brief conversation with the hapless Mayor, stomped off toward his stately home, his face black and stormy.

✲ ✲ ✲

His work settled here, Dorro headed toward Cheeryup's burrow. He was beginning to realize how much he valued her insights—*She's certainly a bright lass,* he mused, knowing that she may well be the smartest child in all of Thimble Down.

Dorro knocked lightly on the door and was greeted by Mrs. Tunbridge, who showed him in. Cheeryup's mother knew that the bookmaster was very good to her daughter and, more than that, paid her well for her library work. Mrs. Tunbridge had also ferreted out details of Dorro's investigations and her daughter's increasing role. As long as there was no danger involved, she would accommodate the additional activities, knowing both how intelligent her daughter was and how the esteemed librarian could help guide her in the coming years. There weren't many opportunities for young women in Thimble Down, aside from working in the trades or as a domestic servant, and she wanted neither for her daughter. "A girl with her wits should have greater challenges than packing groceries or fetching tea," Mrs. Tunbridge often reflected. She knew that their lack of resources meant that university was out of the question, but she also realized that Dorro Fox Winderiver could be the catalyst to a brighter future for Cheeryup—at least brighter than sewing garments alongside her old mother.

"Cheeryup! Mr. Dorro is here!" Mrs. Tunbridge called in her most genteel voice. "Why don't you sit here in the kitchen, sir, while I put on a fresh pot of tea. You and Cheeryup can sit here and discuss your business. And here, I just made some muffins with blueberries from last fall's harvest."

"Thank you, ma'am," rejoined the bookmaster, nodding politely, while also processing the phrase "your business" in his head. *Apparently, Mrs. Tunbridge is aware of my investigatory activities, as well as Cheeryup's role,* he thought to himself. *And I further surmise that she approves of the whole thing. Splendid!*

"Hello, Mr. Dorro," beamed Cheeryup as she joined him at the thick pine table that sat in the Tunbridge kitchen. In her hands was a pair of breeches with a nasty tear in one side. With a needle and thread in one hand and a thimble in the other, the girl quickly resumed stitching up the seam. She was devilishly fast with a needle, noted Dorro.

"Hullo, Cheeryup. You're as gifted a seamstress as your mother," he said, just as Mrs. Tunbridge breezed into the room to pour the tea and set out the muffins. Then she was gone again.

"Well, girl, things are proceeding apace. The Sheriff has hired several Thimble Down lads to act as his deputies, in case things get rough with the elves or they find Wyll hiding somewhere." Cheeryup's eyes flashed when he said that, a fact he duly noted. "You don't, *ermm*, know anything about Wyll's whereabouts do you?"

"No sir. I haven't seen hide nor hair of the boy since he fled. He must be gone." she responded in casual voice, still not making eye contact. But Dorro read her manner quite differently. In these few words and body movements, Cheeryup had indicated that, in fact, she did know where Wyll was and was possibly—and hopefully—in league to keep him concealed. *Good girl!* Dorro elatedly thought to himself, but on the outside, he remained impassive.

"Oh, that's such a shame," feigned Dorro. "We hardly got a chance to know Wyll and—poof!—he's gone from our lives. I would have liked a chance to get to know him better. Wouldn't have you?"

The girl merely nodded, but Dorro was sure she not only knew where he was, but also was keeping him fed, as was her nature. He'd have to find a way to give her some money for food without appearing suspicious, of course.

Dorro then proceeded to regale Cheeryup with the details of his investigations while omitting any news about the letter from his late sister—Wyll's mother, Siobhán. He told her of the possible scenarios of the crime, how the elf Baldar may have killed Bing Rumple in a fit of fury or how he might have met his end by Bill Thistle's greedy hand. It's also conceivable that Bill and Farroot had stolen the gem and were hiding it to sell elsewhere. And lastly, that maybe Wyll did steal it after all and was concealing it somewhere.

"Oh no, Mr. Dorro. That's impossible!" yelped Cheeryup. "Wyll would never do that—he'd tell me. I mean, he *would have* told me, if he were still in the village." She'd slipped up, but hoped that Mr. Dorro hadn't noticed. Of course, he had and was smiling inwardly.

"Yes, I regret his leaving town," said Dorro. "If I could only speak to him again, I'd say how much I believe in him and would like to start over. I think there's much good in Wyll, though he'd have to learn to be more honest with me. But if I ever see him again, that's what I'd say—let's try again."

Cheeryup had a big grin on her face and, involuntarily, jumped up and threw her arms around Dorro's neck. "Oh Mr. Dorro, I'm sure he'd love to hear you say that! I knew deep down you believed in him. We'll get him back someday, I know it."

"I hope you're right, young lady. There's nothing I'd like more. As for the investigation, the question is, how do we find the real thief and lure him into the open?"

Pacing around her kitchen, Cherryup put her hand under her chin and furrowed her brows, as she always did when pondering a problem. The bookmaster, meanwhile, helped himself to a muffin.

"I'm not sure, Mr. Dorro, but what comes to mind is the sight of you fishing at the river. You bait your hook with a worm or a shiny lure, and toss it out there for the fish to gobble down. I don't think a worm would do the job, but maybe something shiny would do the trick."

"Yes! Keep going."

"If the thief stole one gem," continued the girl, "then he might be tempted to steal another one, if you know what I mean. But where would you get another brooch? Moreover, it would have to be larger and shinier than the Telstar. That would attract the attention of a 'bigger fish.'"

"I had a similar thought a few days ago, but I say, Cheeryup, you have given me a devilish idea."

With that, Dorro wiped the remaining muffin crumbs off his chin and jumped up. "I must dash, girl, but your words have been most useful. And oh yes, I owe you some pay from a week or two back."

"I don't think so, sir."

"No, I specifically remember owing you something." He fished into his pocket and pulled out a full gold coin. "Do you have change? Well, no matter. Spend it wisely!"

At that, Dorro flew out the door of the Tunbridge burrow and shot back toward the Perch to work on his new plan. Meanwhile, young Cheeryup stood with her mouth agog staring at the gold piece in her hand. "Mother! I think we can afford to have the burrow white-washed this Spring," she gushed. "And we can have lamb for dinner tonight, too!"

And secretly, she knew how she'd sequester some of these new funds for other uses. There was a boy sitting in the Great Wood who needed a good supper and warm clothes. Cheeryup silently made plans to visit him later that day. But first she had to finish her sewing.

33
Hovering Near Death

heriff Forgo was jolted awake by banging on the gaol's oak door. He stirred from a cot in one of the back cells—he'd been too tired to travel home and this was as good a bed as any. "Wait a minute!" he hollered, staggering toward the front of the building. It just before dawn—the Sheriff could see the soft gray light filtering through the window. "Good grief," he muttered to himself, groggily. "I can't *never* get any sleep anymore."

He unlocked the door and opened it to find a newly deputized Halfling named Bosco, a village lad who, in times past, excelled at annoying the Sheriff in any way possible. But this time there was real worry on his face.

"*Whattya want*, Bosco, you dunderhead?"

"Sheriff Forgo, you must come quick. There's been an accident. Or an attack—I don't know!" said the flustered young Halfling, without a trace of his usual sarcasm.

"It's only by the look on your face, Bosco, that I know you're serious. Because if you weren't, I'd cuff you on the ear before you could blink twice."

"Come, Sheriff, to the Hanging Stoat. *Quickly!*"

Of course it would be that tavern, figured Forgo, *I should have that dump closed for good. Would serve Mungo right, too.*

Bosco had already dashed down the lane toward the tavern. Seeing as how his pony Tom would still be asleep, the Sheriff decided to hoof it. Ten minutes later, he arrived at the Hanging Stoat, completely winded and puffing like an old dog. "Wha ... wha ... what happened?" he gasped. Mungo the barman waved for him to come into the back storage room, the same place where they had placed the severely injured Bing Rumple just a week or so earlier.

In the storage area he saw Mungo, Bosco, and Nurse Pym hovering over a cot (actually, the same one on which they'd lain Bing Rumple so many days before). When the two parted, Forgo saw a horrifying sight—the beaten and bruised face and crumpled body of Dalbo Dall, the old wanderer who lived out of doors. "In the name of good King Borgo!" swore the Sheriff in shock and disbelief. "Is he...?"

"No. He still lives," softly replied Nurse Pym. "But only just barely. Whoever did this to Dalbo probably thought he was dead. He has been savagely beaten from head to toe. I canna be sure he'll live through morning."

"This is unconscionable," said Forgo, his anger rising by the second. "Whoever did this will pay, even if I have to break our own laws and throttle the scoundrel myself."

He took a deep breath. Forgo knew there was little he could do right now. But one idea popped into his head: "Bosco, go fetch the bookmaster."

"Dorro?"

"Yes, Dorro, you blister-brained buckethead! Go wake him and get him here in all speed. Borrow one of Mungo's ponies, if you must. We need him."

Bosco didn't need to be told twice—he'd seen the Sheriff this angry a few times before and knew it wasn't wise to hang around during one of his maelstroms. "Aye-aye, Mr. Captain-Sergeant Forgo, sir!" he shouted, saluting awkwardly and tripping on a bucket while running for the door. "I'll have Dorro back here before you can say, 'Eggs 'n' bacon!'"

☆ ☆ ☆

Less than a half an hour later, Forgo was staring into a cup of lukewarm tea when he heard the sound of a cart rushing up. A few seconds later, the door to the Hanging Stoat was flung open and in stepped a bedraggled Dorro Fox Winderiver, following by Bosco. The Sheriff made a mental note to let Bosco know he was doing a good job later on, all things considered. He might become a worthy deputy after all.

"Sheriff, what is the matter? Your deputy wouldn't divulge any details—only that it was an emergency that required my presence."

"It's Dalbo Dall. He was beaten and left for dead. Yet incredibly, he still breathes."

Forgo noted the look of horror on the bookmaster's face. "Why would anyone do that?" raged Dorro. "Dalbo is one of the gentlest creatures in all Halflingdom. Eccentric, perhaps, but this is a travesty. What is happening to Thimble Down?"

Again, Dorro had to try to stop the torrent of emotions tearing through his mind. If he let it go unchecked, it would disrupt his broader thinking process on the investigation and he couldn't let that happen—they'd accomplished too much to let it slip away again. Moreover, he had a sneaking suspicion that the attacks on Bing Rumple and Dalbo Dall were not unrelated. No, someone is afraid, he thought quickly. Someone is very afraid and has a secret to keep. And they'll do anything to keep that secret safe, including assaulting Dalbo.

"Sheriff, may I see Dalbo?" Dorro asked.

Forgo merely nodded his head toward the back room and said, "Buck up, Winderiver. This isn't pretty."

Dorro parted the curtain and instantly blanched. The elderly Halfling on the cot was hard to recognize, even by someone who's known him his whole life. Dalbo's face was all puffy and purple, with dark-blue welts under his eyes, which were all but shut from the swelling. Yet even from a few feet away, Dorro could hear the slight wheeze of his lungs quietly pumping away.

"By all rights, the creature should be dead," said a weary Nurse Pym. "I've seen brawnier Halflings take a less of a pummeling and die all the same. Dalbo is made of tough stuff."

"Indeed, he is, Nurse."

"Maybe a lifetime of living outdoors has given him extra resilience. Or maybe he's spent so much time up in the Great Wood that their gentle magic hath rubbed off on him."

"Ah, but that's an old wives' tale, Nurse Pym. No one really believes the trees are magic."

"No one? Well, I do, Dorro Fox Winderiver. You canna have attended as many births and deaths as I and not feel the deeper magic of Thimble Down. It's subtle, but it's there. Life comes and life goes, but some beings go on forever, like the trees. And of course, Mr. Dalbo here."

Dorro didn't know what to say. He was a rational-minded Halfling, not prone to believing in such things, yet he didn't want to insult Pym.

"My personal belief," the Nurse continued, "is that Dalbo was once a small tree himself. Yet one fine day, he grew feet and hands, enough to walk around Thimble Down and talk to us mere Halflings. How else could he live outdoors all year long? And have ye looked at his skin? It's cracked and furrowed with deep, tough wrinkles. That's not any skin I've ever seen—that's his bark. So yes, I stand by my conviction. Dalbo Dall ain't like the rest of us. How else could he withstand yon attack, yet still breathe?"

Dorro didn't have any answer, but found her ideas intriguing. He merely said, "Nurse Pym, can I try talking to him? It's very important and I wouldn't ask otherwise. Other lives may be at stake here. Truly."

The Nurse looked wary, but nevertheless, stood up and moved away from Dalbo. She nodded to Bosco and Mr. Mungo, and all three left the room. Knowing he didn't have much time, Dorro walked up to the cot and sat down next to it as quietly as he could. He leaned close to the small, crumpled figure on the cot and whispered in his ear, "Dalbo! Dallll-bo. It's Dorro, the bookmaster. Do you know me?"

Dorro sat back to see if there was any reaction. Sensing none, he bent closer to the beaten Halfling face and spoke a little louder. "Dalbo Dall! It's urgent that we speak. Did you see who did this to you?"

At that, Dalbo's eyes flickered and, suddenly, they opened. The piecing green orbs searched around the room for a second and then fixed on Dorro's face. He had recognized the bookmaster. In return, Dorro gently clasped Dalbo's wrinkled hand. He could see the little creature's lips moving, as if he wanted to speak. Dorro learned in as close as he could and could feel Dalbo's fingers closing on his a little tighter.

Finally, the tiny Halfling forced a sound from his throat. In the softest voice imaginable, Dalbo said: "The good goat ate the star for gold, roots 'n' all."

Dorro, perplexed, said the words to himself, "The good goat ate the star for gold, roots 'n' all? What does that mean? It's nonsense."

Before he could ask more questions, Dorro saw that the old Halfling would not say anymore. Instead, Dalbo had a relieved look in his eyes before they closed again and he fell back into deep slumber. "Nurse Pym!" Dorro shouted. He also chose to keep Dalbo's words to himself—he needed more time to ponder their significance.

The nurse shot back into the room, along with Sheriff Forgo, Mr. Mungo, and Bosco. She waved Dorro out of the way and put her tender hand on the smaller creature's forehead. "I still canna understand why Dalbo is alive. He must have broken ribs and bones galore. Yet he's content to sleep like a wee baby. Barely has a fever, either."

"Nurse, Sheriff, and the rest of you—I need you to listen to me," broke in Dorro. He rarely spoke in such a commanding voice, and everyone, especially Forgo, was completely startled. "Look, whoever attacked Dalbo did it because they wanted him silenced. And that means, if they know he's still alive, he—or she—will try again. And this time, they like won't fail. In his condition, Dalbo could be killed with a feather."

"Sheriff, I know you make the decisions around here, but this time, I need you all to follow mine and all without question. Dalbo Dall's life depends on it. Do you all agree?"

Nurse Pym, Bosco, and Mr. Mungo all looked at the Sheriff, assuming he would blow his stack and tell Dorro to go jump in the River Thimble. Instead, Forgo nodded quietly, giving the bookmaster his full support. All eyes then returned to Dorro.

"As I was saying, Dalbo's life is still in great peril, so we need to do two things—first, we must quickly get him out of here to a safe hiding spot. And more importantly, we need to tell everyone in Thimble Down that the poor fellow died during the night."

Needless to say, everyone's eyes stared fervently at the bookmaster, and there were more than a few slack jaws, too. "More crucially," continued Dorro, his own eyes afire, "this has to become our secret. I need you all to swear you will not tell a soul that Dalbo still lives. No one! Sheriff, take that wooden crate over there, fill it with sacks of flour, and nail it shut! When morning arrives in half an hour, you and Bosco will carry it back to the gaol and tell everyone it contains the body of Dalbo Dall, who got drunk and was run over by a wagon in the fog. Let it sit in front of the gaol for an hour or two; then take it into the Great Wood and hastily bury it in a secret location. No need for a ceremony—just tell folks you have to bury it before it begins to stink the place up."

Forgo and Bosco nodded in agreement. Switching his gaze to the other Halflings standing before him, Dorro unraveled more of his plan, "Nurse Pym and Mr. Mungo, you have an equally important job. You will gently lift Dalbo into the back of the cart outside and take him to Pym's house. If he has any chance of survival, it will be in her capable hands. But we must do this right now, before the sun rises and the folk of Thimble Down begin nosing around, as they are wont to do. And you must do this in complete stealth."

There was a moment of silence, before the bookmaster cackled, "Come on now! We don't have a second to lose and must move Dalbo now. And Sheriff, don't forget to nail down the coffin's lid tightly and bury it with haste. His life depends on it!"

Forgo, Pym, Mungo, and Bosco looked at each other for a few seconds—and then each burst into a grin. The foursome realized they were in the presence of genius.

34
The Metalsmith

ven though it was noon on the same day they'd discovered the severely beaten Dalbo Dall, it felt like the infamous attack had occurred weeks ago. At least it did to Sheriff Forgo and Bosco, who were sitting in the gaol. They were dirty and exhausted from their excursion to the Great Wood, where they buried the coffin that ostensibly contained the "body" of Dalbo. Fortunately they weren't hungry, as Mr. Mungo had already sent over a basket containing bowls of his hearty beef 'n' bean soup and several slices of thick, buttered basil bread, which they devoured instantly. The two Halfling lawmen were just beginning to nod off for a long afternoon's nap. Or so they hoped.

BANG! BANG! BANG!

Forgo and Bosco both leapt up and made ready for a fight. "What the...? Who's there?"

The door to the gaol burst open, as it did many times a day, and in poured a pair from Forgo's latest crop of deputies, Dumpus and Porge. "Sir, we have important news to report!" they said in unison.

"Sweet King Borgo, can't I get any rest?" growled the Sheriff, still groggy from a lethal combination of sleepiness and soup.

"Sheriff, there's strange activity in Bing Rumple's burrow," said Porge, the tall pimply one.

"Aye, sir, one of our scouts said a giant creature had entered the domicile and started thrashing around," added the short squat Dumpus. He winced, expecting the Sheriff to explode any second.

"A giant creature?" asked Forgo, with sarcastic politeness.

"Yessir, Mr. Sheriff. It's one of them elves. The dark one. He's there right now."

"You mean to tell me," continued the Sheriff in his daintiest voice, "that there's *a FULL-GROWN, KILLER ELF IN THIMBLE DOWN! RIGHT NOW?"*

"Errmm ... yes!" chimed Porge and Dumpus in unison, not quite sure whether that was the correct answer or not.

By now, Forgo's face was beet-red and there was steam pouring out of each nostril. "Round up all the deputies and have them converge on the Rumple burrow-hold immediately. Everyone should be fully armed. Bosco, grab some ropes and chains! We're going to war. *NOW!"*

At that, the deputies scattered in every direction, while the Sheriff went to his arsenal cabinet. Therein, he picked up a mace, a short sword, and his beloved cudgel. Over his head he threw a heavy leather jerkin, thick enough to repel a Halfling arrow; he wasn't sure about an elf-made one, however. Even so, his face was set for battle, brows furrowed and mouth clamped shut. In his own mind, Forgo even made a quiet resolution to give up his life if need be. This wasn't going to be pretty. A few seconds later, he stepped out into the warm afternoon air and sucked in a deep lungful of Spring air. Forgo wanted to savor it one last time. Then he turned toward the hillock-home of Bing Rumple, with half a dozen inexperienced deputies scrambling behind him.

✵ ✵ ✵

In another part of Thimble Down, Dorro Fox Winderiver strolled past the various shops and craft houses, seeming to the world like a Halfling who was happily window shopping on a sunny afternoon. Instead, the bookmaster was hoping his plan had worked. According to the latest update he'd received, Forgo and Bosco had successfully brought the coffin back to the gaol and spread the story that it contained Dalbo Dall, who had died of wounds from an apparent wagon accident. A few hours later, the two took the flour-filled crate up into the Great Wood—making sure they were alone and unfollowed—and buried it in a patch of soft earth. The tale seemed plausible enough and, better still, many in Thimble Down believed it.

Meanwhile, Nurse Pym and Mr. Mungo had stealthily carried the gravely wounded Dalbo out of the Hanging Stoat to a waiting cart and brought him to Pym's house in the wee hours of the morning. When he last checked in about two hours ago, via Mungo, the patient was stable, but unchanged. Nurse Pym still wasn't sure he'd make it, but she'd give it her best.

Now it was up to Dorro to craft the third leg of the stool. He stopped in front of a small shop and looked up at its peeling wooden sign:

MR. TIMMO & SONS

EXPERT METALSMITHERY & FABRICATOR OF ALL THINGS

Inside was his old comrade Timmo, who was actually Old Mr. Timmo's youngest son. The elder Timmo had died two decades earlier, and his elder brother had left Thimble Down to find his fortune. Now the younger Mr. Timmo was last in the line, and the quiet shop was all his own. Dorro visited here often in the warmer months since the metalsmith was quite a wizard at creating clever fishing lures, hooks, and devious contraptions of all kinds. *He has an uncanny mind*, thought the bookmaster, stepping through the doorway. *If Timmo ever put his brain to solving crime, I'd have a fair rival 'round here, I would indeed.*

"A-hoy, Timmo. Are you here?"

"Why, if it isn't Mr. Dorro! I knew I'd be seeing ye soon, what with all this warm weather. Are you here to sample my latest lures? I've come up with some real whiz-bangers this Winter, like the Trout Tempter and the Walleye Whacker. And the best of all, the Pickerel Pincer! No fish will be able to resist that one, mark my words."

Dorro had visions of freshly caught fish on a stringer, drifting lazily off his canoe in the River Thimble, while he casted mightily above them, his rod fitted with a lethal Timmo lure! "*Ooo*, the Pickerel Pincer." he thought. "I do like the sound of that one."

Then he pinched himself and came back to the present. "Actually, Timmo, my friend, I'm not here for fishing tackle." The metalsmith looked at him suspiciously. "Really, I'm here on another matter entirely. This one will test the limits of your craftsmanship and skill. Moreover, I need it done today. Timmo, this is your greatest hour!"

Dorro knew he was laying it on thick, but he wasn't half-joking. Timmo needed to rise to the occasion and craft a thing of wonder, and he only had a few hours to do it.

"What can it be, Dorro?" asked the shy metalsmith. "I will do my best, but I'm only a mere Halfling."

"Timmo, my friend, I have the fullest confidence in you. If anyone in Thimble Down can accomplish this task, it's you. And to further tempt you, I shall place three gold coins on the counter as a down payment. For this task will require your finest metals, your shiniest glass beads, and perhaps even little shards of mirrored glass."

By this time, Timmo's eyes were veritably popping out of his skull, and there was an almost-dumb smile on his lips. It was only by sheer dint of self-control that he wasn't drooling. "Tell me more, Dorro. Your wish is my command!"

"I was hoping you'd say that, Timmo. Indeed, your father would be most proud." And at that, Dorro and Timmo lowered their heads across the countertop, and began whispering and chatting. The metalsmith quickly grabbed a piece of parchment and a chalk crayon, and began sketching ideas. "Yes, yes—that's it!" said the bookmaster. The metalsmith wiped his brow a few times, as he knew this wouldn't be an easy job. Yet a few minutes later, the two Halflings shook hands and Dorro left the shop, knowing he'd return within a few hours.

The die was truly cast.

35
Setting the Bait

Forgo and his deputies cautiously approached the Rumple burrow. In the opposite direction down the lane, the Sheriff spied a few more of his novice officers hiding behind a cart and looking quite hopeless.

"*Psst!*" he whispered loudly. The cowering deputies finally took notice and stepped out from behind their cover, oblivious to the danger that was about to strike them. Forgo jerked his head for them to get in position, while waving to the troops behind to him fan out in a half circle, so the entire street was cut off, should the elf decide to run for it. Suddenly, he thought to himself, *Forgo, you daft fool. If there really is a Woodland elf in Bing's house and he decides to get rough, these numbskulls won't live but a minute. He'll pull out his blade and slice a row of them into pieces. And it will be all your fault.*

Realizing the enormity of what was about to happen, Sheriff Forgo puffed out his cheeks, sucked in his substantial gut, and started walked carefully toward the front door. Inwardly, Forgo was girding himself for a massacre of his troops, if there was in fact an elf inside the structure. He stopped about ten feet from the open door of Bing's burrow. It was deathly quiet within.

"Elf! Show yourself."

There was naught but the sound of cardinals and goldfinches tweeting to each other in the branches above.

"Elf! I'm giving you a chance to surrender. Come out slowly and no one will get hurt." (Forgo was, of course, thinking of himself and the deputies here.)

"This is the last time, Mr. Elf, the very last time I'm..."

THHHWWWOCK!

Something silver and shiny whizzed past Forgo's left ear and embedded itself in a wooden lamppost behind him. He turned and saw the object—it was a shiny knife. And not just any knife. It was an elvish blade with an ornate bone handle, gently waving back 'n' forth on the post. At that moment, every hair on Forgo's body stood up and hot adrenaline surged through his veins.

The Sheriff pulled out his sword and widened his stance into fighting posture. The deputies surrounding him did the same thing and he noticed that more than a few of them were shaking with fear. *I don't blame 'em*, thought Forgo, *not one bit.*

But out loud he said, "That was a mighty good throw, Elf, but you missed. Maybe you're not as dangerous as we thought."

The next thing Forgo heard chilled him to the very bone. From inside the burrow came a thin, high-pitched sound. At first he couldn't make it out, but then it dawned on him—the elf was laughing. And laughing in a mocking, heartless way. The elf hadn't missed him with the knife, he realized; he was just playing with him, like a cat before it pounced on a mouse. To his right, the Sheriff also noticed that two of his new deputies were gone. He could just see their bouncing rear ends as they high-tailed it around the corner. "Bleedin' cowards," muttered Forgo.

"I'm not afraid of you, elf. I know you can kill us in a heartbeat, but this is our village and you're breaking the law. Come out and fight like a man—*err*—I mean, like a Halfling!"

The Sheriff waited another second and heard the cold laughter subside. Another second. And another. Suddenly, the door to Bing Rumple's burrow squeaked open a little wider and a dark shadow emerged, standing just inside the door frame. To Forgo, it looked like a demon at the gateway to the netherworld.

"You are brave, little chieftain. But there are many of you and only one of me. Doesn't seem like a fair fight."

"You only have to fight me," countered the Sheriff. "And what are you doing in that burrow anyway? You are an invader in our fair hamlet, sir."

"You know why I am here. It's for the same reason we keep coming back—to recover what is ours, the Telstar. With the thief Rumple dead, I was instructed by our leader Toldir to explore this hovel one more time, in case the brooch was hidden somewhere within. I thought I was quiet enough to remain undetected, but apparently, you Halflings are not as slow-witted as we thought. I congratulate you for that."

Forgo turned his head and gave a nod to Dumpus and Porge, acknowledging their sharp eyes and ears.

"Are you admitting that you killed Bing Rumple? If so, I must arrest you for murder. Step out into the sunlight and come along peacefully. We don't want to hurt you."

Forgo heard another snicker, but then the elf moved. Into the light came his worst nightmare—not only an elf, but the big, dark one named Baldar. *Oh great,* thought the Sheriff.

"I'm afraid, my friend, that I shall not come peaceably. I merely came to retrieve what is ours and if you attempt to stop me I will be forced to retaliate." To prove it, Baldar pulled a long, narrow sword from the scabbard on his waist and lowered his body into fighting stance. He was preparing for battle.

Knowing full well that all his deputies and half of Thimble Down were watching him—including the Mayor and Osgood Thrip, who were hiding behind a rain-gutter spout in the distance—Sheriff Forgo pulled his own sword out and uttered quietly, "As you wish."

And then he charged.

☆ ☆ ☆

Several hours later, it was a typical night at the Hanging Stoat. Beer and cider were being guzzled at prodigious rates, along with bowls of beef stew, plates of pork chops or fish pie, heaps of healthy greens, and thick, delicious loaves of bread. Mungo surveyed the crowd with satisfaction. Granted, the Hanging Stoat wasn't the nicest tavern in Thimble Down, but it suited him fine and made him a comfortable living. He wouldn't trade it for anything in the world. Though, to be honest, he was a bit lonely—it would be nice to have a little company now and again. Almost automatically, his eyes scanned the room and settled on a lady he had long admired. Like the tavern itself, this Halfling wasn't the prettiest in the village, but she was plenty for him. But he was too shy to tell her.

Suddenly, Mungo heard a commotion by the front entryway and, surprisingly, none other than Mr. Dorro stepped into the tavern. "Thrice in one week?" he observed. "That's mighty odd." Moreover, his patrons were beginning to flock around the bookmaster like he was the ghost of King Borgo himself. He moved closer for a better look.

As he approached Dorro, something caught his eye. There were flashes of light, like sparkling rays of moonlight. Mungo also heard the *ooo's* and *ahhh's* of his customers, as if he was wearing something magical. And indeed, he was. For when he got close to Dorro, he saw upon his breast a magnificent brooch, a deftly crafted array of silver and gold, interspersed with gems of bright silver and white—as if the power of the sun had been captured and laid on Mr. Dorro's chest. It was stunning.

"Why, that's bigger than Bing Rumple's brooch!" remarked Huckle MacPine, who fixed wagon wheels and axles down the lane.

"Where did you get it, Mr. Dorro, sir? 'Tis beautiful!" admired Elisabeth Ivy Bluebell, who had just come of age and was visiting the Hanging Stoat for the first time with her parents. With all the commotion and excitement, it would be a night she'd never forget for the rest of her life.

"I've never seen anything like it," crowed Farmer Edythe, who perhaps had one too many ciders in her belly and was rather giggly. She hoped Mr. Mungo hadn't noticed.

With a crowd around him, Dorro decided it was "show time." Using an empty wooden cider-box as a platform, the bookmaster stepped up, prepared for his performance. "Hello friends, it's good to see you all again," he opened, grandly. "I see you've noticed my little brooch. Just a bauble, really."

"Are those real gems, Mr. Dorro?" someone in the crowd asked.

"Why, yes they are. Pure diamonds and crystals from the eastern mountains, reputedly hand-dug by dwarves and gnomes in those distant hinterlands. I can't imagine what they're worth."

"Where'd ja get it?" enthused another.

"Why, from the same place our late friend, Mr. Bing Rumple, got his—from the hunting party of Woodland elves. I visited them in the Great Wood a few days ago and we hit it off famously. They were so delighted by my company that they gave me this gift when we parted. I tried to decline, as it's such a magnanimous offering, but they were insistent. So I gratefully accepted and thought I'd try it out this evening. Oh, and by the way, the elves call this one the Nightstar."

"The Nightstar," said Mr. Mungo foggily, his eyes transfixed on the brooch and its many-faceted gems. "It's like sunlight in a bottle." Looking closer, he noted that this brooch, like Bing Rumple's, also had finely crafted leaves and branches of shiny silver, but had even more gems on it, and even its rim was encrusted with star-making crystals. He'd never beheld such beauty.

Dorro then stepped off the box and said, "I think I'll have a seat and a small glass of sherry. If anyone would like a closer look at this brooch, feel free to come over and ask questions. It is beautiful, isn't it?"

Hoping that he hadn't hammed it up too much, he moved across the room, ostensibly looking for an empty table, but also making sure everyone in the Hanging Stoat got a clear glimpse of the Nightstar brooch. As he got closer to the far wall, however, he saw a table of rollicking Halflings that looked familiar. Indeed, there was Sheriff Forgo, along with Bosco, Dumpus, Porge, and other of his "deputies," apparently having a grand time.

"Good evening, Sheriff Forgo. Why the party? It looks like splendid fun."

"Who *thaid dat*?" slurred Forgo, looking dizzily around the tavern. "Why, it's my ol' pal, Dorro Windy River! Hullo, me bucko…"

He's rather gassed, isn't he? realized Dorro. And indeed, the Sheriff had consumed more honeygrass whiskey than even a Halfling of his girth should. Dorro said, "And what are we celebrating, gentlemen? A rare day of quiet in Thimble Down?"

"Quite the opposite, Mr. Dorro," piped up Bosco, cheerfully. "We're here to honor Sheriff Forgo—he's a hero!"

"Really?" said Dorro, taking a seat and sounding dubious. "Tell me the tale."

"*Hear, hear!*" shouted Forgo groggily and looking at no one in particular. Dorro guessed that his vision was perhaps blurry and he probably didn't even know where he was. He'd figure it all out when we awoke with an exploding headache in the morning—much like cannon going off next to his ear.

"Well, we got a report this afternoon that Baldar, that dark giant of an elf, was in Bing Rumple's burrow," continued Bosco. "The Sheriff was up there in a jiffy, along with all us deputies. No sirree, ol' Forgo wasn't going to let any nasty elf walk into our village and rampage through anyone's home. So he confronted Baldar and told him to be off or face his blade. The elf, of course, threw one of his deadly knives at the Sheriff, but missed, 'cos Forgo was too quick for the blighter. When Baldar realized that he wouldn't give in, the battle began."

"*Hear, hear!*" roared Forgo with that addled grin on his face. "*Thish shizz* the good part ..."

"Um, right you are sir," continued Bosco. "With a cry of 'For Thimble Down,' Sheriff Forgo pulled out his sword and charged the mighty elf right there in front of the Rumple place. Baldar pulled his sword and the two engaged in mighty warfare. We thought Baldar would skewer the good Sheriff like a piece of meat o'er the fire, but no, Forgo held his ground. You could see the elf enjoyed the challenge, as he had a big smile on his face the entire time.

"Really?" said Dorro, still incredulous that the Sheriff would engage in bodily combat. Perhaps he should give Forgo more credit in the future.

"Then it was over just as quickly as it began. Out of the blue, Baldar threw down his sword and put his hands in the air. The elf told the Sheriff he would surrender unconditionally and accept whatever punishment the Halflings judged upon him. O'course, he still had that weird smile on his face, but still, Baldar let us bind his hands and lead him off to the gaol, quiet as a lamb. Forgo had defeated and captured the elf, singlehandedly. And that's why we're honoring the great Sheriff tonight!

"HUZZAH! Hurrah for brave Sheriff Forgo!" shouted all the deputies in unison.

"Hear, hear!" shouted Forgo, right before he crossed his eyes and let his head fall to the table with a loud thunk. The only sound to follow was deep, cavernous snoring.

✫ ✫ ✫

Throughout the evening, many in the Hanging Stoat had been ogling the gem-encrusted brooch pinned on Dorro's left breast and, indeed, more than a few began to secretly covet it. And among them, one Halfling decided—at that very moment—to steal it.

Even if it meant someone had to die.

36
A Burrow Gets Burgled

fter a thoroughly exhausting day, followed by an equally taxing evening at the Hanging Stoat, Dorro finally climbed into bed around midnight. After his performance at the tavern, his mind was weary and his body ready for many hours of sleep. Still, the mission had been successful, and tongues were already wagging about the Nightstar.

Timmo really outdid himself this time, thought Dorro, *In just a few hours, he was able to craft a trinket that looked startlingly real. He's a wizard!*

Indeed, Mr. Timmo had truly outdone himself. The brooch had an intricate mesh of silver leaves and branches, and was festooned all over with shiny gems. Dorro chuckled to himself, as he knew it was a wonderful forgery. The metal leaves were stamped and cut pieces of tin that Timmo painted with a quick-drying silver patina, while the branches were just different-gauge thicknesses of silver wire that were cleverly bent and sculpted into arboreal forms. Timmo was known for his facile hands and sharp eye, and truly proved himself a master craftsman here. And crowning it all was an array of fabulous gems seemingly worth hundreds of gold pieces. Instead, they were merely high-quality glass beads that had been cut into diamond shapes and expertly set into the fake brooch. In the dim light of the Hanging Stoat, the Nightstar looked like the most fabulous artifact ever seen within the borders of Thimble Down.

This brooch was also larger than the Bing Rumple's Telstar, which intrigued the village folks even more and was just what Dorro had counted on. As Cheeryup had suggested many days ago, one way to catch a bigger fish is with a bigger piece of bait, which is exactly what the Nightstar represented. However, time would tell if someone would snatch the bait. The bookmaster felt that it might take some time—word of the new brooch hadn't filtered across Thimble Down just yet. But within the next few days, he was expecting someone to break into the Perch and look for it. It was something he didn't relish, but it had to be done. It was the only way.

He couldn't have been more wrong.

✿ ✿ ✿

Dorro fell asleep quickly and settled into a deep slumber. He dreamt of sitting by the River Thimble, quietly fishing a Spring's afternoon away and napping off and on. At last, he got a mighty bite on his line. He pulled and pulled on his rod, trying to land the giant fish, but this one was powerful and kept diving deeper. Dorro feared the line would break, but somehow, it held and after many hours, he yanked on the rod and the fish broke the surface. "Oh *MY!*" screamed the Halfling in his sleep. "That's not a fish! It's—" And indeed, the creature on the end of the line wasn't a mighty bass or pike, but instead, a behemoth with a tail, fins, and Osgood Thrip's head. And in Osgood's teeth wasn't a hook, but the Nightstar, its gems glittering and reflecting light off the river's surface.

Dorro suddenly bolted upright in his bed, sweating profusely. "What a horrifying dream," he muttered. "Thanks to King Borgo it's over."

Then something else happened. Dorro heard some tapping noises from the front of his burrow. He wondered if a raccoon was scratching about outdoors, looking for some scraps of food or a tasty vole to eat.

CRASH!

The bookmaster froze in his bed, cold sweat on his brow and adrenaline suddenly pumping through his veins. That was the sound of glass breaking, probably one of his front windows. "No, it's too soon!" he thought feverishly. "I'm not ready yet. This can't be happening!"

Dorro then heard more noises—more sounds of glass breaking, as well as scuffling, thumps, and furniture being moved around. Someone was within the Perch and, no doubt, they were looking for the Nightstar brooch. He tried to think quickly. As burrows were built into hills and hillocks, there were no back doors—the only way out was through the front. Furthermore, Dorro didn't have a weapon to defend himself. In his washroom, he would find perhaps a toothbrush or a comb, hardly lethal tools of defense. But he had to move quickly, as the burglar would soon tire of thrashing about his kitchen and front parlor, and move toward the rear bedrooms.

With the thumping noises on the rise, Dorro slipped out of bed and quickly donned his robe. Moving quickly, he scampered into his washroom to look for something— anything—he could use to defend himself. The only thing he found was a large towel next to his bathtub. "Well, it's better than nothing," he decided, knowing all too well that he could be severely injured or killed within the next few minutes.

Dorro grabbed the towel and began creeping toward the front of burrow. In fact, Halflings are good at sneaking around quietly or at least, this one was. Trembling with fear and verily drenched in perspiration, Dorro finally reached his front sitting room and peeked around the door frame. Expecting to see a menacing thug on the other side or—King Borgo save him—an elf, the bookmaster was relieved to see no one. Clearly, the intruder was in the kitchen, opening and closing cabinets and generally making a ruckus. Considering that the perpetrator likely knew Dorro was in the burrow, the fact that he was making so much noise suggested that he didn't consider the burrow's owner a threat. Or worse, he simply intended to kill him. With that realization, Dorro shivered with pure, cold fear.

Slowly, Dorro backed up and crossed the hall into one of rear pantries behind the kitchen. This way, he'd get a look at the assailant and decide whether to either engage him or hide instead. His heart pounding furiously, Dorro tip-toed into the pantry and shimmied up to the door jamb. As slowly as possible, he peered around the corner—there, in the reflection of a single candle's light, was a Halfling, rifling through drawers. More than that, it was large one, if the bookmaster was any gauge of size, and well-built, too. He could certainly give Dorro the thrashing of his life. Perhaps he'd already given one to Dalbo Dall just a day earlier.

At that, the bookmaster decided to crawl back into his burrow and hide. Maybe he could just ride it out. Also, the fake Nightstar brooch was in the pocket of his jacket, hanging by the front door. The assailant might find it and just leave. At least that's what Dorro hoped. As he retreated into the darkness, however, a feeling of shame came over him. The image of Dalbo on that cot, beaten and left for dead, popped into his mind and he couldn't shake it. He couldn't let Thimble Down's well-loved wanderer down.

Dorro stopped in the hall, turned around, and started back toward the kitchen. "Dalbo didn't back down, nor will I," whispered the bookmaster with uncharacteristic

305

bravado. Once again, he sidled up to the door frame and peered around the corner. The big intruder had switched to the other side of the kitchen and was going through some lower cabinets on the inner wall. Dorro swallowed nervously and began to creep into the kitchen. The only thing he had in his hand was the towel from his washroom. Dorro took a big gulp, stepped into the kitchen and threw the towel over the stooping intruder's head.

What happened next was a blur.

The moment the towel covered the hunched burglar's head, he stood up fast, smacking his head on an open cabinet door and roaring in pain. *"GAWRRWR!"* was all he managed before Dorro—either bravely or foolishly— vaulted onto the perpetrator's back and began thumping on his head with his fists. Completely disoriented by this surprise attack, the intruder fell onto one knee and seemed to be losing the battle. Then he gathered his wits and stood straight up with the bookmaster still clinging to his shoulders. The bigger creature reached over his shoulder and grabbed Dorro by the top of his robe. Almost like flicking an ant away with his fingers, he threw the burrow's owner across the kitchen, hard, into a stack of plates that were drying on the counter.

SMASH!

Dorro collapsed to the ground with shards of ceramic falling all around him. His back and spine, which took the impact against the countertop, were wrenched in agony. But he was alert—with the assailant on his two feet, Dorro knew he was an easy target on the floor, even by candlelight. He rolled to the left quickly, just as the Halfling's booted foot kicked out at him. It struck the spot where he had been sitting a half second earlier and smashed a cabinet door into splinters.

Dorro scrambled to his feet and rushed the attacker again, screaming at the top of his lungs, *"FOR DALBO!"* He butted the intruder in the stomach with his head and heard him expel all the air in his lungs. But then the mysterious creature grabbed Dorro by the front of his disheveled robe and lifted him straight off the ground. Flailing weakly at his attacker, the bookmaster knew a fateful punch was headed his way. In his kicking, Dorro managed to topple the candle off the counter and the kitchen was plunged into darkness. This was a pivotal moment, as he felt one of the assailant's punches fly past his ear, missing its intended target—his face—by only an inch or two. Still dangling in the air, Dorro was a sitting duck for the next one. Then his hand grazed something cold and hard overhead. Reacting fast, Dorro reach up, grabbed the handle of a small iron frying pan off its hook, and brought it down hard on the intruder's head.

THUD!

An instant later, Dorro was released and fell to the floor, letting go of the pan as he did. By this time, the kitchen in the Perch had become a raging, tumultuous storm of debris, violence, and noise, as the big attacker screamed and lurched backward, clutching his head in pain. True to form, the bookmaster tried to stand up for another assault, but promptly fainted from a combination of fear and pain. The last thing he sensed before blacking out was the sound of his front door being wrenched open and cold night air rushing into his burrow.

The Battle of the Kitchen was over.

37
The Light Begins to Dawn

***

orro blinked his eyes a few times. *Where am I?* he wondered, beginning to stir in his bed. "Ow!" he cried, as sharp pain shot from his back all the way down his legs. "Wha—?"

"Now settle thee down, Mr. Dorro, you've had quite an evening." He knew that voice. It belonged to Nurse Pym. Now the bookmaster was completely confused. *Why was Pym in his burrow and why did his back hurt so much?*

Nurse Pym stepped into Dorro's line of vision and placed her cool palm on his forehead. "There now, rest easy. You've got bumps all over yon body, including a nasty welt on your back. It was a brave thing you did."

Though still fuzzy, images started flooding back into Dorro's head: the sound of breaking glass, a dark figure in his kitchen, and the sensation of deep, primal fear. Oh yes, there was violence, too. Dorro was fairly sure he didn't win, but at least he was still alive. He looked across the room toward the doorway. Gray, soft light was filtering down the hallway; he figured it was dawn or just past.

"What happened?" he croaked through dry lips. Quickly, Nurse Pym put a cup of water to his lips and let him take a little sip. The cool water gliding down his throat felt wonderful.

"I'll let yon Sheriff explain it. He's been here half the night and worried sick he is."

That's the second time someone had told him Forgo had been concerned about his wellbeing. Outwardly, the Sheriff was as gruff as ever, but the two had certainly bonded during the past week and, who knows, maybe there could be a friendship there. Dorro certainly didn't have many—if any—real friends, but he further surmised that neither did Forgo.

"Well, Winderiver, this is getting to be a regular occurrence between the two of us," said the Sheriff, striding into the room with a big grin on his face. "At the rate we're going, we'll probably meet tomorrow at my funeral!

Dorro tried to laugh, but it hurt too much.

"Settle yourself down, Dorro, yer a bit of a mess this morning," Forgo continued, sitting by the bed. "No need to talk much. I only have a few questions anyway, but here's what I've figured out so far. First, neither of us thought our brooch-thief would make his move this soon.

Yet he did and was unsuccessful on two counts—one, he didn't find the Nightstar. I found it in your coat pocket. And secondly, he didn't count on a fierce counterattack from our placid village bookmaster. As far as I can tell, you fought him off successfully, since you're still alive, and also because there's a frying pan on the floor of your kitchen with a sizeable dent in it. I hope the shape of that dent corresponds to one on the intruder's head."

Dorro nodded his head slightly, causing the Sheriff to grin ever broader. "Good lad! I bet that crook has a bruise the size of a small melon," he cackled. "Did you get a look at him? Obviously, it wasn't the elf Baldar—he's been sitting in my other gaol cell, quiet as a lamb."

"It was very dark," whispered Dorro. "But there was something familiar about him. I can't put my finger on it. I have to think a bit more ..." In truth, there was something *very* recognizable about the intruder, but Dorro's head was still too muddled to figure it out. But he knew he was close to cracking this investigation. He just needed time to sew all the threads together.

"Well, you rest up, Winderiver," added Sheriff Forgo. "Now I have a bit of news for you. Last night, before I departed the Hanging Stoat, Farmer Edythe cornered me for a quick word. I was in a hurry, but I'm glad I waited. She was all flustered and breathless. I thought it was because Mungo was nearby—she's been sweet on him for months—but no, she had something else to say. Osgood Thrip, in her words, as good as confessed to the murder at the table next to hers. Edythe did qualify her comments by saying Osgood didn't outright say "I did it," but did clearly imply that he was part of the plot. It's not real evidence, but it puts your ol' school chum closer to the hot seat."

Dorro nodded again and smiled. This was good news, he knew. As the bookmaster always suspected, Osgood had been teetering on the edge of this case and now he was starting to slip right into the middle. *We are very close to the end*, thought Dorro. And right before he nodded off to sleep again, he had one last realization. *I believe I know who the murderer is.*

And then he slept, deeply and soundly, for the rest of the day.

✧ ✧ ✧

By noon, Sheriff Forgo was back at the gaol, grabbing a nap before the next crisis struck, something he figured was inevitable. This time, the lawman was able to lie on his cot in the back cell for a full three hours before another panicky rap on the door told him his next adventure had arrived. When it happened, he rose much fresher than usual and without the usual grumpiness. He even whistled a few bars of a popular whistle pipe tune as he went to answer the door.

"Sheriff Forgo! Are you in?"

"Why Bosco, me boy, good to see you," said the Sheriff, waltzing into the gaol's front room like he was having a dinner party. "What can I do for you?"

Momentarily baffled by the strangely grinning lawman, Bosco continued, "Um, sir, you need to come outside. We have something to show you."

Still leering, Forgo extended his hand in a manner that implied, "After you!" and the two Halflings exited the small building. What the Sheriff saw, however, was the last thing he ever expected. For there, in the hands of several of his new deputies, was none other than that escaped rascal, Wyll Underfoot. And in another's grip was Dorro Winderiver's young library assistant, Cheeryup Tunbridge—the seamstress's daughter.

"Could this day get any better?" said the Sheriff, putting his hands on his hips and breaking into a huge laugh. "Good job, boys! Where did you flush these grubby little grouse from?"

"Dumpus and Porge saw the girl heading toward the Great Wood twice today, both times carrying a basket," said Deputy Bosco. "The second time, we decided to follow her. After about twenty minutes, we saw her duck behind some bushes. Porge and I snuck over a rise and peered down—that's where he saw the girl with the escaped boy. The younglings were frightened and started to run, but ran right into Dumpus who was a-waiting for 'em. The boy tried to kick his way free, but owing to your previous experience, we stayed well away from his feet.

Moreover, the lad saw that we'd secured the girl with a net, so he gave up soon enough. And here we are."

"Capital, gentlemen! You've done Thimble Down proud," offered a positively beaming Sheriff Forgo. "And I believe you're earned those two gold coins Mr. Dorro promised to whoever found the boy."

"Huzzah for Sheriff Forgo! Hurrah for Mr. Dorro!" they all shouted, equally proud of their achievements. Less enthused were the two children in their grasp. Both Wyll and Cheeryup were sullen and angry, and squirming to get out.

"As for you two little rats, that will require some thinking," said Forgo, tapping his fingers together and looking far less sympathetic. "I certainly hope your dear Mr. Dorro wasn't involved with hiding the boy in the woods. If so, we might have to put him in the cell next to you."

"He didn't know anything about it, you bloated wind-bag!" blurted Cheeryup before she could catch herself.

"*Hel-lo*, this one has spirit, doesn't she?" chided Forgo. "Well, I'm glad your friend Mr. Dorro wasn't an accomplice to your mischief. And did you know that he was savagely attacked last night, right in his own bur-row? I hope neither of you had anything to do with that, did you? I believe young Mr. Underfoot has broken into that property before, *hmm* ...."

That took the fight right out of Cheeryup, as well as Wyll, both of whom suddenly hung limp in Dumpus and

Porge's hands. "Is he alright?" cried Cheeryup frantically. "Will he live?"

"Oh, I expect so, but he won't be moving fast for a while," continued the Sheriff, subtly trying to get the children to offer up more information. "In any case, I need to figure out where to stash you two for a day or two. Normally, I'd let the seamstress's daughter go, but Miss Tunbridge has been involved in too many misdoings lately. I think I need to lock you two birds up where I can keep an eye on you. Unfortunately, our little mule here," gesturing toward Wyll, "drop-kicked the window out of my gaol cell the other day, so I think we'll put you elsewhere. Let me think on this."

A few seconds later, Forgo put his finger in the air, "I've got it! The library is barely a stone's throw from here and, as I recall, Winderiver once showed me the building's rare book room, which he keeps under close lock and key. Bosco, dash over there and tell Mr. Bedminster Shoe that the Sheriff of Thimble Down needs to commandeer that room for official business. He is to surrender the keys to you immediately, though assure him that we won't do anything to harm his precious books and scrolls."

Again, Bosco saluted and sped down the lane toward the library, which was barely a hundred paces away. "This way, we can keep you two safely locked up and maintain an easy eye on you," said Forgo, much like a snake sizing up the little mice he was about to eat. "Deputies, bring these two pests into the gaol for a few minutes and give them some food while we wait for Bosco to fetch the keys."

The Sheriff looked up at the white, fluffy clouds sailing by and smiled. "My, this is turning out to be a simply wonderful day."

38
Lightning Strikes

fter a few days of clear, brilliant April skies, it was beginning to cloud up over Thimble Down. The birds were quieting down and there were threatening, blue-black clouds in the western horizon. Rain would surely arrive within a few hours.

In front of the village gaol stood two Halflings in the midst of a heated discussion. In many ways, their terse talk resembled the thunder and lightning that would soon be upon them.

"Sheriff, please be reasonable!"

"I'm sorry, Winderiver, but the girl was caught red-handed. I had to lock her up."

"But she's just a child. And her mother is absolutely frantic."

"Look Dorro, she and the boy are quite safe and comfortable in your rare book room," continued the Sheriff, a full day-and-a-half after Dorro was attacked and Wyll and Cheeryup were caught by his deputies up in the Great Wood. "We've set up cots in the room, and Bosco makes sure they have plenty of food and drink throughout the day. And legally, I can't release them because I still must discuss their punishment with the Mayor. Don't worry—it will be light, if anything."

Dorro was still not appeased. He was in a considerable amount of pain, too; his back ached just walking to the gaol that afternoon, something Nurse Pym had strongly cautioned him against. But when he heard that Wyll and Cheeryup had been incarcerated, nothing could keep him in his bed.

"Well Sheriff, I'm not happy about this at all. I'll need to see them at once. But first, we need to speak. In private."

Forgo cocked an eyebrow.

"You've got something for me, eh?"

"Yes, I believe I do, Sheriff. Lying in a bed for a day finally helped me order my thoughts. I think I may have a solution to our little problem." Forgo grinned broadly—he'd been waiting for the librarian to have one of his little brainstorms.

At that, Dorro and the Sheriff retreated into the gaol.

✵ ✵ ✵

"Children! It's me, Mr. Dorro. Hurry up, Bosco, you booby!"

Inside the room, Wyll and Cheeryup heard Dorro's impatient voice and the jangling of keys. Suddenly, the door to the rare book room flew open and they sprang to their feet. As had happened more than once over the past few weeks, the three had a joyous reunion. It was beginning to become a habit.

"Are they treating you well? Because, if not I will twist the Sheriff's ear until he screams."

"We're fine, Mr. Dorro," consoled Cheeryup, knowing how worked up the librarian could become. "The Sheriff made sure we're taken care of and Deputy Bosco keeps us well fed. If anything, we'd like to run around outside for a few hours, but it looks like rain anyway and we're content. It's not like we have a shortage of books to read. And poor Bosco isn't a booby."

Wyll nodded in agreement. "In fact, we both quite like him! He's been sneaking us chocolate drops."

"Well, maybe I was a little harsh on the deputy, but I suppose I do get a bit fussy at times."

At that, all three broke out into laughter, knowing well that "fussy" could be Dorro's middle name.

✿ ✿ ✿

It was about four o'clock in the afternoon and the skies were growing darker by the minute. There was a small congregation of Halflings standing outside of the library on the cool grass, all of them looking somewhat concerned and uncomfortable. Dorro and Forgo stepped out of the gaol down the lane and began walking toward them.

It was quite an eclectic group: the Mayor was there, as were Osgood and Lucretia Thrip. Rounding out the strange band were Mr. Mungo, Nurse Pym, Deputy Bosco, Farroot Rumple, and his cohort, Bill Thistle, who wore a rather silly, floppy hat. None of them looked happy to be there, notably the Mayor who was lazy and cowardly, and would much prefer to be in his official burrow, sipping tea and trying not to work too hard. He knew this would be unpleasant.

"Good afternoon, gentlemen," said the Sheriff, "and of course, Mrs. Thrip and Nurse Pym," he added with a cough. The assemblage returned his greeting with nods and dour stares. "We've gathered you here today to have a discussion about the matter of Mr. Bing Rumple, lately deceased, of Thimble Down and brother to Mr. Farroot here. And for that, I'll turn things over to Mr. Winderiver, our esteemed librarian."

"What does *he* have to do with anything?" blurted out Lucretia fiercely. "Shouldn't he be stacking books or something?"

"Actually, Mrs. Thrip, Dorro has been helping out with the investigation and has come to some interesting conclusions," added Forgo. "I think we should hear him out."

"Proceed!" said the Mayor, trying to sound official and not like he'd rather be at home, taking a nap.

Clearing his throat, Dorro began, "First I must apologize to you all, dragging you out of your comfy burrows to be here." They all noticed that the librarian appeared to be in some pain and was leaning on his walking stick. All had heard about his violent encounter the other night, though in truth, some in this group were less than sympathetic. *That's what he gets for meddling in others' business*, a few thought.

"I suppose the place to begin is, well, the beginning," said Dorro. "A week or two ago, Bing Rumple returned to Thimble Down with his brother here and their friend, Mr. Thistle." Dorro looked at the pair and noticed that they were looking at him balefully. "Their return was marked by the fact that Bing was wearing a rather stunning brooch on his chest, one covered with gems and silver—really, nothing of which had ever been seen in our village before. It became all the talk at the Hanging Stoat, and later, news of the gem-encrusted trinket spread through the village like a bad case of the mumps. Subsequent to that, misfortune began following Mr. Rumple—he was hit on the head one evening and collapsed in Mr. Mungo's tavern, apparently the victim of a would-be robbery. Fortunately, he had hidden his famous brooch, the Telstar, and it was not stolen."

"However, troubling reports continued to filter into the village. A day after his attack, Bing ran into town and reported that the Telstar had been stolen from his burrow. Furthermore, there were reports of strange giants seen in the Great Wood. Not long after, the Woodland elves made themselves known. These were the 'giants', as espied by the poor, late Dalbo Dall. We were then told that Bing had been kidnapped—but was he? If that weren't enough, the finale to this saga was the horrific murder of Bing and the discovery of his beaten and stabbed body by myself, the Sheriff, Mr. Mungo, Nurse Pym, Mr. Thistle and, of course, the deceased's brother, Mr. Farroot Rumple."

Everyone in group gravely nodded, giving their ascent that Dorro's interpretation of the timeline was essentially correct. They also cast furtive glances at one another.

"This brings us to the present, when we still haven't found Bing's murderer—or the brooch. Popular opinion would have it that Toldir and his elves were the culprits. Indeed, the Telstar originally belonged to them and—and whether you believe they gave the Telstar to Bing or that he stole it—we have no doubt that the brooch originated with them. And if, by chance, Bing did steal it, they would have real cause to retrieve it, even to the extent of murder."

Dorro quickly glanced at Farroot and Bill Thistle, both of whom looked more than a little uncomfortable. "They murdered my brother, sure as it's going to rain cats and chickens tonight!" protested Farroot. "You even found that elf's bloody knife in Bing's back!" Bill nodded vigorously in agreement, adjusting his silly hat as if to prevent it from falling off.

"That's true, Mr. Farroot, but pray, let me finish. There is in fact an elf named Baldar with a gift for throwing knives with deadly accuracy. And truly, it was his knife found in Bing's back. But I spent time with the Woodland elves and saw a very different side of them—one of honor and restraint. In my opinion, they would not kill indiscriminately, only if they were threatened themselves. And I can't see Bing Rumple posing a threat to these powerful beings."

"Maybe you were under their spell," sniped Lucretia. "I say you were bewitched by those strange elf folk!" At this absurd statement, even her husband Osgood coughed and patted her gently on the arm.

Also trying to ignore her, Dorro continued, "… but even with my opinion, things looked very black for the elves—they had every motive to kill Bing, at least on the surface. However, there was one thing that changed the entire course of this investigation."

"And what would that be, librarian?" sneered Osgood in his most condescending voice.

"That would be …" continued Dorro, clearing his throat once again, "what Dalbo Dall told me the other day. You might also like to know that he's quite alive. I'm afraid I fibbed a few minutes ago, but as Nurse Pym can tell you, Dalbo is improving nicely."

✲ ✲ ✲

At that, the group exploded into irate, panicky voices and frantically waving arms.

"Impossible!" snapped Osgood.

"You said he was run over by a cart and killed instantly!" shouted Farroot.

"You've gone too far this time, Winderiver," growled the Mayor.

"He's correct," said Sheriff Forgo with calm, but forceful authority. "Dalbo did indeed speak to Mr. Dorro and, in truth, Dalbo is alive and continuing to regain his strength. I'm a witness and, to be honest, was part the conspiracy myself. We only spread the rumor of his death to protect him."

Around Dorro and the Sheriff, several of the Halflings looked like their eyeballs were about to pop out of their heads. "Nevertheless, Mr. Dorro will continue with the facts of the investigation."

"Thank you, Sheriff. It's true that Dalbo was near-mortally injured. His injuries were grotesque and horrible. Worse, they were not caused by a wagon. In truth, he was physically assaulted, and I believe, his attackers thought he was dead by the time they'd finished with him. But trust me, Dalbo still breathes."

There were hushed whispers and gasps throughout the group. And still, the sky grew darker by the second, as rain and storm grew closer.

"Just hours after his attack, I was able to speak with Dalbo for a few minutes. The conversation took place in the back of the Hanging Stoat, where Mungo and Bosco had laid his weak, beaten body after they'd discovered him. He said something most curious to me:

"The good goat ate the star for gold, roots 'n' all."

"What are you playing at, Winderiver?" barked Farroot. "Sheriff, can you really be taking this seriously? Mr. Mayor, you must stop this charade!"

"Pipe down, Rumple!" returned Forgo in his most intimidating voice. "Let Dorro finish." The Mayor nodded in agreement. Even Osgood Thrip had the good sense to keep his mouth shut.

Dorro nodded and continued: "Thank you, Sheriff. As I was saying, Dalbo uttered this—at least on the surface—nonsensical phrase. At first I thought it was gibberish, but the more I played with the words in my mouth, the more they made sense to me. Finally, I understood what had happened. Dalbo had been attacked because he had heard something. In fact, he heard two Halflings speaking about something—and that *something* would be the Telstar. He heard the pair discussing how they had murdered Bing for the brooch. Further, they were going to sell it for gold, and then leave Thimble Down in a hurry."

"Well then, out with it!" cried the Mayor, who was growing impatient for his dinner.

"I'm sorry, Mr. Mayor. Of course, Dalbo's silly saying was quite clear, if you start from the end: *'The good goat ate the star for gold, roots 'n' all.'* The word 'roots' is an allusion to Mr. Farroot Rumple and the 'gold' is the brooch itself—the prize. The word 'goat' threw me for a while, but then I tried thinking in silly rhymes and verses like Dalbo always does, which made it easier. For him, a goat would more likely be a 'billy goat' which, when placed next to Farroot's name, is simply bill, which stands for Bill Thistle. So you see, Mr. Mayor, Dalbo was beaten by Farroot and Bill, because he heard them discussing how they'd stolen the Telstar and were making plans to sell it for gold. It's all rather obvious, if you think about it."

The entire group stiffened in shock and bewilderment. But Dorro wasn't done yet. Pulling his pipe out of his pocket and nonchalantly lighting it, he continued.

"The coup de grâce happened two nights ago when someone burgled my burrow, looking for the Nightstar brooch. If you haven't figured it out by now, that one was a fake, cleverly crafted by Mr. Timmo. But I did recognize the burglar, even before I gave him a knock on the head with my frying pan." Dorro took a step forward and snatched the floppy hat off of Bill Thistle's head. There, plain as day, was a giant red welt on the side of the thuggish Halfling's forehead. "I say, Bill, that looks rather nasty. Even though you're a murderer, you should really have Nurse Pym take a peek at it," said the librarian sardonically.

At that moment, there was a huge crack of thunder overhead—something matched only by the lightning speed Bill Thistle pulled a knife out of his belt and launched himself at Dorro's throat.

39
Everything Goes Wrong

*T*he rain was beginning to fall, slowly at first and then building into torrents. The light was fading, too, adding to the chaos.

Even so, Forgo and his deputies were ready. They knew that Bill Thistle would do something the moment Dorro accused him of murdering Bing Rumple. Perhaps they weren't ready for the speed at which Bill could move, drawing the knife hidden in his belt and vaulting for Dorro's jugular vein. It was fortunate, then, that Bosco had spent his childhood in all sorts of mischievous—and accordingly athletic—pursuits around Thimble Down and was rather limber himself. As soon as Bill made his move, Bosco pulled out his own short sword and jumped in to intercept the larger Halfling. And two seconds behind him was Sheriff Forgo with cudgel in hand, moving with surprising speed for a big fellow.

With the wind and rain whipping their faces, the three Halflings collided with crushing impact, Forgo and Bosco barely a match for Bill's rage and brute force. All of the others who had previously been standing on the grass had already scattered in the storm and violence, expect for Farroot Rumple, who drew a blade from within his own clothing and moved to take out Dorro himself.

While Bill was dueling with the two lawmen, the surviving Rumple brother stepped up to the bookmaster and, blade pointed downward, brought his knife down in a terrifying arc. For a quiet bibliophile, Dorro was surprisingly adept at the skill of self-preservation and brought his walking stick up into a defensive posture, holding it horizontally with two hands over his head. Farroot's wrist slammed into the thick wooden stick, causing him to cry out in pain. He somehow managed to hold onto his knife and, switching it to his other hand, took a lateral slash at Dorro. Farroot connected with the bookmaster's cheek, drawing a gash that spurted blood. Dorro screamed and fell to the soggy ground. Pure madness was reigning in a spot that had been quiet and idyllic just a few minutes earlier.

Swiftly, Sheriff's Forgo's reinforcements were on the scene—deputies Dumpus and Porge each had short, stout swords and were moving in quickly to engage Farroot and Bill. Even the normally gentle Mr. Mungo joined the fray, pulling back and landing a punch on Farroot's oily jaw. Less surprising were the Thrips, who fled down the muddy lane shrieking, while the Mayor cringed under a lilac brush and pretended to be invisible. At that precise moment, he began reconsidering his upcoming bid for re-election.

Back in the skirmish zone, Farroot appraised the situation. "Bill, let's move!" he grunted, after realizing they were outnumbered and would be overcome in seconds. The two crooks suddenly sprinted away. The defenders assumed the scoundrels would run off and hide, or skip town entirely. Instead, the two bounded up onto the porch of the library, through its entrance, and bolted the heavy oaken door from within.

Dorro, Forgo, and the rest of deputies simply looked at each other incredulously—they hadn't seen this coming at all. A moment later, they heard the library door being unlatched again and opening slightly. Out ran a pale and panicked Bedminster Shoe, as well as a few library patrons cringing in fear. The door slammed shut and was bolted again. From the outside, the onlookers could observe Farroot and Bill Thistle dashing about the library, closing all the windows and latching them firmly shut.

Sheriff Forgo shrugged his shoulders and looked skyward with exasperation, knowing all too well what was happening. A stand-off had just begun.

✣ ✣ ✣

"Deputies, fall back to the building line. That's an order!" shouted Forgo, preparing the defense for a classic barricaded siege.

"But Sheriff, the children! Wyll and Cheeryup are still in there!" screamed Dorro, his cheek dripping with blood as he got to his feet. "We must save them."

As if on cue, a window on the first floor cracked open a hair, "Sheriff, pull your deputies back. We have hostages and will kill them if you don't follow our exact demands."

"Rumple, if you harm those children, you'll never make it out of Thimble Down alive. Do you hear me?"

The next thing the Halflings saw chilled them to the bone. Even though their visibility was diminished by heavy rain and the maelstrom of thunder and lightning overheard, they could clearly make out a child writhing in Farroot's grip. It was Cheeryup, and the assailant had her pinned to his chest, one arm around her body and the other holding a knife point to her throat.

At the sight, Dorro gasped and cried aloud, "Leave her be, Farroot! She's just a girl. Have you no mercy?"

"*None*, you filthy maggot," was Farroot's icy reply through the roaring rainfall. "Thought you were clever to realize Bill 'n' me stole the brooch. We'll see how clever you feel when you're burying these two little wretches tomorrow morning. Bill's quite good with a knife, y'know. If you don't clear off, I might ask him to do a little target practice. Or maybe we'll just burn your library down, whining children and all." With that, he slammed the window sash down and disappeared.

At that, Dorro began protesting again, but he felt the mammoth grip of Sheriff Forgo grabbing him from behind and dragging him backwards to the nearby blacksmithery belonging to Tom Turner. The rough structure had an entryway with large sliding doors that had been hoisted apart. As well as keeping the rain off their heads, Forgo decided this would be their headquarters for the siege, as it provided him a good vantage point of the library and its environs.

"Stop provoking them, Dorro—you'll do more harm than good. These are dangerous criminals and it's no use taunting them. Farroot is crazier than a raccoon and might just do what he says. We need to give him and Bill time to calm down, and realize what a pickle they're in."

Nurse Pym arrived at the blacksmith's shop and started attending to the bloody gash on Dorro's cheek. At her insistence, he reluctantly sat down on an anvil and let her work. Suddenly, the enormity of what had transpired hit him. "I've been such a fool!" he said, to no one in particular. "I should have known the children were in harm's way. And here I thought I was being so clever and dramatic. An absolute fool, I tell you!"

"Stop wasting your energy, Dorro," said the Sheriff, who had become sober and grave in the face of this growing debacle. He knew their odds of rescuing the children were slim—they were the perfect bargaining chip for Farroot and Bill to get out of Thimble Down. But he wasn't about to let Dorro know that; it would break his spirit.

"We need a plan," he continued. "Bosco, Dumpus, and Porge, I want you to take any deputies we have left and surround the library in case Farroot and Bill attempt an escape tonight. Also Mungo, bring some food. We need to feed them so they don't get desperate. The most important thing, everyone, is not to do anything rash or silly. We need to work in a coordinated manner to free the children. I'm going to say it again—we all need to work *together*."

Yet within his own thoughts, Dorro was already crafting a plan. If it succeeded, he could free the children. *If not* ...

He didn't want to think about it.

40
The Greatest Cast

Outside the blacksmith's shop, the storm raged with crackling thunderbolts, hammering rain on the tin roof. *What a disaster*, thought Forgo. He knew he was as much to blame as anyone for this predicament, but he'd reprimand himself later—those two children were in real danger, he knew. As soon as Mungo showed up with some food, the Sheriff would have a deputy leave it on the library's front porch for the hostage-takers and, hopefully, their prisoners, too. *It's going to be a long night*, he reflected.

Nurse Pym mopped up the blood on Dorro's cheek as best she could and neatly popped a few stitches in there to hold the flesh in place. She was a miracle-worker, even under the most extreme conditions. But if she had known what Dorro was thinking while under her care, she'd have informed Sheriff Forgo immediately. Instead, the bookmaster merely looked at the ground and kept his thoughts to himself.

In short order, Mr. Mungo appeared with several baskets of food, one for the hostage-takers and the rest for the tired lawmen and their helpers. Sheriff Forgo barked out a few orders while demolishing a pork sausage in just a few bites. He and Bosco grabbed another basket and began cautiously approaching the library. He called out, "*A-hoy! Hey!*"

The window sash slowly went up. "What now, ye blow-hard?" asked Farroot, who was clearly tired and in a foul mood.

"Look, we've brought food," continued the Sheriff. "We don't want any trouble. But you need dinner, and the children must be hungry, too. Can I have your permission to put this basket on the porch?"

"This had better not be a trick, Forgo. Do not push me!"

"I swear, Farroot, it's just a basket of food. Bosco here will bring it up and then leave instantly."

The window closed and then the Sheriff gave Bosco a quick nod. The young deputy moved up the stairs, placed the basket down, and retreated. The two Halflings pulled back even further—they didn't want to do anything to provoke the dangerous pair within. The rain was still coming down heavily, but even from a distance, Forgo saw the library's door open slightly, an arm reach out, and grab the basket.

Whew, thought Forgo. At least he'd done one thing right.

✲ ✲ ✲

While the Sheriff was delivering the food, Dorro stood up to stretch his arms and legs in the rear of Tom Turner's blacksmithery. Unbeknownst to all, he had other plans. While all the other deputies were distracted by the actions around the library, Dorro grabbed a short sword from the smithy's rack—a light, nimble blade destined for some lucky customer—and secreted it in his jacket. The bookmaster then walked quietly out the rear of the shop and disappeared into the storm.

✲ ✲ ✲

"Good job, Bosco—you've done well," said the Sheriff when he returned to the blacksmithery a few minutes later. "That was an important first step. We've earned a little of Farroot and Bill's trust. From that we can build a larger plan to rescue the children. Don't you agree, Winderiver?"

Forgo looked about quickly. "Where's Dorro?" he demanded urgently. Most of the deputies threw up their hands, and even Nurse Pym and Mr. Mungo shook their heads. "*Blast!*" roared the Sheriff. He knew exactly what Dorro was up to. And it wasn't good.

☼ ☼ ☼

Dorro had a plan. Of course, it was far-fetched, but it was all he could come up with and he needed to rescue the children, even if it meant a thrashing at the hands of Sheriff Forgo. While the rain was beginning to taper off, the wind still howled throughout the dark Thimble Down night, which he reasoned, provided good cover for his mission. Behind the library was a small shed, where he kept everything from shovels and buckets to rope and tools. Within, Dorro also stowed a few fishing rods, just in case he felt compelled to rush over to the River Thimble to make a few casts and didn't have time to stop at the Perch first. This wasn't his best fishing gear, but it would suffice in a pinch. And today, he was in a pinch.

The noisy wind allowed him to sneak past Deputy Porge, who was cowering in a doorway and trying to stay out of the rain. Using his most stealthy maneuvers, Dorro arrived at the shed in just a few seconds. The wind dampened the sound of him rustling tools around, but he knew exactly where the fishing rods were and, in fact, one in particular. Dorro had taken it out just a few days earlier, when he had a few spare moments. Along with the fake Nightstar brooch, Mr. Timmo had also given him one of his latest lures, the vaunted Pickerel Pincer, and the bookmaster had set it up on the very rod he was holding in his hands.

Although it was dark, Dorro could see the lure in his mind. It was painted bright yellow, with dark stripes like a small baitfish, and had two large treble-hooks in its belly—these had three hooks each and were quite effective at snagging their fishy prey. But tonight Dorro wasn't going for fish, per se, though it prove be the most important cast of his life. Wyll and Cheeryup's lives depended on it.

Sneaking around to the darkest, most remote corner of the library's exterior, Dorro looked up and saw his target. It was a window on the second floor of the building. In fact, this was the very window that Wyll Underfoot had broken into when he camped in the library all those many days ago and they both chose it for good reason. The window had an upper sash that was easy to pull down and thence gain access. Wyll, of course, was nimble enough to climb the ivy trellis alongside the circular building and edge himself along its exterior on each protruding timber. Dorro, meanwhile, would have to use a ladder to get up on the roof and lower himself down via the gutter. *If*, of course, things proceeded as planned.

Standing on the wet ground, his back still aching, Dorro knew he didn't have much time. Farroot and Bill were distracted by the basket of delicious food and wouldn't be paying much attention to the rear of the library, but that moment wouldn't last, so he had to move with speed. Pulling the line of his fishing reel tight, he pulled back and cast upwards into the darkness, trying to snag the window latch. It was like trying to hit a burrow-fly with dart and, accordingly, he missed by several feet. Dorro reeled in the line and tried again. The Pickerel Pincer hit the glass and harmlessly bounced off. Again, the din of the wind was crucial in hiding these noises—otherwise, Dorro would have been sunk. He cast several more times, failing each time. He was now thinking of climbing the ivy trellis himself, though he weighed much more than Wyll and could conceivably crack it and make an awful racket. So he gave the rod one last shot.

Whoooossssh ... CLICK!

The Pickerel Pincer had grabbed something in the dark. Dorro slowly began to reel in the line, not sure if it was the roof or a branch. Suddenly he heard something else—the window latch coming free. *Yes!* he realized, *the lure had found its mark.* Reeling in as tenderly as possible, Dorro was heartened as he saw the upper sash beginning to descend. In a few seconds, the window was completely open. Laying aside the rod, he rushed back to the shed, but was crestfallen to realize the ladder was buried under numerous buckets and shovels—trying to extricate it would create tremendous noise and give the game away. Furthermore, his injured back wasn't up to lugging a heavy ladder across wet grass.

So Dorro made a battlefield decision—he was going up the creaky ivy trellis, despite his size and injury. He put his first foot on the wall-mounted frame and heard it wince under the strain. He also had that small sword stashed in his belt, complicating matters. *There's no other way*, he thought. *Do it for the children, Dorro!* And with that, he began climbing, hand over foot as methodically as he could. The trellis creaked and moaned with the weight, but fortunately, Farroot and Bill were devouring Mr. Mungo's cuisine with relish and took no notice. They even threw Cheeryup and Wyll a few scraps to gnaw on.

Dorro reached the top and knew he must sidle out onto the extended timber ends to get close to the window. They were slick with rain and years of mossy growth, but he didn't have a choice. Holding onto the gutter with his hands, he stepped out onto the first timber and then stretched his foot to the next. Moving his hands along the gutter, he was able to move awkwardly along the wall, but at least he was getting closer to the window. The fourth step almost ended the adventure altogether—Dorro's left foot slipped on the moss. Fortunately, his fingers reacted fast enough and grabbed the gutter, at least long enough for him to regain his footing. Sweating profusely now, Dorro kept moving and finally, he was there, just outside the window.

"Dorro!"

The bookmaster cautiously peered down, only to see a very angry Sheriff standing on the ground, staring up at his bum.

"Dorro, you damned fool," Forgo whispered as loudly as possible. "If you were down here, I'd personally throttle you. What in King Borgo's name are you doing?"

At this Dorro paused. He realized that he didn't actually have a plan past getting into the second-story gallery.

Dorro had figured he would gallantly sweep down the stairs, handily disarm the bandits, and save the children. He forgot about how adept Bill Thistle was with a knife or Farroot with his own blade.

"Dorro—what is your plan?" pleaded the Sheriff again.

Dorro didn't know what to do. He looked down at Forgo and shrugged helplessly. And then the bookmaster did the only thing he could think of.

He slithered through the open window and disappeared into the blackness within.

41
The Battle of the Books

ursing, Sheriff Forgo ran back toward his headquarters in the blacksmith's shop. By the time he arrived, his face was red and, arguably, more smoke was pouring from his nostrils than the nearby forge.

"Drat that bookmaster!" spouted the lawman, drawing everyone's curious attention. "He's in the building." More raised eyebrows. "The *library,* that's what building." Now there were gasps from all around the shed, including Nurse Pym and the absolutely drenched Mayor, who had decided that the blacksmithery was drier than the wet lilac bush he'd been cowering under.

"Alright then—we need to create a diversion and fast. Dorro will need as much as time as we can give him to save those children. Who has ideas?"

Around him, the deputies and others started spouting off thoughts and plans. For the most part, Forgo knew, they were pretty ridiculous, but he liked Mungo's offbeat contribution. It sounded stupid on the surface, but what the heck—he was a desperate man and this was as good as he had. Nurse Pym volunteered to help out and ran down the lane to the seamstress's burrow. Cheeryup's mother, Mrs. Tunbridge, was reportedly catatonic with fear about her daughter's fate, but they all knew she would still help out.

"I need a volunteer, too. Who's up for some real danger and adventure?" He looked around at his deputies; most of them were looking at their fingernails or checking the sharpness of their swords—anywhere but at Sheriff Forgo. But slowly, one hand went up. *Perfect,* thought Forgo. *That one's baby face is just the ticket.*

Nurse Pym returned a few minutes later, huffing and out of breath. And in her hands, was a lovely country dress and bonnet. "Okay Porge, get yer clothes off," barked the Sheriff. "It's time to bring out yer sweet girly side."

✫ ✫ ✫

Dorro couldn't believe the fix he was in. He was a librarian trapped on the second story of his own library and downstairs were vicious criminals holding two children hostage. "How did I get here?" he wondered, but then begrudgingly admitted that it was his own pig-headedness that got him this far. "Sometimes Dorro, you're a real *pip!*" he squeaked to himself.

Edging toward the gallery railing on his belly, he noticed that he had a good view of the first floor. There weren't many candles lit, which would be an asset as he descended the ladder and attempted his rescue. He could see everything from the front door to the circulation desk, as well as the door of the rare book room. And just on the edge of his vantage point, he could see the feet of Farroot Rumple and Bill Thistle, the villains behind this travesty.

Dorro took a moment to count up his assets and liabilities. On the plus side, he was armed; could move quickly and quietly; knew the library inside and out; and best of all, no one knew he was there. On the debit side, he was a poor fighter, a bit of a scaredy-pants, and terribly impulsive. Dorro figured his chances of a successful rescue were about slim to none, but that was better than waiting outside with Forgo and knowing that tragedy could occur at any minute.

Dorro was just about to begin his slow descent via the ladder when he heard the last thing he would have expected.

KNOCK! KNOCK!

There was dead silence from within the building as someone was rapping on the heavily bolted library door.

KNOCK! KNOCK! KNOCK!

Warily, Farroot and Bill edged closer to the front door, their swords drawn and incredulous looks on their faces, as Dorro could see from above. They were whispering between themselves and the bookmaster could pick out random bits: "What's this? One of Forgo's tricks? Be ready, Bill—they may attack at any minute!"

"Who's there?" Farroot finally shouted.

"Hellooooo! Is anyone in there?" It was a young girl's voice, one that Dorro didn't recognize.

"Identify yerself!" repeated the hostage-taker.

"Umm, why, it's Peregrina Pumble. Is the library open? I need to return a few books."

More whispering and eyeball-bulging stares between Farroot and Bill. "Errrr ... we're closed! Come back to-morrow," bellowed Farroot fiercely.

"Oh dear!" said the girl from outside the locked door. "You see, my books are late and I'm afraid that I've amassed a substantial penalty. I would like to square my account today; otherwise, Mr. Shoe told me I'd owe much more tomorrow. Won't you please let me in?"

"Go *away!*" snarled Farroot again, losing patience.

There was a pause. Then the girl began again, "Well, I also want to sign out a new book that I heard was very good. Arabella Turtle told me to read an old classic called *The Adventures of Missy Rabbit & Bumblefoot,* and I thought it sounded delicious. Can I drop off my books and quickly check that one out?"

"*NO*, you may not. Clear off or there will be trouble!"

"Sir, am I to assume that you were planning to take out *The Adventures of Missy Rabbit & Bumblefoot* and don't want to part with your copy? I suppose I don't blame you, but I'd be most obliged if you let me take it out instead."

Dorro chuckled to himself. Farroot was beside himself with rage—he didn't want to have another child-hostage on his hands, but this was too much. How did this one get past Forgo? Trying to sound as sincere as possible, Farroot continued, "Little girl, I have not read *The Adventures of Missy Rabbit & Bumblefoot* since I was a wee lad. And actually, as I recall, it was quite good—I was particularly taken with the antics of Bumblefoot. You know, he made me giggle quite a bit …"

Snapping back to the present, Farroot continued, "Nevertheless, we *ARE* closed today due to special renovations, so you must come back tomorrow. I'll leave Mr. Shoe a note telling him that you won't owe any more for your overdue books. Now, run home to your mama before the storm gets any worse."

More silence. And then the girl spoke again: "But sir—I also have to pee. Can I come in and use the washroom? Please?"

"Look, you dim little lass, you may not know this, but you've just walked into the middle of a hostage crisis."

"Oh dear!" replied Peregrina Tumble. "That's exactly what happened to my Aunt Flea. She had a hosta crisis last summer. The woodchucks ate the poor hostas in her garden every week and she hasn't been the same since. So sad, really."

At this, Dorro began tittering and before he could stifle himself, he guffawed and snorted loudly. Farroot froze—and then slowly looked upwards toward the gallery. He was looking into darkness right at Dorro, but in the black, probably couldn't see him. Yet he realized—this had all been a setup.

"Okay, little girl, how about I open the door and *STAB YOU IN THE HEART?*" he roared. At that, Dorro heard someone leap off the library's front porch and race into the dark evening. Little did he know it was Deputy Porge, dressed up like a Thimble Down lass and scared out of his wits.

Sheriff Forgo's attempt at a diversion had just collapsed.

☆ ☆ ☆

"We've been tricked," muttered Farroot, tilting his head toward the upper gallery. "I just heard a fat pigeon land up in the gallery. Be a good lad, Bill, and *go kill it*."

Dorro knew he was trapped like a rat. He felt cold sweat breaking out all over his body and was paralyzed with fear. With his sore back, he couldn't climb back out to the trellis before Bill would race up the ladder and be upon him. *But wait.* Bill wasn't coming up the ladder. Instead, he was circling the first floor and gazing upwards, trying to get a better view of which deputy might be up there. Dorro watched as Bill began edging himself around the first floor, peering up into the dark in case he could spy the "fat pigeon" before ascending the ladder. There was still not much Dorro could do, plus he was rather insulted at being called fat.

The bookmaster got an idea. It was so obvious, he could have smacked himself on the head, but he'd already made enough of a racket. Instead he peered around himself and waited. And waited. Dorro heard Bill Thistle slowly shuffling across the floor underneath him, closer and closer. Using his quietest moves, Dorro pulled himself into a standing position and reached out toward a nearby pedestal. Just as Bill moved directly under the railing below his feet, Dorro grabbed the 1524 edition of *The Collected Poems of Bodurdo*, a massive, leather-bound tome that weighed at least fifteen pounds, leaned over the railing, and let it fall.

WHUMP!

Dorro peered over the rail and saw the book on the floor, and splayed out beneath were the twisted arms and legs of Bill Thistle. Bill had never seen it coming. On top of the whack from his frying pan a few nights ago, the villain would likely awake with a headache for the ages. *Now that's poetic justice*, thought Dorro to himself. But as usual, he had gotten too giddy for his own good.

"I know you're up there, Winderiver." It was the icy, cool voice of Farroot Rumple. "I saw you there in the candlelight, just briefly. Clever of you to sneak up there, I agree, but I wouldn't want to be you when Bill wakes up. I think he'll have something for you—like a quick knife in the ribs."

Dorro said nothing.

"I can't see you, bookmaster, but can you see me now? I think it's time you came down." Farroot slowly moved into the candlelight. There, held with one arm were Cheeryup and Wyll and across their necks, a steely, glittering sword blade. The children avoided Dorro's eyes. "It would be a shame if I slit their throats and let their blood muck up your charming little library," purred the evil Rumple brother. "Would take you hours to tidy up, don't you think?"

Dorro knew his mission had failed. He stepped over to the ladder, dropped the sword he'd stolen from the blacksmith's shop, and announced sheepishly, "You win, Farroot. I surrender. But please, take me hostage and let the children go! I beg of you."

"You have no bargaining power, Winderiver. Scuttle down here and then we'll deal with you."

By the time Dorro had reached the ground floor, things had gone from bad to worse. Not only was Farroot Rumple holding the children at sword point, but Bill Thistle had risen and was rubbing his throbbing, bruised head. The look on his face was nothing short of murderous.

"Bill, I don't know about you, but I think it's time we got out of here. Grab the idiot bookmaster and let's go have a chat with the Sheriff."

Bill pulled out his own sword and headed toward Dorro. The bookmaster actually wasn't too surprised when the thug lifted the hilt of his blade and brought it down hard on the back of his neck. Dorro staggered to one knee, but didn't lose consciousness, despite the excruciating pain. Dizzy and confused, he felt his body being jerked up and dragged across the floor in Bill's muscular grip. He then felt a rush of cool air and knew he was outside on the library's porch. Lastly, he felt an unmistakable sensation—the cold edge of Bill's blade against his neck.

"*SHERIFF!* Come out—the game is up. And I've caught your spy. It's time we end this." By the sound of Farroot's voice, Dorro knew he was desperate and would do just about anything.

"I'm here, Rumple. Please don't do anything hasty." Sheriff Forgo looked at the porch and saw pretty much what he expected: Dorro and the children being held at sword point by two crazed Halflings. The next few minutes would be crucial, he knew.

"Why did you lie to us and try such a desperate ploy? Seems pitiful for a lawman such as you."

"It wasn't my idea. Winderiver acted of his own accord. This is true, Farroot, I swear!"

Behind the Sheriff, a crowd began to grow in damp night air, now calm after the storm had blown past. Gathered were all the deputies, along with the Mayor, Osgood and Lucretia Thrip, Mr. Mungo, Nurse Pym, Farmer Edythe, and a gaggle of frightened Thimble Downers.

"Maybe you're telling the truth, Sheriff, but this fool of a Halfling must still pay. Bill owes him a 'favor' so I think we'll only have two hostages in a minute. It's up to Bill. And then we're leaving town, so fetch us a cart. *Or else!"*

"Farroot, we can strike a bargain—I know it wasn't you that killed Bing," continued Forgo, trying to turn them against each other. "Surrender yourself with Dorro and the children, and we will be lenient with you. And Bill, you will get a just trial as well. Even murderers get a fair shake in Thimble Down. That is our way"

"YOU'RE A LIAR!"

At that moment, everyone stopped and stared. It was a strange voice—raspy and coarse, but not without force behind it. They all realized who had uttered the words. It was Bill Thistle, whom no one in the village had ever heard speak before.

"I am no murderer, Sheriff, so dare not accuse me of that heinous crime," continued Bill in his strange, gritty voice. "I am merely a thief—gold and jewels are my trade and I truly love their touch and smell. It is my failing, I suppose. But Bing Rumple did not die by *my* hand. I think you'll have to ask his dear brother about that act."

"You filthy traitor!" screamed Farroot next to him. "I should let these children go and slit your treacherous neck instead!"

"I'm sorry, *friend,* but I shan't pay for your evil deed." Bill then addressed the Sheriff. "He killed Bing out of greed and malice. He was tired of his whining and, after I figured out where he'd hidden the Telstar, he bashed him on the head with a fireplace poker. Worse, he stabbed his dead corpus with the elvish knife we had stolen earlier, all in order to divert blame onto those elvish chaps. Me, I just wanted to melt down the Telstar and skedaddle with my share of the gold. I'm no murderer—just a tad greedy, that's all."

Farroot knew the jig was up, but had one last card to play, "Sheriff, I'm still waiting for my cart. I guess I'll be leaving alone with these children. My sword blade is just beginning to scratch their little necks—one sudden move and they'll be dead in my arms. Your call, Forgo!"

"*Don't!* Please, Farroot, we're getting the cart right now!" plead the Sheriff. "And I promise no tricks."

"Good, see that you don't, because—"

Just then, something silver and glittering flew through the air, just over the heads of the Sheriff and crowd, and impaled itself in Farroot's left shoulder—it was a knife! He screamed in agony, but kept his grip on the sword and children. Suddenly, a second blade flew through the air and struck Bill Thistle in exactly the same spot, but this time, Bill dropped his sword and let Dorro fall to the ground.

"*More trickery!*" raged Farroot, blood streaming from his shoulder and soaking his tunic. "Now, my friends, it's time for these young ones to die!"

He laughed mockingly and extended his arm for the fatal slice across Wyll and Cheeryup's exposed necks. But in that merest facet of a second, Dorro leapt to his feet and pulled the knife out of Bill's shoulder. *"Noooooooooo!"* was all he managed to say before vaulting across the porch and thrusting the short blade into the base of Farroot Rumple's throat.

The insane Halfling looked at Dorro with disbelief and shock. Seconds later, Farroot's eyes rolled backwards and he collapsed into lifelessness. What followed was a blur, as Sheriff Forgo and his deputies rushed onto the porch, tackled Bill, and pulled Dorro and the children to freedom and safety.

Thus ended The Battle of the Books.

42
Good is Bad

The following morning, life in that particular stretch of Thimble Down was in complete and utter disarray. Sheriff Forgo and his deputies had cordoned off the library and its soggy environs so they could restore order. Just beyond the perimeter, throngs of Halflings had flooded into the area, as they wanted a glimpse of "the battle" and the dead corpus of Farroot Rumple. Being experienced in these matters, Forgo had Farroot's body covered in a tarp and swiftly moved it to a secret location many hours earlier—actually it was in the rear of the blacksmith's shop, but he wasn't about to publicize that fact. He had more pressing matters to attend to.

"Bosco, *report!*"

The young deputy ran up, breathless. "Yessir! Here's the news. Bill Thistle is in the gaol where he remains under heavy guard. Nurse Pym worked on his knife wound for quite a while. She said it was severe, but he will live. And as you know, Mr. Dorro and the children were escorted back into the library, where the young ones spent the night on those cots in the rare book room. They're quite shaken but healthy enough. Mrs. Tunbridge was allowed in the building and she held Cheeryup all night long."

"Well done, Bosco, well done. And where are the Mayor and Osgood Thrip?"

"The Mayor high-tailed it out of here almost as soon as Farroot Rumple hit the ground, while the Thrips hung about a bit, but then disappeared. I assume they went home."

"That's not surprising," muttered the Sheriff. He was looking out over the Halfling mob pushing and jostling each other to get a better look at the crime scene. It was mildly pathetic, he thought, but in this sleepy village, a fight like this would be big news for months, if not years. However, there was some uproar in the back of the crowd. Something strange was going on.

"Sheriff! Sheriff!"

He saw Deputy Porge running toward him. "Sir, it's the elf!" Just behind him, Forgo saw the culprit cutting through the crowds and making a direct line for him. "Baldar!" was all he managed to say before the big elf stepped over the cordon rope.

"Sheriff Forgo, I'm turning myself in for my crimes. "
"Huh?"

"I'm sure you've already realized it was I who threw the knives that impaled the two evil Halflings last night. I hereby confess. I broke out of your gaol yesterday when I heard the commotion. Further, I must admit I was in your gaol on purpose. I allowed myself to be captured a few days ago so I could be in a central location in case the thieves attempted to sell the Telstar within the village. In fact, Toldir asked me to come into Thimble Down to be 'arrested,' as you quaintly call it. Our plan worked quite flawlessly."

"Buh, buh, buh ...," gibbered the Sheriff like an idiot. "So yer sayin' that it was all part of a plan? Well, *errmm*, I knew that all along." he sputtered. "We wanted you here, too. Glad it all worked out. Of course, you've committed yet another crime and therefore I must re-arrest you for this violent attack, whether it was well-intentioned or not."

At that, Baldar nonchalantly extended his wrists for the deputies to shackle. Porge was about to wrap his wrists in chains when there was another commotion in the crowd. Forgo looked up and saw the rest of the Woodland hunters approaching. Wisely, he waved at Porge to stop at once.

"Well met, Sheriff Forgo" hailed Toldir, the blonde-haired elf leader, raising a hand in salutation and nodding to his fellow elf. "I see that Baldar has helped solve your small fracas. That is well and good. Of course, the more pressing matter is that we need the brooch back. *Now*."

Befuddled, Sheriff Forgo countered, "Well, yes, Baldar did use those flying knives of his to incapacitate two of the criminals, but nevertheless, he did break out of my gaol. Further, he hasn't been tried yet."

Toldir stared at Forgo, unnervingly, with his blazing blue eyes.

"... but, seeing as he was of great assistance to the village of Thimble Down," continued the lawman, turning redder by the second, "I don't see any reason to keep him tied up with a lengthy trial. Owing to the fact that the Mayor has already skedaddled, I hereby by release Baldar from my custody and thank him for services rendered." He finished with an official flourish of the hand.

"That is well," noted Toldir, "but that matter of the Telstar remains. We must have it today, as it is nearly time for us to journey back to our homes in the East. Where is it?"

"Err ... we're just about to wrap up that part of the investigation and hope to have results soon," said Forgo, bluffing poorly.

"I think I can be of assistance here, Toldir," said another voice behind them.

Everyone turned and saw Dorro walking up to the tense group, a bandage on his forehead and fresh red scar on his cheek, but for the most part looking like the same bookmaster everyone knew.

"Greetings, my Woodland companions," said Dorro, bowing low. They returned the greeting with bows and smiles.

"Hail, Wind-and-River, our good friend," said Toldir joyously. "We are pleased to see you, especially if you have news about the Telstar." Turning to Sheriff Forgo, he continued, "We learned not to judge our small confederate here on his appearance—he always seems to have something, as you Halflings might say, up his sleeve."

Dorro basked in the compliment, but as usual, feigned humility and continued. "If you could just give me one half hour, I believe I can retrieve your Telstar. I know you've been more than patient, Toldir, but I beg just a little more of your patience."

Toldir nodded in ascent. Dorro nodded back and began trekking back into the heart of Thimble Down. He had one last mission to perform.

✭ ✭ ✭

Dorro walked through the village for about three minutes and then stopped abruptly. He knocked on a door and waited. And waited some more. Finally, the door creaked up open a few inches wide and the wrinkled face of an elderly woman peered out. "Go away!" she said before slamming the door shut.

The bookmaster sighed and knocked again. And waited.

The door was opened and, again, the peevish face showed itself in the slim gap. "I said *go away*. No one's home."

"I'm sorry, dear lady, but I know your master is at home. And unless he wants me to lead a band of angry elves to this burrow and wreak their terrible vengeance upon it, I suggest you tell him to let me in for a few minutes."

"Wait," said the woman before shutting the oak door once again. Finally, it re-opened and the servant bade Dorro to enter. She led him to the front parlor and left him in the ornate, but cold, cheerless room.

Eventually, he heard footfalls, and Osgood Thrip strode into the room. "How dare you, Winderiver? This is my burrow and I won't have a nosey turnip like you poking in and threatening my housekeeper. *Elves*, I tell you. What nonsense! Anyway, what do you want, before I throw you out?"

"I want the Telstar."

Osgood stopped short. "Don't be a fool. Get out. *Get out*, I tell you!"

Dorro continued, cool as a cucumber, "I know you have it, Osgood, and I won't leave until you give it to me. It belongs to the elves and they shall have it. And I know it's here."

Osgood sneered, "You're bluffing. You have no proof of that."

"You forget about Dalbo. He lives and told me what he heard and saw: '*The good goat ate the star for gold, roots 'n' all.*' You remember that little piece of wit? It told me so much about this case."

"You're as crazy as he is, Winderiver. Or hopefully, as he was."

"I told you and the others what that meant. Or at least, what most of it meant. It was Dalbo's way of saying he'd heard Farroot and Bill—the *root* and billy-*goat*—speaking about how they were getting gold for the star, that is, the Telstar."

Osgood merely snorted.

"The part I didn't explain, however, was the opening image of the 'good goat.' The goat, of course, was Bill, but who was pulling Bill's strings? Why of course, the *good*—as in 'Osgood.' You were behind the whole theft, paying Bill Thistle to coerce Farroot into the crime, as if he needed much encouragement. You had them steal the Telstar for you, which you'd secretly coveted as a prize and planned to sell piecemeal, prying off the gems and smelting the silver down. The gems alone are worth many times what you paid for it. Your wealth would have tripled."

By this time, Osgood Thrip was stonily silent. Dorro kept going.

"What you didn't count on was Farroot's hidden agenda. He'd hated Bing for years and considered him a blight and a burden. Surely, the theft of the Telstar would have earned him enough gold to leave his brother in

Thimble Down and find another Halfling village to settle in, quite comfortably, too. But he wanted more and when Bing wouldn't show him when he'd hidden it, Farroot was driven into madness. As I know now, Bing wouldn't part with the brooch because it gave him something that money couldn't buy—confidence, bravado, popularity, his brother's love and respect—all the things he'd craved his whole life. There is a subtle magic in the brooch. It doesn't have that effect on elves, but on a small Halfling like Bing Rumple, it infused him with power and charisma, which explains why he returned to his former sniveling self after it was stolen."

"Bill and Farroot knew that Bing had hidden the brooch somewhere in the burrow," continued Dorro, now hitting full stride and moving his hands with dramatic flourishes, "They watched him every moment and ultimately, he made a mistake. Bing ventured to his back bedroom once too many times in a single day, checking on his beloved gem out of fear and insecurity. That same night, Bing ventured out to the Hanging Stoat for a drink and was followed stealthily by Farroot. In a dark stretch of lane near the tavern, Farroot gave his brother a conk on the head in order to buy Bill time to search the bedroom. An expert sneak-thief, Bill searched the room all night until he found the Telstar in Bing's 'hidey-hole'—a loose bit of wall paneling that I also discovered when investigating the murder scene a day or two later."

"Which brings us to the darkest chapter of this saga, Osgood, the part you didn't bargain on. I know now that you and Bill were solely motivated by greed, but Farroot's hatred of his brother came from a less sanguine place. Once you put this entire caper in motion, he realized he could use the theft to get Bing out of the way permanently. Sheriff Forgo had ordered the three to leave Thimble Down within a day, yet Farroot certainly had no desire to drag his whining brother with him again. Thus, after stealing and securing the Telstar, he put his own plan into action."

"On the day of their departure, Bing rushed frantically into the village to tell the Sheriff of the theft; this was the moment when young Wyll Underfoot was heartlessly accused of the theft—by Farroot no less—and taken to gaol. And when they returned back to the burrow, the brother picked this moment to smash Bing on the head with a fire poker in the back bedroom, causing his instant, violent death. I examined the poker the next day and, sure enough, there was a greasy mark of blood upon its surface, but I kept that information to myself. In perhaps the most grotesque act of this play, Farroot decided to stick one of the knives they'd stolen from the elves into Bing's back, obviously to implicate Baldar, yet also to buy him and Bill time to prepare their escape."

Osgood laughed, cruelly. "Winderiver, you really are a fool. That is a grand tale, certainly, but you have no proof. None at all!" He laughed again.

"I'm not so sure, Osgood. Granted, you may have the Telstar hidden so deeply in your burrow that it will take us years to find it. But you forget, while Farroot is dead,

Bill Thistle still lives and is in the gaol right now. I'm sure he's ready to tell us the truth in order to get himself a more lenient penalty."

"Thistle is a criminal—no one will take his word. Even if there's a trial, my solicitors can debunk anything he has to say."

"Point taken, Osgood. I suppose, then, you'd rather speak to Toldir or, better, to Baldar himself. He might even show you his trick of throwing knives again. Would you like to see that, Osgood?"

Dorro stood up and made ready to leave. "Since I can't compel you on the strength of my words, I suppose I'll walk back to the library and tell Toldir that the Telstar is in this very burrow and, further, that he and his lads should come get it. It really is a lovely morning to have one's throat slit, don't you agree?"

With that, Dorro spun toward the exit and began to let himself out.

"*STOP!*" It was Osgood, his face grown pale with rage. "You've meddled in my business far too many times, Winderiver. And this time you've cost me a veritable fortune. I shan't forget this—next time, it might be you who winds up with a fireplace poker to the skull."

"I'm not afraid of you, Osgood. Even forty years ago you were an overbearing, pampered prat and you still are. You still don't like it when you can't get your own way. Or when some naughty little boy tugs on Lucretia's greasy pigtails. But there you are—some things never change. And never will."

By this time, Osgood Thrip was seething with anger and hatred, but said nothing. Instead, he turned on his heels and stormed from the room. Dorro waited. And waited some more. Finally, there was shuffling in the dark passageway and Osgood's stooped, miserable housekeeper Martha entered the room. "The Master said this is for you. And for you to let your own self out."

With that, she placed the silver tray in her hands on a small table by the settee and quietly departed. There, on the tray, was a small box covered with a handkerchief. Dorro didn't even blink twice.

He picked up the box and put it in his pocket.

43
Turning Another Page

A few minutes later, Dorro returned to the library grounds where Sheriff Forgo and his deputies were still cleaning up the mess and persuading the last, curious Thimble Downers to go home for lunch. They hadn't found any excitement or dead bodies and were getting bored, though a few enjoyed gawking at the enormous elves. Toldir and his band had been waiting patiently off to the site, minding their own business and saying nothing, but still looked formidable.

Reaching into his pocket, Dorro walked right up to the hunters and beckoned the Sheriff to join them. "Toldir, I have joyous news. On behalf of the village of Thimble Down, I present you with the Telstar and humbly apologize for any and all delays," said the bookmaster, bowing low.

Toldir gently took the small wooden box out of Dorro's hand and looked at it quizzically. He eased off its lid and peered within. A calm smile spread on his face, which made Dorro and Forgo sigh with relief, notably the latter. The elf chief lifted the Telstar out of its soft wadding and held it up for all to see. As if on cue, the sun broke through the remains of the storm clouds and caught the brooch's gemstones in its gleam. Rays of magical light radiated from Toldir's hand and everyone issued a prolonged series of "*oooh's*" and "*ahhh's.*" It was a spectacular vision, as if one of the evening's brightest stars had come down for a quick visit in the daytime.

Forgo turned to Baldar and added, "And I have something to return as well—the pair of knives that you used to incapacitate the villains. I think we've seen one of these blades many times already." He held one of the knives up and everyone recognized its carved bone hilt clearly—this was the same knife used in the slaying of Bing Rumple. "It's ironic that this is the same knife Dorro withdrew from Bill's shoulder and used to stab Farroot. Kind of a cruel twist of fate—like it wasn't an accident or something."

Dorro got a cold shiver down his spine, while Toldir and Baldar nodded in grave agreement. Suddenly, the rest of the elves stood to leave.

"Toldir, are you leaving us?" asked the bookmaster.

"Nay, Wind-and-River, we shall tarry a few days in the Great Wood, as we have grown fond of its streams, hills, and woodlands. There's little wonder why you

Halflings revere it so strongly. And what will you do next, Wind-and-River?"

"Oh, I suppose I'll get back to the library in a day or two, and finish the translations of Bodurdo I've put off so long. Plus there's a young lad I need to spend more time with—my nephew."

Next to him, Forgo raised his eyebrows. "Huh?"

"I didn't tell you, Sheriff? Turns out that Wyll Underfoot is my sister's son. I just found out myself. He and I shall be having many long talks soon. Hopefully, Wyll shall also be staying in Thimble Down for a good, long while."

"And what of the villain Bill Thistle?" asked Baldar eagerly. "Did I hear that he will survive?"

Forgo piped up, "He will survive indeed. Now the question is, what to do with him? He's an accomplice to murder—as well as a kidnapper—and therefore will likely be exiled, but that's for the Mayor to decide. There are some distant Halfling villages to the east. They welcome our exiles as they need every warm body to work the fields and defend their hamlets from goblin attacks. They lead a rough life out on the frontier. Then again, there isn't a caravan headed that way for many months, so Bill may enjoy the pleasures of my gaol for most of the summer."

Toldir coughed and said, "Excuse me, Sheriff Forgo, but would you consider letting our Woodland elves escort your prisoner to one of these villages. We are grateful that you brought the Telstar safely back to us and accordingly, would be more than happy to provide him safe passage to his new 'home.'"

"Now say, Toldir, you may be onto something there," said Sheriff Forgo, scratching his chin, yet with a gleam in his eye. "Let me talk to the Mayor about it this week. If he's agreeable, and Nurse Pym gives us the okay to let Bill travel, I will accept your offer."

He extended his hand for Toldir to shake. Indulging this strange Halfling ritual, the elf chieftain merely laughed and returned the shake heartily. Soon, everyone was laughing, elf and Halfling alike, relieved that the worst was over.

It was time to return to better things.

✧ ✧ ✧

Dorro stepped up onto the library porch and into the circular building. There, as usual, was Bedminster Shoe, who was cleaning up after the traumatic events of the previous day. "Why Mr. Shoe, let me help you with that."

"That's okay, Mr. Dorro, I'm almost done and I couldn't leave this fine institution in such a state. We'll have patrons back here tomorrow and they like a tidy library to read in."

"You are a marvel, Mr. Shoe, simply a marvel," beamed Dorro.

"Of course, I do consider this *work* time," smiled the scribe.

Dorro burst out laughing, "Why, of course, Mr. Shoe—I shall happily pay you for this and all the many other hours you've put in recently. I'd guess you have a small fortune headed your way!"

"I'm sure whatever you pay will be most satisfactory," said Bedminster, resuming his work. "But of course, I want to be first in line to interview you, Sheriff Forgo, and the others about this investigation for my files. You know how insistent I can be."

"I do indeed! I promise you a full exposition in due time. Now, off to see the children."

Dorro toddled back across the library until he found himself on the structure's back porch. There, sitting quietly on rocking chairs were Wyll Underfoot and Mrs. Tunbridge. Asleep and curled up on her lap was Cheeryup, who was profoundly content in her mother's arms. Dorro stepped out and in an instant found Wyll hugging him tightly across his midriff.

"You should have told me, Wyll. I found your mother's letter."

The boy looked up with tears in his eyes. "I didn't want to be a burden, Mr. Dorro. I wanted to earn my own way."

Dorro paused and then spoke: "That's admirable, boy, but the cat's out of the bag now. You may be Wyll *Underfoot*, but let me remind you that you're half Winderiver, too, and that means that you'll be honest with your old uncle from now on. Furthermore, they'll be no more sleeping in trees, rare book rooms, or garden sheds—you'll have a proper bed and a proper wardrobe back in the Perch. Certainly, I'll give you plenty of chores to keep you busy, aside from schoolwork, but you have the family name to uphold in Thimble Down. We Winderivers stick together, y'know!"

"*Uncle?*" This time it was Cheeryup's voice, as she had just awoken from her nap.

"Yes, isn't it wonderful?" beamed Dorro. "An old fox like me with a new pup in the house. I can hardly believe it!"

Once again, the girl ran jumped up and the three of them hugged long and mightily. "I say, children, I think this calls for a party. What do you think?"

Wyll and Cheeryup both screamed *Yes!* and grinned with excitement. "Wyll, you go tell Sheriff Forgo and his deputies that they're invited to dinner at seven o'clock sharp this evening. *Oh*, and don't forget Mr. Timmo, too. Cheeryup, I want you to invite Mr. Mungo, Mr. Shoe, and Nurse Pym, if she can leave Dalbo Dall for a few hours. Also ask Farmer Edythe—Mungo will more than enjoy that, I'm sure," added Dorro with a knowing grin. "By the way, I spoke to Pym earlier, and Dalbo's making a tremendous recovery. Maybe he really is a tree. Wouldn't surprise me in the least! And Mrs. Tunbridge, you're required company, too."

She blushed and nodded happily.

"Now, as to the feast. I have a giant smoked ham in my food cellar that's been waiting for an occasion such as this. I'll stop by the Bumbling Badger this afternoon and purchase all manner of apple and blueberry pies and aromatic herbed breads. Lastly, I'll ask Mrs. Fowl up the lane for some of her pureed root vegetables and meat pies. And we'll top it all off with wine, cider, and delicious, sweet apples from last fall's harvest. I think you know where to find them, eh, Wyll?

The boy blushed and grinned sheepishly, nodding eagerly all the same. They were the same apples he'd stolen all those weeks ago.

"All right, children, I think we have everything in place for our party. But wait, that's not the right word—it's more than just a mere party." Dorro paused for a second and then brightened.

"I know. Let's think of it as the beginning of our *next* adventure."

The End

Acknowledgments

The author wishes to thank his wife, family and friends;

Pat James for kick-starting the project; Laurie Baxendell for expert graphics and

Jane Carroll for expert editing; Harvey Newquist, Rich Maloof, and the GFF set.

ENJOY PETE PROWN'S MUSIC AT:

CDBABY.COM/ARTIST/GUITARGARDEN

Made in the USA
San Bernardino, CA
19 December 2013